P9-DTP-337

The Heist

The Heist

Michael A. Black

Five Star • Waterville, Maine

First Edition
First Printing: June 2005

Published in 2005 in conjunction with Tekno Books
and Ed Gorman.

Set in 11 pt. Plantin by Christina S. Huff.

Printed in the United States on permanent paper.

Library of Congress Cataloging-in-Publication Data

Black, Michael A., 1949–
  The heist / by Michael A. Black.—1st ed.
    p. cm.
   ISBN 1-59414-277-7 (hc : alk. paper)
   1. Chicago (Ill.)—Fiction.   I. Title.
  PS3602.L325H45 2005
   813'.54—dc22   2005004994

Dedication

To my Dad, to the memory of the real
Tony Carduff (CPD), and to all the rest of the
brave men who served on the USS Fuller,
APA 7 during World War II.

And
To my fallen comrade,
Detective William "Wally" Rolniak, Jr.,
Riverdale, Illinois Police Department.
Rest in Peace, Brother.

Chapter 1

Friday, April 10, 1992

8:50 A.M.
Steady ripples of the current collided with waves fanning from the bow of the tow and barge. About one hundred feet up the river Johnny "the Mink" Osmand stood by the metal railing of the Michigan Avenue Bridge and watched the boat's progress. A cigar smoldered between his thick fingers as he leaned against the railing, seemingly unconcerned about the crowds of downtown workers who had to step around his jutting figure on the busy walkway.

The Mink was a stocky man in his mid-sixties; the silvery mane, which gave him his nickname, swept back from his forehead above eyes as cold and unforgiving as the water far below. He looked down at the murky grayness and spat. The river slapped against the bow of the tug, and for a moment Osmand wondered what it would feel like to be swallowed by the dark wetness, his hands tied behind his back, concrete blocks wired to each ankle, and fighting the hopeless need to breathe as he sank. Would he have the strength to hold his breath until he passed out, or would he succumb to that dizzy panic and just open up, letting the icy, strangling flow wind its way into his lungs?

The Mink wasn't anxious to find the answer, and he hoped the decision he'd made this morning wouldn't cause him to end up beneath that gray-green water looking up.

He licked his lips and drew on the cigar, catching a glimpse of the big, round-faced clock on the Wrigley Building across the way.

Eight-fifty.

More people pushed past him, and Johnny glared at them. After checking his watch again, for the fourth time in the last five minutes, he looked up to see the tall man's head bobbling along above the rest of the pedestrians. The corners of Osmand's mouth twisted downward into an ugly scowl.

"Fox," he yelled.

The tall man turned, his brows furrowing slightly.

"Over here," Osmand repeated with an undercurrent of impatience. Above the two men, carved into the limestone corner of the bridge, a colonial soldier grappled with a Blackhawk warrior in bas-relief. Neither combatant looked as angry as the Mink.

Reginald Fox strolled over, his topcoat slung over his left arm, a finely crafted leather briefcase dangling from his right. He was three decades younger than the Mink, and half a foot taller.

"You're late, counselor," Osmand grunted.

"Sorry," Fox said. "But I didn't get your message till this morning. Why all the secrecy?"

Instead of answering, Osmand cocked his head toward the cement steps that led down to the docks, where tourists could get boat rides up the river to the lake. They moved down the stairs, but at the midpoint, Osmand turned into the enclosed section that housed the gritty ambiance of Lower Wacker.

The lawyer sighed, but followed. The cement walls and ceilings of the enclosure amplified the sounds of the passing cars and trucks. A foul odor hung in the chilly air. When Osmand stopped, Fox set his briefcase down and began to put on his topcoat.

"Johnny, what the hell's going on?" Fox asked, as the shorter man hailed a taxi stopped at the light.

"Making sure we ain't tailed," Osmand said.

"Tailed? Johnny, come on. We're due in court at ten."

But Osmand was already getting into the cab. Fox rolled his eyes. With some difficulty he folded his lanky frame into the rear seat.

"Where to, gentlemen?" the cabbie asked, a trace of New Delhi in his accent.

"Jewelers' Row," Osmand said, reaching over the seat and handing him a five. "And we're in a hurry."

The driver nodded and pulled out into traffic, cutting to make the Wabash Street ramp. Fox gave Osmand an imploring look.

"Johnny, please. Tell me what's going on?"

"Aww, shut up," Osmand said. "Why do you think I pay you the big bucks?"

They took the cab over to Wabash, and Johnny told the driver to pull over by the El tracks.

"Come on," Osmand said, starting toward the upper platforms.

"If you think I'm going on the El . . ." Fox protested weakly, but he went along.

"For a young guy, you sure ain't in no kind of shape," Osmand said, going up the stairs. "Shit, when I was your age, I was a rock."

"I prefer to use my mind rather than my body," Fox said. "Now where are we going? I told you, we've got to be in court at ten."

"Then we better move our asses, right?" Osmand said. He stopped abruptly and surveyed the people coming up to the platform behind them. Fox stopped next to him, puffing slightly, and Osmand figured that the crack about not being in shape had stung the lawyer. "I thought you played basketball for that fancy college you went to? What was it? Harvard?"

"Princeton," Fox said, his breathing slipping back to a semblance of regularity. "Look, Johnny—"

But Osmand appeared in no mood to listen. He continued to stare at the people ascending the stairs. After a few more minutes, he motioned for Fox to follow and they went to the stalls. Osmand shoved a bill under the window toward the attendant and got two tokens. He pressed one into Fox's hand as they went through the gates. On the other side he paused again and looked back. Fox seemed to know better than to say anything. He followed as they went up the stairs to the third level. Out on the platform, they waited for the next southbound train. The outbound side was practically deserted. A few people joined them as the train began clattering into the station. The El darted in, slowing to a stop. Its doors popped open and disgorged groups of people. Osmand and Fox waited for a path to clear, then got on. So did the few others who'd been standing next to them. Osmand scrutinized the other passengers carefully, then, at the last second before the doors closed, he pulled Fox's sleeve and they jumped off the train.

Fox sighed heavily as Osmand watched the El rumble off. The platform was now completely deserted, the last of the commuters having already hurried through the gates. Osmand nodded toward the exits.

When they reached street level, Osmand looked around one more time, then chuckled softly.

"Come on," he said. "We got a stop to make, then we can go to court." He inhaled deeply, then let out a long breath. "Ain't nothing like the sweet smell of fresh, free air."

"Laden with exhaust fumes," Fox said.

They walked up the block past the jewelry shops that lined both sides of the street.

"You talk to them about the deal?" Osmand asked.

"I told them that we'd consider it," Fox said.

Osmand frowned. The lawyer had an irritating way of sounding condescending whenever he spoke. Like everybody else was just a cut below him. Johnny turned into the Wabash entrance to the Pittsfield Building and Fox followed him through the ornate revolving doors. Inside the lobby Osmand walked over to the tobacco shop and bought three cigars. The two men exited on the Washington Street side and went the half-a-block east to Michigan Avenue. Johnny stopped again, making a show of leaning into one of the crevices of entrance to light his cigar.

"We're gonna go into the bank two doors down," Osmand said in a hoarse whisper. *"Capisce?"*

"Is *that* where we're going?" Fox said, his tone lapsing into petulance.

It was an expansive building, full of Plexiglas stands and shiny silver pillars. Inside, a young black man in a security-guard uniform eyed them and pointed to the No Smoking sign. Johnny reluctantly stuck the smoldering cigar into the white sand of a standing gold ashtray. For an older bank, it was exquisitely furnished. The tellers were lined up like a picket fence behind a chest-high counter fashioned from black marble. Beyond that, a dozen or so secretaries were seated at expensive desks on the perimeter of a series of glass-walled offices. Osmand steered Fox to the down escalator. The lower section was equally sumptuous, with miniature Art-Deco statues standing sentry on ornate pedestals. Osmand went toward the west wall where a pretty girl of about twenty-five sat behind a partition, the flat, polished onyx top matching her ebony complexion. She stood and smiled as they approached and held out her hand. Behind her were rows of small steel drawers. Osmand showed her a flat, silver key. The woman looked at it and went to one of the drawers, flipping up a stack of cards that were filed in staggered succession. Leaving the cards flipped up to that spot, she returned to the counter and put a white slip of paper on the flat surface.

"Good morning, Mr. Orlando," she said. The gold nametag above her left breast said DIANE. "How are you today, sir?"

"Fine, honey," said Osmand, scrawling Joe Orlando on the line. She took the paper and went back to the card file to compare the signatures, made a quick notation on the card, and flipped it down again.

"Oh, Miss," Osmand said. "I'd like to put my attorney on my card, if it's all right."

Diane smiled, running her polished red fingernail along the stack of cards again, and once more flipped them up. This time she removed a beige card.

"Certainly, Mr. Orlando," she said. Then to Fox, "If I may see some identification, sir."

Fox set his briefcase down, shifted his topcoat to the other arm, and took out his wallet. He selected his driver's license along with a business card and snapped them onto the countertop with a precise click.

"Co-renter or a deputy?" she asked Osmand.

"As a deputy I'll have full privileges only if something happens to Mr. Orlando, correct?" Fox said quickly. Diane nodded and looked back at Osmand.

"I guess it don't matter none, as long as he can get in it if I'm . . . indisposed." He looked at Fox. "Co-renter's fine." Diane made the notations on the card then showed Fox where to sign. When he was done, she smiled at him and replaced the card. After grabbing a ring of keys, she indicated that they should move around behind the counter and over to a large vault door. Both men watched her as she walked in front of them. She was dressed in a tight blue dress, and her nylon pantyhose swished slightly as she moved.

"Nice ass," Osmand muttered to Fox.

The vault door was standing open, its huge, concentrically-formed steel rings attesting to its thickness and solidarity. The back of the door was Plexiglas, so that the large steel rods of the locking mechanism were visible. On the lower portion of the right side, a horizontal row of numbers were displayed down to the second, showing that the electronic time-lock had now been open for one hour and fifteen minutes. They passed through the row of vertical steel bars on the other side of the door. Inside the vault were rows and rows of safety deposit boxes of all sizes. All the doors were gold-colored and numbered in vertical succession. Osmand and Fox followed Diane to the section of the largest boxes. She placed the key from the ring into the first lock. Osmand handed her his key and she inserted that one into the second lock. She gave both a half turn and the steel door opened. As she drew the black metal box from its resting place, the weight caused her arms to sag slightly. Osmand reached forward and grabbed it from her.

"You know where the rooms are, don't you, sir?" Diane asked. Osmand nodded. "Just call me when you're ready, gentlemen." She watched them carefully as they moved out of the vault toward the examination rooms.

Osmand set the box on the table.

"Shut the fucking door," he said. Once it was closed, he reached in his coat pockets and removed two bricks of bills, which were rubber-banded together. He opened the lid of the box. Several more stacks of bills were visible. The top bill of each carried the picture of Benjamin Franklin.

"How much you got in there?" the lawyer asked, eying them.

"Never mind how fucking much I got in there," Osmand said in a guttural whisper. "This is all I want you to be concerned about." He reached in the box and took out a VHS cassette tape in a plain, white cardboard package.

Fox stared at it, then looked at Osmand.

"You want to tell me what it is?" he asked.

Osmand smiled. So broadly that the gold crowns of his molars were visible.

"Insurance," the Mink said. "The best fucking insurance in the world."

Chapter 2

Monday, April 13, 1992

6:38 A.M.

Anthony Cardoff looked at the reflection in the mirror for a few seconds before slapping on the lather. It was the only time he really felt old: when he saw his reflection. His beard had turned gray a long time ago. So had the hair. But at least he still had all of it. He ran the edge of the safety razor under the hot water and began scraping, listening to the disc jockey read the traffic and weather report for this fine spring morning. No rain predicted. That was good, even though this was April, and it was supposed to rain in April. He turned on the shower and adjusted the temperature as he thought about how soon September twelfth would be coming. This would be his last summer. As he was drying off, he caught a glimpse of himself in the full-length mirror on the back of the door. His tall body still had its leanness, despite being only five months away from the department's mandatory retirement age. But at sixty-one he still managed to take down an occasional door with the raid team.

The kitchen of his old house had a linoleum floor, and it was cold against his bare feet. He checked the coffeemaker and went into the bedroom to finish dressing. This was when he really missed her: the mornings, when he saw her photo on the dresser. It had always been such a special time for them, her making breakfast as he got ready for work. He'd always

15

meant to take an early retirement, so they could spend some quality time together. Travel. Do the things they always planned on doing. But the expenses delayed it at first, getting the kids through college. And after his transfer to the Organized Crime Division, something he'd dreamed of his entire career, he couldn't just up and leave the department. Mary had understood and had supported him completely. They'd have time, she said, and he always felt they would, too.

Then suddenly time ran out.

She'd left him quickly, mercifully lingering only a few months after the tumor was discovered. After that it seemed pointless to quit. Why retire when there was nothing left for him? He'd buried himself in his work, becoming what the newspapers called the pre-eminent authority in the Police Department on the Chicago Outfit, or the mob. After several successful prosecutions, he was selected to head the special, multi-agency taskforce that would hopefully end the career of the current *capo di tuti capi,* Salvatore "Vino" Costelli.

The coffeemaker hissed, and Tony heard it from the bedroom. He slipped on his shirt and went back into the kitchen, taking a cup from the cupboard and filling it with the steaming brew. He liked it black, a throwback to his time in the Navy, when an old CPO had told him if he learned to like it black, he'd never miss it if there was no cream or sugar. He tried to limit himself to three cups a day now, a far cry from his early days on the force when he'd need nine to ten cups just to get through a midnight shift. Sipping the strong coffee as he walked back into the bedroom, he was reminded of the first time he'd ever seen Salvatore Costelli.

It had been a cool spring night, and Tony, who was still considered a rookie, had just gotten his permanent assignment to District Twelve, the wonderfully quaint area around Taylor and Halsted known as Little Italy. The V. A. Building was down the street, along with the massive construction project that would one day be the University of Illinois Hospital and Circle Campus. Lining the streets of the area were all kinds of family-owned businesses: pizza shops, shoemakers, grocery stores. He'd parked his squad car in the mouth of a nearby alley. D'Angelo's on Carpenter had the best Italian beef in the city, and he rarely missed a chance to eat there. After devouring the spicy sandwich, he was walking out with his cup of coffee when he heard the disturbance.

At first it just sounded like loud voices. Nothing unusual for this area. Then a woman screamed. Tony dropped his coffee and ran toward the sound. Down the block, in front of Casio's Shoe Repair, he saw three figures. Two men and a woman: Mr. and Mrs. Casio and a stranger. The stranger was a short, heavy-set man in a navy blue, pinstripe suit. His black hair was slicked back, and he wore sunglasses even though it was dark. Mr. Casio was hunched over, holding his face. Blood dripped from between his fingers and puddled on the sidewalk. The stranger stood in front of them, his right hand concealed by his leg.

Tony unsnapped his .38 as he ran up and screwed it into the stranger's left ear.

"Let me see your hands," Tony said.

The stranger turned his face toward him and smiled. It was a fat face, made more massive by the oily pompadour. The man looked to be in his mid-thirties in the glow of the street lamp. On his right cheek was a V-shaped birthmark that descended onto his neck. Tony saw a glint of light, and something scudded onto the sidewalk by the man's right shoe. A straight-razor. Pushing the stranger roughly over to the wall, Tony told him to put his hands on the building.

Mrs. Casio was speaking in frantic Italian and trying to tend to her husband, who kept pushing her away with his blood-covered hands. Tony could see that Casio had a cut across the bridge of his nose that was bleeding badly.

"I'd better call for an ambulance," Tony said. "You're going to need stitches."

Mrs. Casio said something Tony didn't understand.

"No," Mr. Casio said, continuing in his broken English. "I be all right. No ambulance." Tony stooped and picked up the straight razor from the sidewalk.

"Is this what he cut you with?" he asked.

But instead of answering, Mr. Casio just shook his head and said something to his wife in their native language. The blood was beginning to congeal on his face, but still ran from the wound. Tony took out his handcuffs and reached for the stranger's right arm.

"Tony, no," Casio said, placing his bloody hand on Tony's forearm.

"Huh?" Tony said. "This guy cut you, didn't he?"

"No," Casio said. "I fall down. That's all."

"Bullshit," said Tony.

"Tony, please," Mrs. Casio implored. "Let him go."

The man had been leaning against the wall with his arms outstretched. Now he relaxed a little and straightened up. Turning, he faced Tony and smirked.

"Tony, huh? You a *paisano?*" he asked.

"Shut up," Tony said, then turned back to Mr. Casio. "Did he threaten you or something?"

Still fending off his wife's probing hands, Mr. Casio looked at Tony for an instant. There was sadness in his eyes, and something else. Fear, maybe?

"I gonna go back inside my shop now, Tony," Mr. Casio said. He turned to go. Tony was dumbstruck. He reached for the injured man, just as he felt the stranger's hand grab his wrist.

"Hey, *goomba*," the man began, his voice somewhat conciliatory.

A split-second later Tony's left fist smashed against the man's jaw, about where the birthmark was, and the greaseball went down in a heap on the sidewalk. Tony had boxed in the Navy, and had reacted out of instinct as much as anything else. The guy was out cold, as Tony snapped the cuffs on him.

"Tony, no. You no do," Casio said, as Tony ignored his pleas and called for a paddywagon. "It's no good. You don't know who he is."

But he found out. The man's name was Salvatore Costelli, a small-time crook working his way up the Outfit's ladder by collecting street tax from all the merchants. Tony charged him with Unlawful Use of a Weapon for having the straight razor and threw in Resisting Arrest for good measure. Mr. Casio refused to sign any complaints. When it got to court a month later, Costelli walked in with a high-priced lawyer who conferred with the State's Attorney in a low voice. Ten minutes later Costelli pleaded guilty to a reduced charge of Disorderly Conduct, and was given a fine-only sentence.

Tony looked on in disgust, but felt a tinge of satisfaction upon seeing that Costelli talked through clenched teeth. His jaw was still wired shut. As they turned to walk down the center aisle, the procession stopped in front of Tony's chair. Costelli looked down at him coldly, then drew the corners of his mouth up in what was supposed to pass for a smile.

"Hey, *goomba*," he said, as he reached out and patted his open palm against Tony's cheek. "Maybe next time, huh?"

The next time never came for Tony. Salvatore worked his way up the mob ladder very quickly after that, graduating to made-man, lieutenant, and finally to the top man. It was in December of 1988, during one of the Outfit's power struggles, that the bodies of his two biggest rivals were found dumped in a field on the South Side, their skulls crushed by what the Medical Examiner termed "blunt trauma."

The phone rang, jarring Tony from his reverie. He set the cup down and went to answer it, thinking that the incident with Costelli seemed more like last month than almost thirty years ago.

"Tony?" It was Arlene Casey, one of the federal prosecutors on the taskforce.

"Yeah," he said. "I was just getting ready. What's up?"

"I got a call from downtown," she said. "Court's been canceled."

"Canceled?" Tony said. "Why?"

"I don't know," she said. "Something about a power problem downtown. They were real vague."

Tony let out a slow sigh.

"And we were supposed to have our little meeting with the Mink, too," he said.

"That's why I called," she said. "I put a call into Reggie's answering service to see if we can meet with them later."

It bothered him when she referred to that asshole defense attorney Fox as "Reggie." But, then, she was young and didn't look at things from his perspective.

"Want me to pick you up?" he asked. He knew that Arlene, who lived in Skokie, hated the hectic drive into the city.

"And have you drive all the way up here from the South Side? No, of course not. I guess I can take the El."

"No, don't do that," he said. "I can call Ray to stop by for you. He lives in Roger's Park." Ray Lovisi was his partner on the P. D.

"Oh, that's okay. I don't want to bother Ray either," she said. "I can call Kent and have him pick me up. He's a lot closer."

The Heist

Kent Faulkner was the third party in their special taskforce. An FBI agent. He was handsome, tall, broad-shouldered, and, of course, he was young, too. Young enough, Tony thought, to make a play for her. Something he would do if he were Kent's age. But Faulkner was either too stupid or too shy to make the move. So far.

"Okay, just promise me you'll stay off the El," he said. "It could be dangerous. Remember the kind of people we're dealing with."

"Yes, I promise, Father," she said, the good-natured sarcasm evident in her voice. "I'll meet you at the office."

He hung up the phone thinking about how much Arlene reminded him—maybe too much—of his Mary. The way she'd looked when they first met and decided to get married while he was home on leave from the Navy. Forty years. It had passed so quickly. Too quickly. If he'd only known then what he knew now.

The sun was barely coming over the tops of the buildings when Lincoln Jackson trotted up the stack of cement blocks that substituted for stairs in front of his uncle's "office" trailer. It was sandwiched between two dirty-looking brick buildings, a tavern and a beauty salon, at 115th and Michigan. The metal sign fastened adjacent to the door read: Bartwell Construction.

Linc opened the door and went inside. A burly looking black man stood behind a desk made out of two-by-fours and plywood. Papers were strewn over the top of it, and Henry Bartwell was hunched over, sorting through them. To his left was a grease-spotted Dunkin' Donuts bag. On his right was an extra-large Styrofoam cup of steaming coffee.

"Morning, Uncle Henry," Linc said.

"You seen that invoice for them pipes?" the big man asked without looking up. Sweat was starting to form on his bald head.

"No, sir, I haven't," Linc said. He stopped in front of the desk and watched the man's thick black fingers rifle through the stacks of papers. His uncle looked up over a pair of half-glasses perched on the tip of his nose.

"Well," he said with exaggerated impatience, "you gonna help me look for it, or what?"

Linc grinned as he began sifting through the loose sheets. He was a big man, too, in his late twenties, with a short-cropped fade hairstyle, and skin like cream-colored coffee. He grabbed a piece of paper and held it out to his uncle. "This what you looking for?"

Henry glanced at it, snorted, and grabbed the paper.

"You wanta tell me what it is you want?" he asked.

Linc grinned again.

"What makes you think I want something?"

"Because I know you," Henry said, lowering his huge body into a leather swivel chair. It was the only bit of luxury he allowed himself in his trailer-office. The chair squeaked loudly as he leaned back. "When you come in here, nice as you please, and give me that 'Morning, Uncle Henry,' you always wants something." He stared at Linc over the flat-topped rims of the glasses. "That shit might have worked when you was in the Marines, but don't try to bulljive me. Now, what you need?"

"I need," Linc said slowly, "a favor, I guess."

Henry's left eye narrowed slightly, but he said nothing.

"I need a little time off today," Linc said.

"Time off," his uncle repeated. "Busy as we is, you want time off."

"I wouldn't ask if it wasn't important."

"What's more goddamn important than us meeting our deadline?" Henry's voice boomed. "This is the Deep Tunnel Project. It ain't gonna dig itself, boy. You know how hard it was for a minority-owned firm to get a piece of that action?" When Linc neither spoke nor flinched, his uncle seemed to relent slightly. "Oh, hell. How much time you need?"

"Just an hour or two. I gotta take Rick down to the V. A. hospital."

Henry's brow creased and he pulled in a deep breath through an open mouth.

"That white boy again? Why can't his own people take him? And besides, don't he have a car? Where's that Eagle Talon I seen him driving?"

"It's in the shop," Linc said. "I sort of promised that I'd help him out."

"You know, I done what you asked. I gave him a job when you two came home from the Marines last February," Henry said. "And all that motherfucker's done since I hired him has been to call in sick every other week. He ain't given me but a half-dozen good days' work since I hired him. Now he's got you running around playing his *nigger* for him." He paused intentionally, as if to gauge Linc's reaction.

"It ain't like that, Uncle Henry. We been through a lot together. And now he's just sick, that's all. It ain't his fault." Linc's voice hardened. *"And I ain't no man's nigger."*

Linc saw that his fierce flare of pride brought a smile to Henry's lips. He'd been testing him after all. Henry had always taken a special interest in him when Linc's mother, Henry's sister, had died.

"Okay," Henry said, taking in a deep breath, and letting it out audibly. "I guess it'd be all right. But you gotta promise you'll make up the time. And, boy, I'm telling you right now, I can't keep carrying your friend on the books if he don't get better fast. Hell of a note, anyway, keeping a white boy on when there's brothers standing in line wantin' work."

"Any of them save my life?" Linc asked, defiance creeping into his voice. That night in Israel flashed before him: the ferry overturning, men screaming, the cold water reaching out to engulf him. Flailing arms, panic, more screams. The dark water seemed to be pulling at his legs, forcing itself into his mouth. He'd never learned to swim, and in that second, when the ferry capsized, he knew that he was going to die. Death by drowning. Blackness seemed to be crowding out all the light. Then, all at once, he felt an arm snare his head, snaking around his neck . . . his face feeling the air, and a voice telling him to be cool, as he felt himself being propelled through the water. When they got to the dock, someone hoisted him upward, and for the first time he got a clear glimpse of the person who'd rescued him. A white guy pushing off into the water again, going after another drowning Marine.

Linc and Rick Weaver became inseparable after that, living in the same bunker for the next six months in the Saudi desert. They found out they had a lot in common: both were big and bad, both came from Chicago, and both had the same MOS, advanced recon, attached to the combat engineers unit. They spent the war waiting to go, champing at the bit, after having seen action in Panama.

And then it was over in little more than a hundred hours.

They were given a parade when they got back to the States. But six months after they'd come marching home, the Corps told them they were being "RIFed." Reduction In Force. Conversion to a peacetime world. After nine years in the Marine Corps, the government had suddenly decided that warriors were no longer needed. They couldn't believe it. Discarded. Like yesterday's newspaper after the job was done. It was a bitter pill to swallow. They'd seen more than a few of their comrades die in the Corps. Was this all it meant to America? Was this all that they'd meant? Maybe it was time for a payback . . .

When Henry had given Linc a job in the family construction business, Linc talked his uncle into hiring Rick too. It seemed like a good way to pay him back. Then Rick started to get sick.

"They still ain't found out what's wrong with him?" Henry asked, his voice penetrating the perimeter of Linc's thoughts.

"They're saying now it might be some kind of parasite. Something he picked up in the desert."

"Well, I'm just glad *you* didn't get it. Check in with me when you get back." Henry turned his attention back to the invoice, and picked up the phone. "Now if you'll excuse me, I gots a business to run."

Linc smiled broadly, and flipped up the collar on his Desert Storm field jacket as he turned to go. For all his gruffness, Uncle Henry was really just a big pussycat.

The phone rang in the den of Salvatore Costelli's River Forest home. Salvatore, called Vino because of the reddish birthmark on his right cheek that was roughly shaped like a wine glass, leaned forward in his easy chair and stubbed out his cigar in the ashtray. He picked up the receiver and listened intently as the voice on the other end spoke.

"That coat's going on sale."

"When?" Vino asked. He brushed some cigar ash off the front of his gold-colored satin bathrobe. He felt the birthmark flame to red.

"Don't know yet," the voice answered.

"Okay. Keep me posted." He hung up and stood. Vino Costelli was not a tall man, but he made up for it in bulk. In his younger days he'd been as strong as a bull. Sort of like Rocky Marciano: short, but with big arms and hands. Even now he still had a chest like a barrel. He clasped and unclasped his hands as he thought of his most trusted lieutenant, the Mink, going over to the other side. Bending over and spreading his cheeks for the "Gee." His mouth twisted down into a scowl as he crossed the room and snatched the Louisville Slugger baseball bat from the rack on the wall.

It was made of finely polished ash, the heavy tape wound around the handle now dirty-gray with age. Vino sighted down its length, a faint smile tracing his lips. Then he crouched into a batter's stance, leaning forward just like he'd done as a boy in the Catholic Youth Leagues. It was the same bat he'd used as a kid to hit the home run to win the citywide championship. And it was the same bat that he'd used years later to hit "the Grand Slam," as he always called it. The night three-and-a-half years ago when he'd bashed in the skulls of Maxie Campo and Bugsy Volpone. Just like Big Al, Scarface himself, had done in the twenties to those pricks who'd dared to cross him. Right at the dinner table, the blood splattering all over that white tablecloth. The Mink had been his right-hand man in those days, setting up the whole thing at his own house, no less. And now the rat bastard was selling out.

I can't fucking believe it, Vino thought.

He snapped the bat in a wide arc, imagining a ball streaking far into left field. In his mind's eye the ball bounced in the green grass, and, as it rolled to a stop, it became something else. It became Johnny the Mink's head.

Chapter 3

Monday, April 13, 1992

7:15 A.M.
When Linc got back to the apartment Diane was sitting at the kitchen table sipping a cup of coffee. She was in her bra and pantyhose and he grinned broadly as he saw her.

"Hey, baby, wanna play?" he said.

She smiled and told him that she had to finish putting her makeup on.

"I don't have a lot of time before I have to get to the train," she said, brushing away his playful fingers.

"You look great to me, Miss Cassidy," he answered, going to the phone. He picked up the receiver and punched in a number. After four rings there was a weak hello.

"Rick? It's Linc, man. How you feeling?"

"All right, brother," Rick said, but his voice sounded otherwise. "Where you at?"

"I spent the night at Diane's."

"You still coming by as planned?"

"Yeah, I'll be on my way soon," Linc said. He hung up and went into the bedroom where Diane was now pulling on a white silk blouse.

"I love the way silk feels against my skin," she said.

Linc reached under the front of it and cupped her breasts. "How's *this* feel?" he asked, easing his fingers under her bra.

27

"Will you stop," she chided. "I have to get to work."

"We got time, baby."

"You gonna explain to my boss why I'm late?" she said, pushing his hands away and tucking the blouse into the top of her pantyhose. She went to the bed and grabbed her navy blue skirt. Linc leaned against the wall and watched as she slipped it over her well-developed ass.

"You going to take Rick up to Hines?" she asked.

"Yeah."

"Good, then drop me at the Metra station on the way." She reached out and placed her right hand on Linc's shoulder for balance as she pulled on cotton socks and stepped into her shoes. They were white Nikes with the laces tucked in by the tongue. She stooped to pick up her heels, which were in a plastic tote bag by her purse, went through a final check to make sure she had everything, then turned and smiled at Linc. He gazed back at her dark face.

"You sure do look great this morning," he said.

"Meaning what? That I don't look great every morning?" He was almost taken aback, until she leaned forward and kissed him. She just used her tongue, he noticed, so she wouldn't mess her lipstick.

"You coming by the bank later, right?" she asked.

"Yeah, after Rick picks up his medicine," Linc said hesitantly.

"I told you that he came Friday, didn't I?" she said. "Brought some fancy-looking lawyer with him. Put him on the box list, too."

"Uh-huh."

"So, you guys are gonna check it out, like we planned, aren't you?"

"Just like we planned, baby," Linc said, grabbing her and pulling her to him. He crushed his lips against her mouth, kissing her long and hard. At first her hands went to his shoulders to push him off, but stopped a millisecond later and just lightly rested on his muscular arms.

It was close to eight as Tony pulled down the driveway to the underground parking at the Dirksen Federal Building. One of the security guards walked over toward him, waving his arms.

"Building's closed," the guard said, his breath coming out in a frosty cloud.

"I work in there." Tony flashed his badge.

The guard glanced at the Chicago star and gave a half-smile.

"Sorry, but there ain't nothing I can do. No power. They can't even raise the door." He gestured toward the massive overhead door at the bottom of the sloping driveway.

Tony frowned, but before he could speak Ray Lovisi appeared and knocked on the passenger's side of the unmarked. Tony reached over and unlocked the door. Ray, who was hatless and clad in a tan overcoat, quickly slid in.

"About fucking time you got here," he said. His nose and cheeks were red. He'd obviously been standing outside for a while.

Tony nodded to the guard, who stepped away as the car started to swing around to make a U-turn in the driveway.

"What's the matter," Tony said, wrestling with the wheel, "this nice April weather too much for a tough guy like you?"

He grinned as he said it, because Ray, who was only about five-nine, prided himself on being tough. He'd boxed Golden Gloves, and many a bigger man had fallen after underestimating him.

"April, Jesus, it still feels like December, but at least . . ." Ray said, rubbing his hands together.

"At least what?" Tony asked.

"At least they're predicting that it's gonna warm up," Ray said after a moment. But Tony knew Ray was probably going to say, "At least I ain't old," but had thought better of it.

"Go on down the block to the Italian Village," he said.

The Italian Village was a restaurant on Clark, half a block east. Tony angled out into the traffic on Dearborn.

"We gonna catch breakfast?" Tony asked.

"Nah," Ray said. "Believe it or not, half the fucking buildings around here are without power. Some kinda flood or something."

"Flood? I don't see any water."

"Me either," Ray said. "But then again, we been going to court for near onto three months on this fucking case and I ain't seen no justice, neither." He looked over at Tony and grinned. Despite his "boxer's nose," Ray had a rugged handsomeness about him. "Anyway, Arlene and Faulkner are waiting for us at the restaurant. Supposed to meet Johnny the Mink and his mouthpiece there at nine-thirty."

"Oh yeah?" Tony said. Now it was his turn to grin. "You think he's gonna cut a deal?"

"I'd say so," Ray said. "Probably realizes he's outta options."

"I hope so," Tony said. "I certainly hope so."

When Johnny Osmand and Reginald Fox arrived at the restaurant they were uncharacteristically clad in hats, which nonetheless did little to disguise who they were. Osmand's short, square body next to the lanky Fox made them look like a real-life version of the old comic strip characters Mutt and Jeff. The Mink's head twisted back and forth warily as he eyed his surroundings. The restaurant was unusually crowded for this hour. It looked more like a lunchtime crowd than a midmorning one. Fox spied the four legal eagles sitting at a table and pointed them out to Johnny, who pulled away and went to a vacant booth in the smoking section. Fox followed.

"Looks like the Mink wants to sit by himself," Ray said, following Fox's progress toward the booth.

"We got more time than money," Tony said. He smiled at Arlene. She was dressed in a conservative black suit, with a pale yellow blouse. Her brown hair was spread over her shoulders today. In court she usually kept it pulled back in a severe French-braid. Tony always thought she looked like a kid when she had her hair pulled back.

Faulkner, who was also watching with obvious interest, leaned over and whispered, "Should I go over and see if they want to talk?"

"They want to talk, all right," Tony said.

"Otherwise they woulda told us to go scratch our asses," Ray said. He grinned as he glanced at Tony, who frowned on using rough language around Arlene.

Tony glanced at Faulkner. God, he looks like a stuffed-shirt, he thought. Blue suit, white shirt, Florsheim shoes . . . You think he'd have the guts to at least wear a red tie, or something. He took a deep breath and smiled to himself. The fed's tie was a bland-looking blue and gray.

"But if we sit over here, and they're over there," Faulkner said with growing bewilderment, "how're we going to accomplish anything?"

"Just wait," Tony said. "Let 'em order some coffee first. They'll make the sign." He picked up his cup and then set it back down, realizing it was now empty and he'd already gone beyond his three-cup-a-day limit.

When the waitress came to refill their cups about ten minutes later, she set the pot down and dug into her pocket.

"The gentleman in the booth wanted me to give this to you," she said, placing a folded napkin on the table. She picked up the pot and left. Tony unfolded the napkin. On it was scrawled: *Only Cardoff and the broad can come over.* Tony felt Arlene leaning against his arm to read it. He glanced at her surreptitiously, seeing her fine profile and catching a whiff of her perfume. Ray reached over and took the napkin from Tony's fingers.

"Who the fuck does he think he is, writing something like this?" he said angrily. He crumpled the napkin in his fist.

"Take it easy, Ray," Tony said. "Maybe this'll work out better. You and Kent can watch our backs while we talk to them."

Ray grunted an agreement.

Tony stood, and he and Arlene walked over to Osmand's booth. The inside of the restaurant had become even more crowded, especially in the smoking section where a cloudy haze hung in the air. There were no windows in this area and lighting was subdued, causing an almost clandestine ambience. At the booth the Mink extended his hand, but Tony didn't take it. Realizing this, Osmand twisted his palm upward, pointing it toward the seat across from him. Ignoring the gesture, Tony slid into the booth next to Osmand. Arlene sat beside Fox.

"You thought things over, Mink?" Tony asked.

Johnny smiled as he bit into a big Italian pastry. With his mouth full, he said simply, "Yeah."

"Let me say that we've taken your offer under advisement," Fox said. "We're willing to talk particulars, if we get an informal agreement worked out as a matter of record."

"Neither of you are wearing a wire, are you?" Osmand

said, while continuing to chew. It was one of those elongated, hard pastries with lots of icing on the top.

"Huh-uh," Tony said derisively. "Why, you wanta search us?"

"Nah, your word's good enough," Osmand said. "You I know, Cardoff. Shit, we've known each other for what? Ten, fifteen years now? I know you ain't gonna fucking lie to me. We're cut from the same cloth, you and me. Just different suits, that's all."

Tony didn't say anything. Neither did Arlene. Her eyes moved from Osmand to Tony. The Mink took another bite, then looked at her and smiled. There was dough wedged into the gumline around his upper teeth.

"Run it by me again," Osmand said, reaching for his coffee.

"The standard deal," Arlene said. "You plead to three of the fourteen counts, and serve eighteen months. Of course, you could get a suspended sentence in exchange for your co-operation and testimony."

"You got any idea how long I'd last if the word got out that I was gonna spread my cheeks for you?" Tony looked at him sharply, and Osmand shrugged. "Sorry, Miss, I guess I ain't used to talking to no lady."

"That's okay, Mr. Osmand," she said. "But you do understand that we would be offering you refuge in the Witness Protection Program."

"Yeah, yeah, I know," Osmand said.

"I have a problem with pleading to three counts," Fox interjected. "Can't we go with a blanket of immunity if my client does decide to cooperate?"

Before Arlene could answer, Osmand cut her off. "Just shut the fuck up, will ya?" he said to Fox. Then, turning back to Arlene, he apologized again. "Sorry, Miss. I know my manners ain't the best in the world. But before we make any final decisions, I'd like to run one other thing by you."

Arlene nodded.

Osmand leaned back against the cushion of the booth, folding his hands in a steepling gesture on the table in front of him. He exhaled before he spoke.

"Suppose I had a way for you to nail somebody . . . big. Real big." He said the last words quickly. "Then maybe there'd be a way for me to just kinda disappear on my own, without having to testify at all." It was more of a statement than a question.

Arlene looked at him with steady eyes. "I'm not sure I know what you're saying, Mr. Osmand."

Osmand seemed to think for a moment, before choosing his words.

"You know, some kinda evidence . . . rock-solid evidence that somebody did something."

"I'm afraid your vagueness has me a bit confused." Arlene glanced at Fox for clarification. Fox only shrugged and looked up at the ceiling.

"Johnny, without knowing what this evidence is," Tony said, "we can't really evaluate it."

Osmand worked his tongue over his upper teeth while he considered Tony's last statement. Then he reached in his inside coat pocket and took out a thick cigar. Unwrapping it, he rummaged in his pocket for his lighter, flicked it, and held the flame to the end.

"Cardoff," he said, after exhaling a prodigious mouthful of smoke, "you remember back when Campo and Volpone got their skulls smashed in?"

Tony nodded.

"Who you figure done 'em?" Osmand asked, drawing on the cigar again.

"Who do you think? Vino."

Osmand licked his lips. "So tell me. Why ain't you never arrested him for it?"

"You know as well as I do," Tony said. "Knowing something and proving it are two different things. Why, you willing to finger Vino for doing them?"

A wide smile spread across Osmand's mouth. He leaned forward, and spoke in a low whisper.

"Suppose I tell you that I got the whole thing on videotape," he said. "Recorded by a pro. Better than you guys coulda done it."

Tony's eyebrows raised reflexively. Flashes of Costelli on TV wielding the proverbial blunt object danced through Tony's mind. Vaguely, he became aware of Arlene saying that she'd have to discuss this new development with the chief federal prosecutor.

"And naturally, we'll have to see a copy of the tape first to prove its authenticity," she added.

"Huh-uh," Osmand said, shaking his head. "If I give you the tape first, then you don't gotta do nothing for me."

"Where's it at, Johnny?" Tony asked.

Osmand just looked at him and smiled while shaking his head slightly.

"Don't be stupid, Johnny," Tony continued. "If Vino gets word that you've got something like that . . ."

"It's in a safe place," Osmand said. "And that's where it's gonna stay, until we finalize the deal. You make any moves on me in the meantime, you'll never see it."

"What about Vino?" Tony asked.

"He tries to pull any shit, Fox'll turn the tape over to you," Osmand said. "But anyway, Vino don't know dick about it. It was just like that old show, 'Candid Camera,' you know?" He grinned again. Some of the pastry still clung to his gumline.

"So you go ahead and run it by the head man, but I want the deal in writing. You can work everything through him." He pointed at Fox, then leaned back and puffed on the cigar some more.

Fox leaned forward and said that they would be waiting to hear from them. As he and Arlene stood, Tony watched Osmand staring at him, a simpering grin still stretched on the Mink's face, the big, partially-smoked cigar dangling from his thick lips. Tony leaned forward over the table and snatched it from Osmand's mouth.

"One more thing. Mink," Tony said, bringing his face close to the other man's. "Don't you ever think that you and me are cut from the same cloth." He straightened up and plunged the ash-covered end of the cigar into Johnny's coffee.

Chapter 4

Monday, April 13, 1992

Midmorning

As Linc waited for Rick in the parking lot of Edward Hines Veteran's Hospital, he drummed his fingers on the steering wheel of the pickup and felt bad about telling the lie to Uncle Henry. But it couldn't be helped. He and Rick needed time to make another recon. And it wasn't really a total lie anyway. Rick *did* pick up some kind of parasite or something during Desert Storm, and it was making him sick. And they *were* giving him medicine at the V. A. Hospital. It seemed to be working. So he wasn't really lying to his uncle, just fibbing a little bit. After all, he could hardly go in and tell Uncle Henry that he and Rick needed the time off so they could put the final touches on their fantasy plan of breaking into a bank.

He first got the idea for the heist about two months ago when he and Diane were in bed, watching the news. They showed this old gangster motherfucker walking out of the Dirksen Building after being indicted. All the newsmen were running after him, following him down the street, filming him and asking him questions. But the dude was cool and just ignored them. Linc laughed out loud, and when Diane glanced at the TV to see what was so funny, she froze.

"What's wrong?" he asked.

"That man," she said. "I think I know him."

"Him?" Linc pointed at the screen as they flashed a blow-up of an old mug shot of Johnny "the Mink" Osmand while the anchorman gave more details of the indictment.

"He's got a safety deposit box at the bank," Diane said. "Only it's under a different name. I'm sure that's him, though."

"Ain't that a trip," Linc said as he turned over on his side to grope her.

But she wasn't having any of it, her eyes still glued on the TV.

"I wonder," she said, "what he's got in that box?"

And it quickly developed into an obsession with her. She searched through all the card files until she was sure of the box number. It was one of the large ones. The man, who used the name Joe Orlando, had rented the box three months before she'd seen him on the news and had visited it twice a week for the past three months. Always in the morning, almost like clockwork. He never stayed in the examination room more than a few minutes. Sometimes he had a briefcase with him. Other times not. But the box always felt heavy when Diane pushed it back into the slot. And, each time she secured the door with the two keys, her belief of what was in it became stronger.

"It's got to be his stash," she said one night to Linc. "I'll bet he's got a million dollars of dirty old cash in that damn box."

"So what," Linc said. "You work around that kind of money every day, don't you?"

"It's different," she said. "That box's got mob money in it. Collected from all the suckers they done hooked on that shit they sell."

Linc laughed out loud. "What difference does it make, anyhow?"

"Honest folks don't keep cash in a safety deposit box, for

one thing," she told him. "It ain't allowed. He's probably got it stashed under this false name so the government won't find out about it. I bet he's gonna make a run for it after he collects his cool million."

"You sound like you'd like to steal it."

She turned to look at him before answering, and when she did he saw something in her eyes. Something strange that he'd never seen there before.

"Don't you see? If there was a way we could get into that box . . . get that stash . . . he wouldn't even be able to tell the cops."

"But I'm sure he'd tell *somebody*. Man like that got to have a lot of real bad friends that I sure as hell wouldn't want on *my* black ass."

"If we had that kinda money they wouldn't be able to touch us, baby." Her eyes twinkled. "We could be on a beach somewhere in the Bahamas drinking rum punch."

And that was how it started. The plan. It began to take real shape when Linc was talking to Rick while they'd been working on the tunnel project. Rick had casually mentioned that he knew a little something about locks. Could he pick 'em? Linc inquired.

"Sure," Rick said. "My uncle was a locksmith. He raised me after my parents died, and I used to work with him when I was in high school."

"Could you pick, say . . ." Linc asked with a smile, "a safety deposit box?"

"There ain't a lock made that can't be picked if you've got the right tools," Rick said. "But the biggest problem with something like a safety deposit box lock would be the time factor. It would take a while. Even the banks just drill them when you lose the key."

Linc let it go, putting it off as just a pipe dream. Something to fantasize about. Even after Diane came home with all that information on the box and the bank he remained skeptical. Then in mid-March Uncle Henry had them go assist on a special dig for a broken gas main in the North Loop. The city engineers met them and were very specific about where to sink the holes. When Linc asked them what the fuss was, one of them mentioned the tunnels.

"Tunnels?" Linc said. "Around here?"

"Sure," the engineer said. He was a brother, too, an older guy who liked to talk. "You guys got a few minutes I'll show you."

And he did. Linc and Rick went with him into the building where the broken main was, and went down into the sub-basement. At the bottom there was a long corridor that ended with a solid metal door. The building-guy pulled out a heavy key and used it to unlock the big, case-hardened security lock. When the door was opened, the engineer shined his light into what seemed like an endless tunnel about eight feet high and seven feet wide. The walls were thick cement and angled up from the floor in sort of a bowed triangle.

"Go ahead, feel those walls," the old city worker said. "That's craftsmanship. That there's cement-work. Over a foot thick."

Linc ran his hand over the cold wall.

"How long these been here?" he asked.

"They was built around the turn of the century," the old guy said, pulling his pipe out of his pocket and packing it with tobacco. "Used to use 'em for coal in those days; then when everybody went to gas . . . say, if there's a gas leak maybe I ought not to light this, eh?" He chuckled. "Anyways, they been used for everything from mail delivery to cable TV."

"How far does it go?" Rick asked.

"Hell, it goes all around under the whole Loop," the old guy said. "More than fifty miles of tunnels. They run under every major building downtown."

Linc and Rick looked at each other, the germ of a shared idea suddenly gleaming in their eyes. That night Linc went to the library and found a book named *Forty Feet Below*, by Bruce Moffat, that told all about the tunnel system. Linc was surprised to find that one of the branches went right under the bank where Diane worked.

In that moment, the plan began for real.

Rick had been just as disgusted as Linc about being dropped from the Corps after the Storm. "The politicians trot us out when they need some blood spilled, then forget about us after the battle's won," he said. So it didn't take much to sway him over. That's when the plan started to take shape. Just like it was a military operation. They scouted the bank and the vault section, invisible in their construction coveralls and dangling tool belts. It helped that Diane was working, which gave them the run of the place because she was the assistant in charge. She showed them exactly which box it was, standing guard as Rick slipped a blank key into the lock several times. They checked the door to the tunnel, descending into the sub-basement, which they estimated to be about forty feet down. Nobody paid much attention to two guys, one black, one white, who came back a few days later dressed in construction-type clothes and went down to check the basement.

But there were three major stumbling blocks to the plan. One was the constant stream of people who were always coming and going by the vault. Rick said that he would need at least fifteen to twenty uninterrupted minutes to make the impressions and file the replacement key. There was way too much traffic during business hours. It might be possible after hours, but there were all kinds of sophisticated alarms that detected motion in the area. Even if somehow they could neutralize the alarm system, the vault itself was locked with a time-lock.

So the plan kind of faded into that realm of fantasy, where they kept planning it, but in their hearts knew that they'd never really be able to pull it off. Still, they went through all the various phases: scanning the top of the bank building from the roof of the taller structure next door, finding out which windows were the washrooms, figuring where they could tie off if they had to rappel down to the roof of the bank. But those three blocks—the people, the alarms, and the time-lock—seemed insurmountable. Diane kept harping on it, like it was all she could think about. Linc more or less humored her, pretending that he was really serious about it. And deep down in his gut he also had the feeling, after all the shit he'd been through in the Corps, that somehow there really was a way to do it. Some kind of way.

Linc was lost in his daydreams when the passenger's door of the pickup opened and Rick slid in. He was wearing his Desert Storm field jacket, just like Linc was, but it hung much looser on Rick. He was about the same height as Linc's six-two, but not as big through the shoulders. His pale skin had lost all the tan he'd acquired in the Gulf and now had an almost sickly pallor. He grinned at Linc as he slammed the door.

"Shit, that was quick," Linc said. "What'd they do?"

"Another shot of antibiotics," Rick said. "Just like when you catch the clap."

"You want to stop for coffee?" Linc asked.

Rick shook his head.

"Might as well get going then," Linc said, starting the truck. "Anyway, we got plenty of time. I told Uncle Henry we'd be a couple of hours. Sure didn't take you long."

Rick nodded quickly.

"I caught that same nurse I met last time and she got me in and out."

"How'd you manage that?" Linc asked with a grin. "You fucking her or something?"

"Better hope not. I wouldn't have been in and out so fast then, partner," he said. Rick leaned back and stretched out, putting his head against the back of the seat. Linc noticed that his buddy was still sweating profusely, just like when Linc had picked him up.

"You want me to turn down the heat?" Linc asked, reaching for the dash control, although it wasn't really hot in the truck.

"No, it's cold," Rick said. He closed his eyes and took a deep breath.

This boy's still sick, Linc thought. It was just another reason why the plan would probably never come together. He turned on to Roosevelt Road and headed east toward First Avenue and the Eisenhower. When they got to the expressway, he got on and headed east again, toward the Loop. Linc was amazed at the traffic coming west from downtown. Usually it was heavier going into the city this time of morning, but this looked like afternoon rush hour, and it was barely ten o'clock. He got off at Halsted and made his way up to Chicago Avenue, careful to stay off any of the boulevards with the truck. But as he drove toward Wabash, he couldn't believe what he was seeing. The whole street was teeming with cars, taxis, buses, and trucks. They were all heading for the expressway entrances. And there were cops everywhere directing traffic. People were crowding on buses. Big yellow

Streets and Sanitation trucks rumbled north on Canal Street. Cops directing traffic made quick, jerking gestures for drivers to get out of the way as fire engines worked their way through the traffic toward Michigan Avenue.

Linc looked at Rick, who'd opened his eyes and was also staring in disbelief.

"Would you look at this," Linc said. "Ain't this a trip?"

A cop on the corner of Wabash and Randolph waved for him to go west with the rest of the exodus. Linc rolled down the window as he crept through the intersection.

"What's going on, man?" he asked.

"Keep going," the cop yelled. "Head for the express-way."

"But we got a delivery to make," Linc said.

"Not today you don't," the cop yelled back. "The Loop's being evacuated. Now move it."

Linc fell into place with the rest of the traffic. He and Rick looked at each other.

"Maybe the Russians are coming," Rick offered.

"Naw, we's their asshole buddies now," Linc said. "Gonna put their whole country on general assistance."

As the traffic inched along, he turned on the radio, switched from WGCI to one of those AM all-news stations, and listened. The announcer was repeating the same message about every ten seconds or so: Due to an unexpected series of water-related emergencies, all business in the Loop was being canceled today. He went on to advise all commuters and drivers to stay clear of the downtown expressways because of major gridlock.

Linc tuned through the channels until he got one where two guys were just talking. One of them was asking the other guy questions about the cause of the emergency and how long it was expected to last.

"Well at this time we're unsure of the extent of the flooding," the guy being interviewed on the radio said. He sounded like some sort of city spokesman. "We have crews down at the river now, trying to assess the problem."

"What are they planning to do?" the interviewer asked.

"It's our plan at this time to try to plug the leak with sandbags; however, it's unknown exactly how long this will take, or even if it will be effective."

"And coming so close to the Easter shopping holiday, how badly will some of the downtown businesses be hurt?"

"I estimate it will hurt some, but I'm confident that the problem will be corrected shortly," the city official said, "and we'll be able to get back to normal business soon."

The radio reporter thanked him and then gave a quick summary update.

"Once again, many stores and offices in the downtown section of the Loop have been closed due to a water-related emergency. All persons are being asked to stay away from the area until further notice, and the police department has issued an emergency parking ban for the entire downtown area. Many buildings are without power, so if you don't have business down here, or even if you do, stay away."

"Looks like we gonna be late for work anyway," Linc said, inching the truck forward.

Rick looked over and saw a policeman by a squad car, hooking a leash onto his K-9.

"Yeah," he said. "But now at least we got an excuse."

Vino had been watching the squirrels chase after the peanuts he'd been throwing in his back yard, when Tommy Del Bianco opened the gate. Tommy was one of his lieutenants who'd worked his way up the ranks. A relatively young guy, he did what he was told and didn't ask questions. Vino liked that. He also liked the fact that Tommy wasn't the sharpest pencil in the box, because when somebody was too bright, then you had to start worrying about them.

"Mr. Costelli," Tommy said. "Bobby's back."

"Take him into the den," Vino said. "I'll be right in." He tossed a couple more peanuts toward the squirrels and watched them scurry. Then he turned and went up the back steps. Inside the house he stopped and sipped a spoonful of the sauce that his wife had left simmering on the stove. Not totally satisfied, he added a pinch more salt before going into the den. Bobby Mallory, Vino's number one surveillance man, was seated in front of the desk. Tommy stood off to one side.

Vino nodded to him as he walked in.

"Get us some coffee, Tommy," he said.

Tommy's dead-pan eyes showed no expression as he left the room. Vino sat behind the big mahogany desk and turned his attention to Mallory.

"So what you got for me, Bobby?" Vino asked.

Mallory flipped up the top of his little notepad and read off the following: "At seven o'clock he left his house in his white Lincoln and headed downtown. He arrived at—"

"Cut the shit," Vino said. "What I want to know is, what happened in court. Did he meet with the Feds?"

"Yes and no," Mallory said, starting to smile, then quickly losing the grin. "The court got canceled. All the court. The whole building's closed down. So is most of the Loop."

"Huh? How come?"

"There's some kind of flooding problem downtown," Mallory said. "It seems that there's a leak in the tunnel system over by the Kinzie Street Bridge—"

"I don't give a fuck about that," Vino said, cutting him off again. "Did he meet with the Feds?"

"Uh-huh," Mallory nodded, flipping through his notes.

"At the Italian Village Restaurant. They set this up through Fox's answering service. Met there at nine o'clock."

"So tell me what happened."

Mallory smiled.

"I can do better than that," he said. "The joint was so packed I got in the booth next to them. I taped the whole fucking conversation. Got a lot of background noise, but you can make out most of it." He reached in his pocket and took out a small recorder. After setting it on the desk, Mallory handed Vino the earplug and set the recorder up to play. Vino listened to the tape, his face hardening into a scowl the more he listened. Then suddenly, he jerked, like somebody'd pinched his gut. He punched the stop button and pulled out the earpiece.

"You listen to this?" Vino said, his voice soft, almost inaudible.

"Yeah," Mallory said.

"You think he was fucking with them?" Vino asked. He was starting to sweat. "About that tape?"

Mallory shrugged.

Vino pressed his fingers to his temples and closed his eyes. He took a deep breath and exhaled.

"Bobby, what's the name of that guy in New Orleans?" he said. "You know who I'm talking about? The one they call The Regulator."

"Germaine," Mallory said. "Vincent Phillip Germaine."

"Yeah," Vino said. "Go make some phone calls. I want him up here right away. And keep the tails on both of them. I wanna know if either of 'em even farts too loud."

"Okay, boss," Mallory said, and started to get up. Tommy walked in with two cups of coffee on a tray. Mallory sat back down and reached for one of the cups. Vino was around the desk in an instant, raking his right hand across the tray, scattering the cups over the carpet.

"I said go make them calls!" he screamed. "What the fuck's wrong with you?"

Mallory's mouth drew into a thin line and he was up and moving toward the door without a word. Vino turned his gaze on Tommy.

"Clean this shit up," he snarled. He stormed back to the desk and sat down again, putting his head between his palms. It felt like some big hand had closed over his balls and was just starting to squeeze.

Early Afternoon

When Linc and Rick finally got to the construction site, it was well after noon. They parked the truck and tried to hurry to the dig, but everybody had broken for lunch. Henry stood there, arms akimbo, looking down his nose from under his yellow hard hat, watching their approach. Linc smiled, but the expression on his uncle's face told him that there'd be hell to pay.

"And just where the fuck you two been?" Henry asked, making an exaggerated display of looking at his watch.

"Sorry," Linc said. "We got held up in traffic. The whole Loop's been shut down. It's just like rush hour."

"I don't give a shit about the motherfuckin' Loop," his uncle said. "We been running short-handed the whole morning on this dig 'cause I expected you two would be here sooner, rather than later."

"Sorry," Linc said. Rick echoed the sentiment and started to say it was all his fault, but Henry cut him off.

"No, it ain't *your* fault," he said. "It's mine." He gave them both a few more seconds of the evil eye, then said, "Everybody else is on lunch. You two get your asses down there and start laying pipe."

Linc and Rick both hustled over toward the big pit, its

sides reinforced with wooden planks. As they were getting their hard hats and equipment belts on, Henry ventured over toward them and asked softly, "You feel up to this, Rick?"

"I'm okay, Henry," Rick said. "Thanks."

Henry just nodded and walked over to his on-site trailer. He glared at the group of workers, who were still sitting around on the empty wooden cable spools, then stepped inside and closed the door. As soon as the door had swung shut, several of the men sauntered over to Linc and Rick. Booker Cole led the group. He was a huge black man, with the massive shoulders and arms of someone who'd spent his life doing laborer's construction work. When he wasn't in jail.

"Want some?" he asked Linc, holding out a brown bag with a bottle inside.

Linc shook his head. Cole didn't offer any to Rick.

"My uncle find out you drinkin' that shit around this heavy equipment—" Linc started to say.

"Your uncle ain't shit," Cole spat. "He know I do mo' fucking work than you and this honkey buddy of yours put together."

"You better watch what you be sayin'," Linc said.

"Why, you gonna do something about it, nigger?" Cole took another swig and stepped in closer. Linc just stared at him.

"See me after work, motherfucker," Linc said. "Then we see."

Cole spat on the ground close to Linc's boot, then backed up a step and smiled. He was missing a front tooth.

"After work you ain't gonna have ol' Uncle Henry to protect you," he said, doing his best "sissy imitation."

"Back off, man," Rick said. "You're outta line."

"Don't you even talk to me, you white motherfucker!" Cole said.

Rick started to move forward, but Linc put his hand on Rick's chest. Cole's lower lip thrust out as he drew back the hand with the bottle.

"Come on, nigger," he growled.

Linc smiled disarmingly and shook his head. Then his left lashed out, smashing into Cole's face. Linc stepped to the side and grabbed the bigger man's right arm, pulling it up and back, twisting the brown bag out of his hand. Cole stumbled backward, lurching to try and maintain his footing. He managed a roundhouse swing at Linc, who only had to move his head slightly to avoid the blow. Linc slapped Cole's face with a flicking left jab, then snapped a right hand over the top that sent him onto the seat of his pants.

"You want some more?" Linc asked.

Cole licked his lips with a bloody tongue, then shook his head.

"Good," Linc said.

"What the fuck's going on here?" Henry said, walking briskly over to the men. "Whose is this?" he asked, kicking the bottle in the bag lightly with his toe. Nobody spoke as Henry looked at each man in the group. His gaze centered on Cole, who was getting to his feet, dusting himself off.

"I tripped," Cole said.

"Like hell," Henry said. He looked at Cole, then back to Linc. "That right?"

Linc nodded.

"Then all you motherfuckers can get back to work," Henry boomed, walking back toward the trailer. "Lunchtime's over, as of now."

The men started gathering up their stuff. Rick pulled close to Linc and said, "I think that was a mistake. I don't trust that guy." He nodded at Cole. "He might make trouble for us later."

"Booker knows better now," Linc said, slipping on his helmet.

Henry bellowed out to him, "Phone call," and looked at his watch.

Linc bumped his shoulder into Cole's, but the larger man did nothing. Running to the trailer, Linc grabbed the cellular phone that his uncle had left sitting on the steps.

"Linc, it's me," Diane said.

"Yeah, baby, what's up?"

"We are," she said, her voice vibrant with excitement. "Have you heard what's happening downtown?"

"Yeah, we got caught up in the traffic."

"And they sent all of us home early. There's no power or alarms or phones or anything," she said, stressing the last few words.

"Nothing?" he said. "Because of the flood?"

"Yeah," she said. "The lower basement in the bank's filled with water. And you know what else?"

"What?"

"If there's no power, then there's no time lock. It won't re-set. And the battery back-up system's only good for twelve hours." The rapture in her tone was almost palpable. "It's just like a miracle for us, baby."

Oh. Lord, he thought. *Oh, Lord.*

After talking with Linc on the phone, Diane took the bus down to the Sportmart way down on Ninety-Fifth Street. She had the list that Linc and Rick had drawn up weeks ago when they first started planning it. All fun and games, like they never expected to actually get the chance to really do it. Like the punks who talk shit that they've had so many women; then, when they get their drawers off, they're really cherries.

The bus lurched as the driver slowed so he could pick up another chump. Diane watched him get on, fishing the exact change out of his pocket. Who did they think they were, demanding that you had to get exact change before they'd let you ride on their stinking bus? She held onto the metal pole, still standing because there were no seats, and none of those assholes sitting down could even spell "gentlemen," much less stand up and give her their seat.

Well, fuck this, she thought. Once they got the money, she'd never have to ride on the motherfucking bus again. Just settle on some island in the Caribbean and play the rich bitch. Everybody'd be calling *her* Lady Di then. The thought brought a smile to her face that lingered as she got off and went into the store. After grabbing a cart, she collared one of those walking salespeople and made him help her find everything on the list. Not that he seemed to mind. He was a young white guy, barely out of his teens, and kind of cute. He seemed taken with her, too. She'd never been with a white boy, unless you counted that fat, middle-aged motherfucker Fielding at the bank. But even that had been worth it to get her promotion to assistant of the vault department. Amazing what a couple blowjobs could do. But she was through with all that too, now. It was time to think of other things, like what she was going to do once she had all that money. If she got tired of Linc, there'd be time for lots of men. Whatever kind she wanted. But one thing she knew for sure. Once this thing was over, she'd never want for another thing in her life. Not ever.

"How many feet of this nylon rope you want, ma'am?" the sales kid asked her.

"Whatever it says on the list," Diane answered.

"It says three thousand feet. You sure you want that much?"

"If that's what it says," she said, thinking she'd probably have to take a cab home with this load of shit.

The kid scratched his head and began measuring it off.

"I'll see how much I got here. Might have to go in back. This for rappelling or something?" he asked.

"What?"

"I was just wondering what all this stuff was for," he said. "You got D-rings, lanterns, flashlights, and batteries on this list. You going mountain climbing or something?"

Diane smiled her prettiest smile before she answered. "Treasure hunting," she said. "We're going treasure hunting."

Chapter 5

Tuesday, April 14, 1992

12:35 A.M.

Linc lay naked on top of the covers next to Diane, who was curled against him, her fingers gently rubbing his chest. He reached up to the headboard and grabbed the remote, bringing the volume up slightly as Arsenio Hall made his last-minute quips about who'd be on tomorrow night's show. The re-broadcast of the ten o'clock news would be next and Linc wanted to be sure he caught it all.

He and Rick had driven downtown in Uncle Henry's pumper-truck, sort of half-assed hoping that something would happen to spoil things so they wouldn't really have to go all the way and break into the fucking place. Something happened, all right. There were motherfucking cops on every corner, walking big-ass police dogs around. They hadn't even gotten up to the place when one of the honkey cops directing traffic at a roadblock flagged them down and gave them the third-degree.

"What you guys doing down here?" the cop had asked, shining his flashlight into Linc's face.

"We're supposed to be doing some pumpin'," Linc said, pointing his thumb back toward the generator and pumping machinery in the back of Uncle Henry's truck.

"You got your work permit?" the cop asked.

"Didn't know we needed one," Linc said.

"Yeah. You gotta get that before I can let you through here."

A big Commonwealth Edison truck rumbled up to the roadblock and the cop waved it through. Linc and Rick looked at each other.

"Okay, officer," Linc said. "We'll go back to the boss and tell him he got to get his shit straight."

The cop grinned and stepped back.

"You do that," he said.

That was when they realized that they needed to fine-tune their plan.

The credits faded and they announced that the following was a re-broadcast of the ten o'clock news. Linc and Diane both sat up as Bill Kurtis and Linda MacClennan came on and began talking about the flood. After a quick explanation of what seemed to have caused it—some pylons were driven into the wrong place near the Kinzie Street Bridge, flooding the old freight tunnels under the city—the picture shifted to one of their reporters in the street. Against the backdrop of scenes that showed the chronology of the disaster, the reporter described how the Loop was virtually shut down by midmorning.

"That ain't no lie," Linc said.

Diane shushed him, shooting an angry glance his way before looking back at the TV. Linc frowned in silence as she perked up and fixed her eyes on the screen. She sure was acting strange since this flood thing. Like breaking into this fucking bank was the only thing that mattered anymore, badgering him every second about doing it. Christ, he wished she'd leave it alone for a while. He stared at her a moment more, before he, too, turned his attention back to the newscast.

"So can we expect things to return to normal anytime soon?" he heard Bill Kurtis ask the on-scene reporter.

"It looks really doubtful, Bill," the other guy said. The

camera focused on the Kinzie Street Bridge area, still all lit up with people swarming around it like busy hornets.

"There. See?" Linc said. "I told you they wasn't gonna get things straightened out anytime soon. Now will you just be cool."

She kept staring at the TV, shaking her head.

"I sure hope you're right," she said after awhile. "We ain't never gonna get another chance like this. I mean, it's all just so perfect." She turned and looked into his face, studying his eyes before she spoke again. "You are sure you and Rick will be able to do it, aren't you?"

"Quit worrying, baby," Linc said. "You're talking to the man who done whupped old Saddam Hussein's ass." He stretched his arms around her and rolled her on her back, then began kissing her neck. "The next time we make love," he said, his hand reaching down to spread her dark thighs, "we'll be doin' it on top of a million bucks."

11:46 A.M.

Tommy Del Bianco glanced up at the video flight monitor showing the arrival times of the various airlines into O'Hare. Delta 245 was due in from New Orleans at 11:40 at gate K-10 of Terminal Three. The little blinking light next to the flight number showed that it had already landed. Tommy extinguished his cigarette and went down the corridor toward the gates. He had to remove all his keys and coins before going through the metal detectors, and the fact that he wasn't packing his piece disturbed him. So did the fact that the boss had sent for this out-of-town asshole from Louisiana. What the hell, did the old man figure he couldn't handle it? He made up his mind as he strode down the long corridor that he wasn't going to take no shit off this guy, no matter if the boss had sent for him or not.

The Heist

What the fuck, he thought. This cracker's coming into *my* back yard to handle things, making it look like I don't know what I'm doing.

Christ, that was enough to piss off the Pope.

At the gate, people were already starting to come through the doorway from the plane. Most of them stretching and looking around for someone to meet them. Tommy stepped up and leaned both elbows against the information desk, then decided that this pose didn't look tough enough. Maybe he should be standing straight when this fucker walked off the plane. A tough Chicago guy. Yeah, that was it. He straightened up, slipped on his sunglasses, and pressed a cigarette between his lips.

"I'm sorry, sir, but there's no smoking in this area," some uniformed black broad said to him. Tommy turned and started to tell her that she could go fuck herself, then remembered that the boss had told him explicitly not to do anything that would call attention to himself or the visitors. Tommy just smiled and mumbled an apology, replacing the cigarette into his pack. Suddenly he heard a voice say: "At least y'all had the good manners not to say, 'What are you gonna do, arrest me for smokin'?' like that gal did in that *Basic Instinct* movie where she forgot her panties." The voice seemed to glide slowly over the vowels, like a man contemplating the weight of each syllable. Tommy glanced up and saw the owner of the voice moving toward him. The guy was about forty, but pretty fit-looking. He was somewhere around six feet, but his hair, which was completely white and slicked back into a pompadour, made him look taller. His suit was dark gray and he had on cowboy boots and one of those western-type string ties. The guy stuck out his right hand and Tommy shook it, suddenly aware of the power in the southerner's grip.

"Am I correct in assuming that y'all must be Mr. Del Bianco?" the man said.

"Yeah," Tommy said. "All of me is."

If the guy was pissed that Tommy had just made fun of the southern accent, he didn't show it. He just said, "I'm Vincent Phillip Germaine." After he finished shaking hands with Tommy, Germaine made this little half-step backwards and held out his other hand, palm-up. "And this is my good friend and associate, Mr. Queen."

Tommy looked past him and saw an enormous black guy in a dark brown suit with close-cropped haircut and a chest about the size of a refrigerator.

"Pleased to meet ya," Tommy said, extending his hand to show how he wasn't intimidated by some big nigger-helper. The black man just glanced down at Tommy's hand, then back up to his face, his eyes looking like two huge brown marbles in his dark face.

"Mr. Queen, or Gumbo as I like to call him, prefers to keep his hands free at all times," Germaine said with a smile as Tommy slowly let his outstretched hand drop.

"Yeah, right," Tommy answered. He turned and started walking back down the corridor. "You guys got luggage, follow me," he said over his shoulder.

After claiming two black suitcases on the lower level, Tommy led them over to the escalators. In front of the terminal they walked past the porters who eyed them expectantly, and Tommy flagged down a taxi. Germaine and Gumbo got in back. Tommy opened the front passenger's door and gave the driver his best sneer, just in case the fucker was thinking about saying something about him riding up front. The driver, some fat-faced white guy, kept his trap shut, except for asking them where they wanted to go. Tommy gave him the address. The cab eased into traffic and picked up speed as it crested the ramp leading to the expressway.

Germaine glanced out the window at the fading airport and the heavily industrialized scenery of the surrounding area.

"I always enjoy coming to your fair city, gentlemen," he said. "In many ways it reminds me of my home." His voice seemed to drip mint julep, and Tommy frowned to himself as he thought again how wrong the boss was for thinking that he needed these out-of-town clowns to handle things.

The cabbie took Irving Park Road to Harlem and fought traffic pretty well until arriving at their destination, a restaurant on Diversey. Tommy paid the fare and got out. He lit up a cigarette and looked around as the cabbie opened the trunk for the luggage. When the cab had taken off, Tommy pointed to a dark blue Lincoln Town Car with tinted windows in the rear, parked near the doors to the restaurant. The men moved toward it, and Tommy fished out the keys and hit the alarm-deactivation button. He went to the driver's side and said, after taking a drag on his cigarette, "It's open."

Germaine slipped into the rear seat and Gumbo managed to squeeze his body into the back too. He put both shoulder bags on the front seat next to Tommy, then situated himself off to the right so the view in the rearview mirror wouldn't be blocked. Tommy went south on Harlem until he got to Grand Avenue, then turned west. Who did these fuckers think they were, sitting in back and treating him like some kind of flunky, he thought as he drove, periodically glancing in the mirrors to make sure no one was following them. Occasionally he would catch sight of the big man in the back seat. Germaine continued to rattle on.

"As I mentioned before, I always enjoy coming to this city," he said. "There's so much history here. The first atomic bomb, Al Capone, the Untouchables, the Democratic National Convention of sixty-eight . . . Of course you look a might young to remember that one."

Tommy smirked. Maybe he'd get a chance to show this shit-kicker some real moves before this whole thing was finished. He swung the Lincoln into the driveway of a factory and jerked to a stop. A uniformed security guard peered out the window of the gate shack as Tommy lowered the driver's side window. The guard nodded and went out to open the gate, which was a cyclone-fence mounted on heavy metal hinges that swung inward. Three strands of barbed wire ran along the top of the fence all the way around. A brick building was set perhaps fifty feet away, across an asphalt parking lot. The building had windows along the front side, but they were covered with metal grates and their surfaces showed the reflective mirror-like finish of one-way glass. Tommy drove up to a foyer that had an expansive overhang. The sign on the front of the building said Franklin Meat Packing. Tommy got out and went to the front doors. Germaine and Gumbo trailed behind him.

Inside, the foyer section was set up like a waiting room. Several offices were visible beyond a long, cubicle-like station. A uniformed female security guard, a pretty redhead, sat behind the desk watching them come in. She smiled as they entered and said that Mr. Costelli was waiting for them. Tommy grinned and gave a little wave for Germaine to follow him. He started down the hallway to the left that led to the offices. At the end of the hall he stopped and knocked on the frosted glass of the door. A voice made a garbled sound from inside and Tommy twisted the knob and went in. Germaine and Gumbo followed.

Salvatore "Vino" Costelli was inside leaning over in the middle of the room, a golf putter in his hands. Spread out before him were several white balls and one of those portable holes for putting practice. He tapped the ball by his feet and watched it roll across the green carpeting toward the hole, then twist off to the side at the last second. Vino straightened and looked over at the men who'd entered.

"Any problems?" he asked.

Tommy shook his head.

"You change cabs like I told ya?" Vino asked.

"No, but I checked, boss," Tommy said quickly. "Nobody was behind us."

Vino's face flushed darker for a moment and he reached forward and slapped Tommy's face. Then he jerked back, his forehead and neck reddening, to match the bright blotch on his cheek.

"*Chooch!*" Vino said. "Next time do it like I fuckin' tell ya. You think we're dealing with fuckin' amateurs? These Feds smell blood, they pull out all the stops." He turned and flung the putter across the room, watching it crash into the wall; then he stripped off his golf gloves. "Go out and help Gloria watch the cameras, for Christ's sake." He waited until Tommy left the room before turning to the big white-haired man who'd been standing there with his hands in the pockets of his suit jacket the whole time. "You Germaine?"

"Vincent Phillip Germaine at your service, sir," he said, moving forward, extending his hand. Vino grasped it. "This is my friend and associate Mr. Queen," Germaine added, cocking his head toward Gumbo. Vino just nodded. The black man did the same, but made no move to go toward him, which was all right with Vino, who wasn't about to shake hands with no shine.

"Mr. Moretti told me you had a rather pressing problem that needed our immediate attention," Germaine said.

"Yeah, yeah," Vino said, moving around behind his desk

and taking out a cigar. He offered one to Germaine, who took one, and to Gumbo, who only shook his head slightly.

"Moretti speaks real highly of you. I heard they call you 'The Regulator,' " Vino said, sitting in the big leather chair and lighting his cigar.

Germaine, who'd been smelling his cigar with an expression of delight, smiled as he took out a gold butane lighter.

"A little title bestowed upon me for my considerable efforts to handle any problem with the utmost efficiency." He flicked the lighter and twirled the cigar end in the flame. "Ahh, an excellent blend of tobacco, sir, for which I thank you." He blew out a prodigious cloud of smoke, then sat back in the chair in front of the desk and grinned congenially. "Now, Mr. Costelli, why don't we get down to brass tacks, as they say?"

Vino considered this, pursed up his lips, and began.

"I got this lieutenant in my organization," he said. "The guy's been like a brother to me. We came up through the ranks together. His name's Johnny Osmand, but we always called him the Mink, cause of his hair." He paused to draw on the cigar, then shook his head slowly before he went on. "He's under indictment. The Feds. Now I got it from a good source that he's getting ready to flip."

"And you wish for him not to do that?" Germaine said sympathetically.

"I wish I had the motherfucker's balls in my hand right now," Vino said, raising his hand up and clenching it into a quick fist. He held the fist in front of him for a moment, then dropped it. "But it ain't that simple."

Germaine raised his eyebrows.

"He's got something on me," Vino said. "Something I need to recover, before I can do anything."

"And what is this item?" the southerner asked.

Vino looked down and scratched his forehead.

"It's a videotape," he said. "You know, one of those cassettes from a VCR."

"I see," Germaine said. "Well, I will need to find out more about Mr. Osmand, as well as the services of two or three of your best men, a car, and some other sundries."

"Yeah, whatever you need, you just tell Tommy," Vino said. "There's just one other thing."

Germaine looked at him attentively.

Vino leaned forward and spoke in a guttural snarl: "I wanta *nail* the motherfucker myself. Right here."

1:30 P.M.

Tony punched out the familiar rhythm on the speed bag with rote skill. It gave him immense pleasure that, after all these years, he could still keep a pretty decent beat going. Not like his Navy days, but what the hell, that'd been some time ago. So what if he'd lost maybe half-a-step. He glanced at the wall timer and saw that he had about ten seconds left, so he went from double strikes to single ones, increasing the speed of the bounce-back. When the buzzer sounded, he let his arms fall and stepped back.

"Lookin' good, Tony," a voice said from behind him. It was Nate Wells, one of the guys from Gang Crimes South. Nate was in his early thirties, as tall as Tony, and with a body that looked like carved ebony. He held up his open palm and he and Tony exchanged a high-five. "Mind if I work in?"

Tony grinned and shook his head. Nate began pulling on his bag gloves, the muscles in his dark forearms standing out like steel cables.

"Haven't seen you in a while," Nate said. "Was wondering if you'd pulled the pin, or something."

"Nope, not till September, anyway," Tony said. "Then I'll have to."

"Well, even LeRoy had to leave when his number came up," Nate said, referring to LeRoy Martin, the Police Superintendent who'd recently stepped down after reaching mandatory retirement age. "But you look good. Been comin' here regular?"

"Yeah," Tony said. "Me and my partner usually come in the afternoons. After court."

"You still in Organized Crime?"

"Uh-huh. How about you? Gang Crimes?"

"Yep, workin' the Roseland area now," Nate said. "Shit, it's getting real bad. Fuckin' gangbangers getting to be just like the new Mafiosi."

Tony thought about saying that he could remember when the Roseland neighborhood was one of the jewels of the South Side, but didn't want Nate to take it the wrong way because the area was predominantly black now. Instead, Tony moved over to the heavy bag and began working jabs and hooks into it. Nate, in the meantime, had begun pounding on the speed bag, his dark arms working like pistons, flashing so fast they were only a blur. Tony thought of his own recent performance on that apparatus and suddenly realized that he'd lost more than just half-a-step. Maybe it *was* time for him to step down. Let the younger guys take over the long fight. He smacked a double jab into the bag, then followed up with a right cross, left hook combination. Then another left hook, with everything behind it. Just like the one that had broken Vino Costelli's jaw so many years ago. No, goddamnit, he'd finish it. Take Vino out before he stepped down. It was something he had to do. The timer showed twenty seconds left, so he moved in close, set his legs, and worked a flurry of body punches to the heavy canvas surface. When he finished, he stepped back and saw Nate staring at him.

"Shit, man, you really tearing into that motherfucker, whoever he is." A broad grin spread over Nate's face. "Anybody in particular?"

"Vino Costelli," Tony gasped out.

"The ol' Godfather himself, huh? Got him in your sights yet?"

"Maybe," Tony said, still out of breath. "Got one of his made-men ready to flip."

Nate nodded approvingly.

"That's the only way," he said. "Got me a snitch working both sides of the fence too. Used to be in with the gangs real tight. Did some time, now he's out. Convicted burglar on probation. Got caught shoplifting some Jack Daniel's. He got him a little drinkin' problem. So I been squeezing him to keep me posted on the activities of the local shitheads."

Tony's beeper went off, and he stripped off the bag gloves and pressed the acknowledge button. It was Arlene's private line. He tapped Nate's right glove and went into the locker room to the pay phone. Fishing a quarter out of the pocket of his sweatpants, he dropped it in and dialed.

She answered on the first ring.

"Arlene, it's Tony. What's up?" He strained to hear over the raucous conversations of the other men.

"Hi. Where are you? Sounds like you're in a bar or something."

"No, Ray and I been going over to the old Police Armory Building to work out every afternoon. Usually we stop on the way home, but since everything got canceled today, we came early."

"Wow," she said, the admiration evident in her voice.

"That's what I should be doing. I'm gaining so much weight sitting around all day."

"Naw, you look great," he said, forming a mental picture of her. He paused.

"Well, I just wanted to tell you that Fred's okayed the deal for Osmand," she said. "It's just a matter of working out all the formalities and waiting for things to get functioning at the Dirksen Building. Isn't this flood thing unreal?" She punctuated the question with a giggle.

Tony thought of how her laughter sounded like musical chimes. So much like Mary's used to.

"Any idea as to when that may be?" he asked.

"They're hopeful that they can get the elevators working by Wednesday or Thursday," she said. "The first floor, basement, and parking area aren't going to be in full service until they can plug the leak, but they said that things on the upper floors should be operational. This is the first time I can ever remember the city being shut down like this."

Tony could remember other times. During the riots of the sixties. He shuddered at the memory and hoped he'd never have to go through another one of those.

"So all I have to do is get ahold of Reggie and work out the details," Arlene said.

"Not by yourself, I hope," Tony said.

"Oh gosh, no," she said. "If they want to meet, I can always call you or Kent."

A fat lot of good that idiot would be, Tony thought. But he said, "You're going to keep me posted, right?"

"Of course I will," she said. Her voice seemed to soften and she said something else, but it was rendered indistinguishable by the intrusion of the computerized operator's voice: "Five cents more, please." Tony fished in his pocket for more change, but came up empty.

"Arlene I couldn't hear you," he said quickly. "I'm out of change."

"I said—" Her voice was cut off again by the automated: "Please deposit five cents for the past one minute."

He could hear Arlene's laugh again, then she quickly said, "Tony, I'll talk to you later. Don't worry."

The connection was broken and as he hung up, he wondered what it was she'd said. He sighed, and headed back out to the gym area. Ray was in the ring sparring with one of the guys from the raid team. The guy was probably close to a half-a-foot taller than Ray and had a big, rangy build. He was trying to keep Ray off by using a piston-like jab, but the little Italian was adept at slipping under it, cutting off the ring, and punishing the bigger man with sharp body blows. They made a thwacking sound each time one connected. Tony winced, knowing the power in Ray's short, swift punches. He walked over to the edge of the apron and watched. Ray ducked inside again and pummeled his taller opponent with a flurry just as the round bell rang. They paused and slapped gloves. The big guy spit his mouthpiece out and said he had to go. Tony smiled up at his partner as the other man bent, with considerable effort, to step through the ropes. Ray moved to the corner right above Tony and rested his arms on the bands of the turnbuckle.

"That was quite a performance," Tony said, grinning.

"Shit," Ray sputtered. He spit out his mouthpiece and held it in his sixteen-ounce glove. "How about holding the focus pads for me?"

"Sure." Tony grabbed the two flat pads out of Ray's ditty bag on the table next to the ring, and went up the three steps. His partner stepped on the bottom strand of rope to lower it a little. While Tony was working his hands into the focus mitts, Ray squatted, reaching through the ropes to toss his mouthpiece down onto the bag. He stood up, glanced at the ring timer which was coming up on the ten-second warning, and nodded at Tony. "Ready?" he asked. Tony slapped the pads together and began dancing backwards toward the center of the ring. Ray followed him and worked his jab into the extended pad.

"So who beeped you?" he grunted.

"Arlene."

"Oh," he sent another jab at the pad. "No wonder you ran outta here so fast. Quickest I seen you move all day."

When Tony said nothing, Ray grinned wolfishly and worked a three-punch combination.

"So what did she want?" Ray asked.

"Looks like the Mink's gonna go for the deal. Foreman's okayed it. Soon as things get back to normal, we'll probably work out the details. The way I figure it, they'll probably want to keep it a secret and convene a special grand jury so we can get the indictments, then grab Vino's ass before he gets wise and takes off."

Ray paused and crossed his hands in front of his waist, signaling Tony to do the same so Ray could simulate body punches. Tony crisscrossed the pads and Ray pelted them.

"So is that all?" he asked. "She say anything else?"

"Nothing important," Tony said. "Why?"

"I was just wondering if she wanted to jump your bones or anything."

Tony pursed his lips. "You oughta consider keeping that mouthpiece in when you do this. You're wasting too much energy flapping your jaws."

"Well, did she?"

"Will you knock it off," Tony said somewhat petulantly. "She's young enough to be my daughter, for Christsakes."

"No she's not," Ray said, then flashed the wolfish grin

again. "She's young enough to be your *granddaughter*." He leaned back and Tony swept the focus pad in an arc at Ray's head, allowing him to duck back to slip, then bore in with a counter-combination. Ray seemed to sense that Tony had been stung by that last remark, and tried to soften it slightly. "If you were from the projects, that is. You know, if you woulda had a kid when you were twelve or thirteen, or something."

Tony showed no reaction to the wisecrack.

"Hey, Tony, I was just kiddin'," he said, pausing to drop his hands. "Okay?"

"No, it's not okay," Tony said. "You drop your hands like that in the ring again, even an old man like me will drop you."

Ray instantly put up his hands and bore in, throwing quick, short punches at the pads.

"Maybe you ought to ask her out," he said. "No kiddin'. Really. Age doesn't mean shit nowadays."

"It does to me," Tony said. "Besides, she's got the hots for Faulkner."

"That wimp," Ray snorted. He threw two more punches as if to punctuate his statement. "You're twice the man that fucker is."

Tony held one of the pads up flat so that Ray could work the uppercut. He moved in and belted the pad toward the ceiling.

"Watch it when you do that," Tony said. "You're steppin' in to throw it. That leaves you open for a counter right."

Ray nodded, threw a couple of jabs, then moved to the side.

"Maybe if I can get into good enough shape, I'll enter the Police Olympics," Ray said. "Have to lose about ten pounds to get back down to middleweight."

Tony glanced at the clock, saw there were only about fifteen seconds left, and held up each of the pads. Ray, knowing this meant that it was the end of the round, began to alternate punches as fast as he could for the entire time, until the bell rang. Then he dropped his hands and grinned.

"Got a good one that time," he said. "Thanks, Tony."

Tony nodded, resting his arms on top of the ropes. Ray came over next to him.

"Say, partner," he said. "You ain't pissed off at me for kidding around a little, are you?"

"A little of your kidding goes a long way," Tony said.

Ray considered this, then said, "What I was getting at was being lonely. I know Arlene likes you, and what I meant was that it ain't no big deal nowadays, if a guy your age wants to—"

"Can it, would ya?"

"Yeah, I will," Ray said, drooping one of the oversized gloves over Tony's shoulder. "But when all is said and done, don't say I didn't try to tell you."

Tony heaved a sigh.

"In fact," Ray said, "I'm just gonna say one more thing."

"Only one more? Are you sure? Let me call the Guinness Book of Records."

Ray smirked.

"Like I said. I'm only gonna say this once." He glanced at Tony and his face seemed to take on a look of seriousness. "Maybe you ought to consider getting yourself a dog." The infectious grin spread over his face again.

"What do I need a dog for?" Tony asked. "You keep giving me all the shit I can handle."

Ray laughed and leaned over the ropes next to his partner.

"Well," he said. "Once the Mink flips and we get that special grand jury indictment, we'll be looking at putting Vino away by the end of the summer. Then the only thing we'll have to worry about is planning the best damn retirement party in the history of the department for you."

"I hope," Tony said with a sigh.

"Whaddya mean, you hope?" Ray said. "It's practically a done deal now. All over but the crying for Vino, only he don't know it yet. The Mink's gonna flip; all we got to do is keep him on ice till he testifies, and the Feds'll do that. What could go wrong now?"

Tony shrugged.

"You know what Yogi Berra used to say," he said. "It ain't over till it's over."

3:00 P.M.

Reginald D. Fox finished packing his heavy leather brief-case and leaned forward, placing his fingers and thumbs on the desktop. Had he forgotten anything? He hadn't, he decided, and flipped the case shut. As he slipped on his over-coat, he glanced at his Rolex. Three o'clock. It would feel good to get out of here early for a change. Maybe he could even beat the rush-hour traffic if he got to his car soon enough. Then he remembered: the Loop was still shut down. There really wasn't any rush hour to speak of. His office building, in the North Loop, was one of the few that was open. He could afford a leisurely walk to the parking garage. All he had to be concerned with was which of his girlfriends he would take to dinner. He didn't even have any pressing court cases tomorrow. Just an appearance in Bridgeview on a DUI case and a minor drug case in Markham. He pressed the intercom and spoke to his secretary.

"Tina, I'm going for the day."

"Okay, Mr. Fox," the box answered back. "Do you have anything else for me after I finish these briefs?"

Fox picked up his briefcase in one hand and pocketed his

portable phone with the other. It was a small gray model that folded together to conveniently fit into a coat pocket. He moved to the door of his office and opened it before he answered her.

"No, but if you're free tonight I'll take you to dinner," Fox said in a heavy whisper as he moved through the doorway. Tina blushed slightly. She was an attractive strawberry blonde in her late twenties. When she'd been hired, Mr. Leopold had told her that it was strictly against the rules to date any of the partners. But that hadn't stopped Fox from hitting on her.

"Uhhm, why don't you call me later?" she said coyly. He could tell she was giving him her most promising smile.

"I just may do that," Fox said as he moved through the reception room and toward the foyer. If I can't get ahold of anyone better, he thought.

Fox let the heavy frosted glass door slide closed behind him and walked jauntily down the marble hall toward the elevators. This flood hadn't turned out to be such an inconvenience after all. He'd been able to stretch out the Osmand deal with the Feds, because they couldn't finalize anything until they had things running at the Dirksen Building. That way, at least, he could soak the Mink for a few more days of legal representation. The Gee would probably end up picking up the tab, once the old fart turned Government Witness. They'd have to, because they'd have to hide him, that was for sure. And the beauty of it was that the bad boys couldn't do squat to him, because they knew that anything Osmand had told him was protected by lawyer-client confidentiality. He might even end up getting to represent the big man himself. But that might not be such a good idea, either. These gangster types scared him a little. He reached out and pressed the down button.

The Heist

As he waited for the elevator, another man came out of the washroom at the end of the hall. The door was always kept locked for security reasons. The man let the solid wooden door swing shut behind him and moved toward the elevators.

Must have his own key, thought Fox. The man, who was an innocuous-looking, overweight guy in his fifties, sauntered up beside him and pressed the down button again. The guy smiled at Fox, then turned his attention to his newspaper. The metal doors slid open and both men got in. Fox pressed the button for the lobby; the other man glanced at this approvingly, and returned to his paper. Fox felt the drop of the elevator and debated whether or not to give Tina the treat of going to dinner before he screwed her. When the elevator opened, Fox got out and went straight through the revolving doors and onto the street. It was cool for April, but at least it hadn't rained. He strolled toward the parking garage, noticing that the man who had descended with him in the elevator was now pressing the digits of a cellular phone as he trailed along in the same direction as Fox.

Fox frowned as he walked by the booth in which the attendant sat, slumped over a *Penthouse* magazine. Probably his big thrill for the day, Fox thought. A fat lot of good *he's* going to do to keep out the riffraff who want to break into cars. Fox was glad that he had an alarm on his Jaguar, but would an asshole like that even take the time to call the police if he did hear anything? Not that they'd break their asses getting there anyway, with all the other stuff going on in this city. It was getting to be just like a war zone.

He got to his silver XJ-6 and, taking out his keys, pressed the alarm deactivation button. He was just getting in between the cars when a black van pulled down the aisle and stopped in back of his car. Fox could see that the driver was a huge black guy with an enormous Afro. The passenger's door opened and a white guy with prematurely gray hair got out.

"Excuse me," the white guy said, "but are y'all leaving?"

"Yeah," Fox said, setting his briefcase onto the passenger seat. "Be out in a second."

"Looks like you got a scratch here," the guy said, pointing to the left rear fender. His voice had a southern twang to it. "Maybe we shouldn't park here after all. Might not be safe."

"What?" Fox said, his brow furrowing angrily. If there was a scratch he was going to have that fat asshole of a parking attendant's job. He went back to look. "Where?" he asked bending over. "I don't see anything."

"Do you see this?" the man asked. Fox heard a snapping electric sound and felt something sting him in the ass. His whole body jerked and went limp. It wasn't that he was unconscious, just limp. Like when his foot fell asleep and he couldn't move it. Kind of tingling. But this was his whole body. Fox tried to speak, but it came out garbled. He saw something in the man's hand move toward him again. He was holding something black. It zapped and a bluish crackle appeared between two electrodes. Then Fox felt himself being lifted and carried toward the van. The side door opened and the black guy tossed him onto the floor of the van like a sack of potatoes. Another figure got out of the van, stepping over him gingerly, and Fox heard the door slam shut. The floor was hard metal and had no carpeting.

All at once the white guy who'd zapped him was lifting a tarp and Fox was enveloped in darkness. Dust seeped into his mouth and nose, but he was still too disoriented to even cough or sneeze. He felt the van moving and tried to scream, but only a gurgling sound came out. The van stopped and Fox heard muffled voices; then the vehicle started moving again. Slowly he flexed his fingers, then his arms. They felt prickly, but he could move. Just then the tarp was pulled off his upper body and he looked up at the man sitting on the fender well. He wasn't holding a stun gun now. He was holding a large caliber snubnosed revolver. The guy was wearing a brown suit and his whitish hair was slicked back away from his face. He spoke in the same slow, southern drawl.

"The sensation should be returning to your arms and legs now, so I just wanted you to be forewarned not to try anything . . . dumb." He paused before the last word, as if to emphasize it. "Or instead of another six-thousand volts, you'll get a little taste of this." He brandished the chrome-colored weapon briefly, then pointed it back at Fox. In his other hand the guy held a cellular phone, into which he punched a number. The man smiled beatifically as he placed the phone to his ear. "Yeah, mission accomplished on this end, Bobby," he said. "I assume you got the car out with no problem?" Then nodding, he said, "Very good. Proceed to the rendezvous point." When he terminated the call, he smiled down at Fox.

"Mighty nice automobile, those Jaguars," he said. "I myself prefer to buy American, however."

"Is that what this whole thing's about?" Fox managed to say. "This is one of those car-jackings? Christ, you can have it, just let me go."

The man's mouth twisted up at the ends into what passed for a lips-only smile, and he said, "A car-jacking? You know, I've heard about those, too. But this . . ." he paused again, "is not really a car-jacking, *per se*. It's more of a lawyer-jacking, wouldn't y'all say so?"

Fox heard some heavy chuckling from the front of the van and swiveled his head. It was the big black son-of-a-bitch he'd seen before, only now his head was practically shaved, and a huge Afro wig lay on the floor next to the driver's seat.

Oh, my God, Fox thought. *Oh, my God.*

11:36 P.M.

"What if it's the same cop as last night?" Rick asked, staring ahead at the empty streets. The checkpoint was only about three blocks away now.

"Last night we went to the one at Randolph and Canal," Linc said. "This one's at Canal and Jackson. That's five blocks."

"Yeah, but suppose the guy switched checkpoints or something," Rick said nervously. "Suppose somehow he sees us."

Linc bit his lower lip, then forced a smile.

"You know what the chances are for that?" he said. "Slim and none, and slim left town."

Rick was silent for a moment. "You know this is crazy, don't you?" he said. "We can still call it off at this point. I mean, the stuff we've done up till now, it's all just bullshit. But if we go up there and get caught . . ."

Linc was disturbed to see Rick this shaken. What the fuck was wrong with him, anyway? But he did have some doubts of his own, too. When they'd planned everything, it had seemed almost like a game. Just for fun. But he knew how fast things could get real.

"If we can't get through, we can't get through," Linc said, kind of hoping that maybe they wouldn't be allowed in again, and he'd at least have an excuse to tell Diane why they couldn't get it done. "Then we just turn our asses around and head for home."

They could see the flashing lights of the checkpoint ahead of them now. Out of the corner of his eye, Linc caught the purple and black glow of a Dunkin' Donuts sign and braked suddenly.

"What's wrong?" Rick asked.

"Got me an idea," Linc said, turning toward him with a grin. "You know what they say about cops and donuts."

The pickup slowed to a stop as the cop flashed his Kel-light at them. He was a middle-aged white guy, sort of thick around the middle. Behind him the lights of his blue-and-white oscillated slowly. The squad car had been parked diagonally in the middle of the intersection, effectively challenging all northbound and eastbound traffic trying to enter the Loop area. As the cop walked over to the truck, Linc saw him shivering from the chill in the spring air. Rolling down the window, Linc gave him his most ingratiating smile.

"Sure is a piss poor night to be out workin', ain't it?" he said.

The cop nodded.

"Com Ed," Linc said, ducking his head to show the yellow hard hat that they'd taken from the Commonwealth Edison truck that they'd broken into earlier. At the same time Rick pointed to the emblem on the bright yellow coveralls they'd also taken from the truck. "We got sent on a coffee run," Linc said. "In fact," he reached into the Dunkin' Donuts bag on the seat between him and Rick, "How you like yours, officer?"

The cop looked at him for a moment, then shined the flashlight onto the side of the door where they'd taped the black-C-overlapping-the-red-E emblem that they'd razor-bladed off the real Com Ed truck.

"Cream and sugar," he said.

"You's in luck," Linc said, grinning broadly. He held up a hot paper cup, with an apple-cinnamon donut on top, the steam curling up from the hole. The cop reached over and took it, muttering a thank-you.

"Don't mention it," Linc said. "Compliments of Commonwealth Edison, working for you." He pointed his index finger at the officer, who, taking a bite out of the donut, waved them through. Linc glanced in the sideview mirror as they drove forward, then looked over to Rick. The grin on his face was as expansive as Linc's own.

"See, what'd I tell you," Linc said. He patted the side door of the truck. "If the rest of this thing goes as smooth as that, we'll be done before that dumb motherfucker's coffee gets cold."

Chapter 6

Tuesday, April 14, 1992

11:55 P.M.

Once they got past the checkpoint they were amazed at how deserted the city streets were. No traffic, but lots and lots of cops. Squad cars prowling around, flashing lights at everything that moved. One spotlight beam shot out and swept over the truck, but vanished as soon as it hit the Com Ed emblem.

"Pretty smart idea I had, huh?" Linc said with a grin. He glanced over at Rick to see how his partner was holding up. Rick's face looked taut in the semi-darkness, his lips drawn into a tight line. He'd had the same look just before the balloon went up and the ground war started in Kuwait. But that had turned out to be a piece of cake. A fucking turkey shoot. Virtually no resistance. Hopefully, this would go just as smoothly. As they approached the intersection of Dearborn and Adams, there was another checkpoint. Beyond it the huge buildings reposed in an eerie twilight, back-lit by the lights along Michigan and farther down in the North Loop area. The cop from this checkpoint got halfway out of the car, shined his flashlight over them, then got back in his squad car, motioning them through the intersection with a quick wave.

"Good thing," said Rick. "We're out of coffee."

Linc smiled. It was good to hear him joke. He shot another

glance Rick's way, making sure his friend wasn't taking sick again. His face was glistening with sweat, but, hell, so was Linc's. No, Rick looked all right. Those antibiotics that they'd given him must have done the trick. Linc cut down to Washington and passed through another police checkpoint without incident, this cop not even making an attempt at getting out of his car. They must have been depending on the outer perimeter to screen most of the incoming vehicles. Sloppy, but understandable. After all, it was the second day of this and they were probably dead-tired. Or maybe they were running the license plates of all the cars coming in, which was also cool, since they'd removed the truck's regular plates, belonging to Uncle Henry, and put on the plates they'd taken off the Commonwealth Edison truck they'd raided. Uncle Henry's truck was an off-white color, and, with the stolen emblems, looked just like the real thing.

Linc drove toward the lights of Michigan Avenue, directly to the east of them. All along the curbs oversized hoses sprayed steady streams of water into the gutters. The night hummed with the percussive dissonance of the sputtering portable generators and pumping machines. Linc cut into the wide mouth of the alley that ran behind the row of buildings. As the truck splashed through a large puddle of standing water, he cut off the lights and coasted up to the building adjacent to the bank. The maze of heavy metal Dumpsters and garbage cans formed various caverns. Linc pulled the truck up so it was under the fire escape that crept up the back of the structure like a metal vine. He shut the engine off and put some pilfered papers along the dashboard to cover the VIN, just in case some enterprising cop managed enough gumption to get out of his squad car and run a check on it.

"You think I should leave the flashers on?" he asked Rick.

"Let's wait. I'll turn 'em on when I get back down. No sense drawing attention to ourselves right off the bat."

Linc nodded in agreement. Why not play it that way: cautious on the way up, then nice and ballsy. If they immersed themselves in the role, they'd seem less suspicious if they were stopped. They put the yellow hard hats on the seat and slipped on the black stocking caps that could be rolled down to completely cover their faces, except for their eyes. Rick opened the door on his side and got partially out of the truck. He shone his flashlight up at the dangling black stairway of the fire escape. It was suspended by heavy metal springs at least twenty feet off the ground. Another latch, which was held in place by a pin, added further support. Rick got back in the cab and licked his lips. Linc looked over at him expectantly.

"Like I said before, it still ain't too late to call this whole crazy fucking thing off," Rick said.

"You bailing on me?" Linc asked.

Rick's gaze fell momentarily, then he looked back at Linc.

"Just wondering if it's right, that's all."

"Right?" Linc said emphatically. "Is it right that they recruited us, trained us, sent us off to the wars, then, once all the shit's done with, told us they don't need us no more?"

Rick said nothing. Linc went on.

"Look, man, the beauty of it is, we ain't really rippin' nobody off here."

"No?" Rick smirked.

"No. We just collectin' on a debt that's owed us. The money's dirty. Drug money. Mob money. Belongs to us just as much as anybody else. And if we don't take it, the government will, if they find it." Linc looked up and down the alley. "If not them, then some Mafioso will end up with it. We put ourselves on the line so many times, and look how they treated us. It's time we done something for ourselves. For you and me, bro. Use all that training to set us up for life."

Rick was silent for a moment more, staring down at the ground. Then he looked upward.

"You'll have to boost me up," he said. "It looks pretty high."

Linc grinned.

They rolled the windows of the truck down and used the doorframes to step onto the roof of the truck. The metal popped and groaned, denting under their combined weight. Linc did a semi-squat and bent over.

"We gonna owe Uncle Henry a new roof," he muttered.

"We get outta this one we'll buy him a new truck," Rick said, climbing onto Linc's back. He looped his legs over Linc's shoulders, and Linc straightened up, cautious not so much because of the added weight, but to maintain his balance. Rick again shone his flashlight up toward the metal arm. It was still about three feet above him.

"Gonna need something to reach it," he said.

Linc slowly squatted again, allowing Rick to slip off him. Rick jumped down into the open bed of the truck and fished around for the rope and grappling hook. Once he had them, he joined Linc on the cab's roof again and straightened out the line. When it was untangled, he took the grappling hook in his right hand and, after a furtive glance around, gave it an underhand toss. It hit the metal rods with a clank and bounced down toward the truck. The sound echoed in the darkness of the alley. They both crouched instinctively and surveyed the area. Nothing moved. Rick re-coiled the line.

"Want me to throw it?" Linc asked.

"Huh-uh," Rick said. "The first one never counts, anyway, remember?"

Linc smiled. That had been what Rick had said to him

while they both sat shivering under the blankets at the port that night in Israel. Right after Rick had saved his life, then gone back to pull another two GIs out of the cold, dark water as the capsized ferry began to go down. Linc had asked him why he'd taken the chance to go back again and again with all the confusion and danger in the water. "I had to," the shivering white boy had told him with a grin. "The first one never counts."

Rick gave the hook another looping toss. This time it caught with a metallic clank. Rick pulled the line taut, glanced around again, then nodded. Linc bent and squatted once more. Rick mounted him and this time, using the rope for balance, kept climbing up onto Linc's broad shoulders until he was standing on them.

"It's just another foot, or so," Rick said in a hoarse whisper. "Can you manage it?"

"Does a bear shit in the woods?" Linc grunted, grabbing one of Rick's feet in each of his powerful hands. Linc braced himself, then lifted, pushing Rick upward as he went hand-over-hand up the thin line. The truck roof made another series of groaning protestations, and Linc started to feel the strain of the lift in his back. Then suddenly the weight disappeared as Rick was able to grab the lower rungs of the fire escape. Linc swayed at the sudden loss of weight and tumbled backwards in the bed of the truck. He landed hard on the pumping equipment, while Rick swung in mid-air. Linc watched him kick his legs to give himself that last bit of manufactured thrust. Doing sort of a modified pull-up, he managed to lever his upper body onto the edge of the bottom of the iron platform.

"I'm there," he whispered. "You okay?"

"Yeah," Linc said, getting back onto the roof. He snatched his big knapsack and strapped it on his back as Rick removed the pin that permitted the hinged iron stairway to descend. The rusty metal made the most noise so far, sounding almost like a siren's wail in the dark serenity. But with all the noise on the streets from the pumps and generators, they figured it wouldn't be noticed. Linc grabbed the fire escape and went up the steps quickly, but as stealthily as he could. It was fifteen floors to the top. They made the trek with deft, strong strides, neither going excessively fast, nor noisily. As they turned at each juncture, they peered up and down the alley, looking for roving police. But so far, no one had come from either end. At the tenth floor Rick began to get a little winded. Linc asked him if he needed to rest a minute.

"I'll rest once we've got the whole thing over with," he said.

They continued upward at a slightly slower pace, but still taking the steps two-at-a-time. Another two stories and they'd be at the top. Linc started to feel the strain in his legs, too. A burning through the thighs. He glanced at Rick, who, despite breathing heavily, was matching him stride for stride. They paused at the last platform before the top. Their military training took over and Linc crouched, scanning the ground, while Rick sneaked his head up over the edge to survey the rooftop. Moments later he flashed a thumbs-up gesture, and both men scrambled over the parapet. They stood on the roof, and from their vantage point they could see over both Michigan and Columbus to the blackness of the lake. Twisting vapors of steam rose from the water. The street lights were on along the Outer Drive, but the rest of the lighted skyline that they knew so well—the fluorescent mosaic of tall buildings—was conspicuously absent. Hulking black shapes against a velvety sky had taken their place. It looked like just a few scattered blocks in this downtown section where the power was out. The wind whipped across the roof, sending a chill up Linc's spine. It felt a lot colder up here than it had on the ground.

The roof was flat, with a crenulated four-foot-high section running along the sides. Tiny whitish pebbles crunched under their boots as they walked over to the air-conditioning vents.

"Think these'll be strong enough to tie off on?" Rick asked.

Linc went over and pushed against one of the big metal sides with his gloved hands. It felt solid. He nodded, then turned around, so Rick could get into his pack. Rick took out a long coil of black nylon rope, a D-ring, and a five-foot length of white nylon cord. He busied himself uncoiling the rope, slipping a foot-long, heavily woven sleeve over the untangled end of the rope, and then tying it around the jutting base of the massive air conditioner. Linc looped the white nylon around his waist, through his crotch, and up around each leg, forming a "Swiss seat." He tied the ends together in a secure square knot, then pressed the D-ring over the front strand. Rick brought the coils of the rope over to the edge of the building, fitted the heavy nylon sleeve over the edge of the parapet to prevent any chafing to the rope, and then, fashioning a long loop, dropped the rest of the tangle over the side. He still held the two ends of the rope. Linc walked over and adjusted his gloves as he looked down at the roof of the adjacent bank building several stories below them. The area between the buildings was a narrow expanse of murky darkness.

"You ready?" Rick asked.

Linc nodded and snapped the black nylon rope through the D-ring. He put his mini-mag flashlight between his teeth and through clenched jaws, said, "I'll signal you."

He went to the edge, placing one leg over, pausing to look down before swinging the other leg over. He was so far up that he couldn't even see the semi-gloom of the alley below. He'd never rappelled from a building this high before. Probably just as well he couldn't see the bottom, he figured, and straightened out, perpendicular against the wall of the building, but keeping both strands of the rope held out in front of him. Rick held the double strand, too, waiting to let Linc control the descent, then take over the belay at the signal. Linc took his small mini-mag flashlight out of his mouth and tested the brightness of the bulb. Rick nodded and Linc stuck the flashlight back between his jaws. Then he shoved off and felt his body glide in space, his descent controlled by the friction of the rope moving through the D-ring.

Bouncing off the wall, he sprung out again, thrilling to the glide. His feet tapped the wall, and this time he paused, checking his location. He'd gone down maybe three stories. The roof of the bank was perhaps another forty feet below him. Using more caution, he descended once more and came to a stop maybe twenty feet above the roof of the bank building. He turned and surveyed the distance between the two buildings. It was fifteen feet at the most. Bending his legs, Linc flexed and shoved off hard, stopping himself as he alighted on the bank's roof. Standing on the edge, he coiled up the line and took the flashlight in his hand.

Two quick flashes. Rick signaled back with his. Now it was his turn to come down. Linc backed up, giving the rope enough play so that Rick could rappel easily. When he got within sight, Linc merely backed up, pulling the line so that Rick landed lightly on the roof of the bank, too.

"How was the trip?" Linc asked in a hoarse whisper, slapping Rick's shoulder.

"Piece of cake," Rick said. But Linc could tell by his stride that his legs were weak. Rick pulled the rope taut and walked over to this building's air conditioning units. Finding a flat piece of metal on the unit closest to him, he deftly tied off the line from the other roof. Then he took out another heavy nylon sleeve and began threading a second coil of rappelling rope through it. He and Linc walked to the other side of the angular metallic structures. This roof was covered with pebbles, too, and their feet made the same crunching sounds as they worked, looping a double strand of the rope around the base of the farthest unit. After tying the rope securely to one of the support beams, Linc and Rick drew out the line to the edge and placed the sleeve on the cornerstone. Linc glanced over the side and counted.

"Fifth floor. Ain't that right?" He didn't really have to ask, because they had counted it several times in their previous reconnoitering, but he wanted to hear Rick's reassurance.

"Right," Rick said. "Fifth floor, third window from the left." He shook his head slightly, as if trying to snap off the fatigue like perspiration.

"You gonna be able to make it back up there?" Linc asked, nodding toward the adjacent building.

"I'm a Marine, ain't I?"

"Ex-Marine," Linc corrected.

"No such thing," Rick shot back with a grin.

Linc grinned too, placing the flashlight between his teeth once more. He was slipping the line through the D-ring again and giving the rest of the line to Rick, so he could belay when the time was right. Linc stretched out perpendicular to this wall, and then sprang outward. His descent this time was slightly more cautious, because he had a shorter distance to go. He paused at each story until he was just above the fifth-floor window that they had identified on a previous trip as the women's washroom. With the toes of his boots on the upper edge of the window, he positioned himself just right, and slowly lowered himself until he was hanging directly in front of it. Linc used his left hand to secure the rope, and then, with his right, carefully took the flashlight out of his mouth again. He held it upward and pressed the button twice.

Rick responded with two flashes of his own, and Linc felt the rope stiffen as his partner took over the belay, effectively holding Linc in his present position, while giving him free use of both hands. The hardest thing about rappelling in assault-style was letting go of the rope with both hands, since the grip on the rope was what controlled the descent and prevented a freefall. To relinquish it, the rappeller had to be able to trust his life to the partner above. With only a second's hesitation, Linc released his grip on the rope and stuck the mini-mag back in his mouth, this time with the lens facing toward the frosty glass of the window.

He took out his knife and pressed the blade into the space between the upper and lower windows. Neither one budged. Linc wiggled the knife until he had it worked in pretty far, then reached into his pocket for a thin piece of wood to use as a shim. As he withdrew his clumsy gloved fingers, several of the shims fell away, twirling into the darkness. Linc swore, but that was why he'd brought an extra supply. More carefully this time, he took the glove off his hand and probed his pocket again. He worked several shims in between the two frames, then used his blade to try and pry back the lock. It wouldn't budge. Something had to be binding it. Bracing himself, he stuck the blade between the frames once more and twisted slightly. The shims dropped out and cascaded downward. Linc blew out a slow breath, aware that Rick must be getting tired holding his suspended weight for so long.

He decided to go to plan B. It was a little more risky, but what the hell. Besides, they were fighting the clock. Linc folded the knife and slipped it back into its scabbard on his belt. He wiggled his fingers back into his left glove, then he reached into the pocket of his black fatigue pants and took out a window-glass punch. The panes were divided up into four smaller sections, each framed by its own wooden border. Placing the tapered end against the glass above the area where the lock was. Linc cocked the mainspring, but he hesitated momentarily before releasing it.

The breaking glass would make a certain amount of noise, he thought, but hell, nobody would hear it. And a broken window this high up, no one would even be around to notice it until the bank re-opened. From what Diane had heard, that wouldn't be for at least another two days. He released the punch and the glass shattered with an echoing ping. Linc scraped the rest of the shards out of the frame and put the punch back in his pocket. The window lock twisted easily. He took out the knife again and stuck the blade between the base of the frame and the sill, then pried upward to raise the lower portion of the window. Swinging his right leg in and straddling the sill, Linc swept the light around the inside of the washroom. It was empty. He leaned back out of the window and signaled Rick with three quick flashes. Rick acknowledged with his three, and Linc disconnected the rope from the D-ring and pulled the rest of his body inside.

Rick felt the line go slack, then saw Linc's three flashes. Just in time, he thought. A sickening feeling swept over him and he almost collapsed against the roof. But something held him up. Maybe it was fear. Or adrenaline. Or maybe it was something else. Maybe it was knowing that this crazy thing had now gone too far to even think about backing out. His partner was inside and would be working his way down to the tunnel entrance. Rick knew he couldn't stop now.

Gathering up the rope, he wound it up, stuck it in his knapsack, and went back to the brace to which he'd tied the line from the other roof. Undoing it, he moved to the edge and, flipping the rope as he walked, managed to whip it over the corner. The rest of the rope was still tied off on the roof of the first building from which they'd descended. The next maneuver was going to be tricky and he paused to take a couple deep breaths. The cool night air failed to energize him. Instead, the enervating feeling continued to escalate. His bowels felt loose. And his stomach was suddenly overflowing with bile. Turning his head Rick bent over and puked. The stench of the puddle assaulted his nose, as he felt the sour taste in his mouth. He spit a few times, and straightened back up.

At least I managed to feed the pigeons, he thought as he turned back to the task at hand, mentally rehearsing what he had to do. He was going to have to swing over to the adjacent building, steady himself, then begin a downward rappel. But instead of going straight down, he needed to walk around the corner of the building until he could reach the fire escape. It didn't seem difficult when he thought about it in those terms. Just a few small steps. He tried to forget he was twelve stories up. The only hard parts were the initial jump, which he had to cushion with his legs as he landed, and the walk-around. There was a chance that the sleeve might have slipped and the friction would be wearing the rope away as he moved. That would mean he'd fall to his death.

I could quit now, but then Linc would have to go it alone, he thought. Then he wished Linc were going it alone. How did he ever get hooked up in this crazy scheme?

Figuring that he'd dawdled long enough, Rick slipped the dark nylon cord through the D-ring and moved to the edge of the building. Instead of getting out perpendicular to the edge, as Linc had done, Rick cautiously swung his legs out over the parapet, facing the wall where he had to go. Tightening his grip on the rope with both hands, the left one in front of his face and his right at the small of his back, Rick took a deep breath and swung forward. He sailed through the blackness for a few seconds before his boot-soles smacked into the bricks of the adjacent wall, expertly doing a little bounce to minimize the shock. After steadying himself momentarily, Rick walked several steps to his right. The corner was only a few feet away. He went down a few more feet, then stopped and walked to the right some more. He was at the corner now and the rope still felt strong. Of course, they all felt strong until . . .

Pushing those thoughts out of his mind, he walked around the corner and downward at an oblique angle toward the metal structure of the fire escape. About ten more feet and he'd be there. He continued his slow walk, the rope still feeling taut in his grasp. It was a good thing he had plenty of line.

A shock wave of terror shot through him as a snapping twitch vibrated down the rope. Then it felt secure again. All the sideward movement was causing it to twist. Rick steadied himself and took a couple of deep breaths, not daring to look down. He was perhaps five stories below the rooftop of the bank. The one he'd swung off of. All he would have to do, after he got to the fire escape, was go back up to the roof of this building and retrieve the rope from the original tie-off place, then get to the bank's tunnel entrance. Sounded simple, but he had to get there first. He continued his angular descent. Finally, after about seven minutes of cautious climbing, he reached the cast-iron banister.

Getting on the fire escape, Rick knelt and rested for a few minutes. Got to keep moving, he thought, for he knew that once he stopped for any protracted length of time, he was dead. Or very well could be. After unsnapping the rope, he untied his Swiss-seat and stuck that and his D-ring in the pack. Glancing upward, Rick saw that he had to climb up at least a dozen floors. But it was better than doing the rappel in the dark with no one on belay, that was for sure. He took the stairs as steadily as he had with Linc before. On the roof, he quickly untied the rope from the air conditioner, and placed the coil into his pack. Then he headed to the fire escape and began the careful, but steady trip down to the alley. He paused occasionally to watch for cops, but nobody came near the truck. Suddenly, when he was about two stories up, he saw a blacked-out patrol-car turn into the far end of the alley. If they caught him on the fire escape it would be over. There was no way he would be able to explain why he was up there. And they would surely stop to check out the parked truck.

Rick descended the remaining two flights on the metal stairs as fast as he could. He lost sight of the squad car and, praying that they hadn't seen or heard him, got to the final section that lowered to ground level. Fearing that movement of the large metal platform would be too noticeable, Rick slipped off the knapsack and dropped it down into the darkness. Then he gripped the bottom of the metal railings and lowered himself down, hanging there for an instant, before letting go. The drop must have been about fifteen feet, and he landed between two Dumpsters, rolling as he hit, to cushion the impact, but still feeling the tremendous shock shoot up through his legs.

Managing to struggle to his feet, Rick staggered to the passenger's side of the truck. He fumbled for the keys, then remembered that they'd left the windows down. He tore off the stocking hat, slipped on the yellow hard-hat, and began stepping into the Commonwealth Edison coveralls.

The Heist

The squad car was suddenly beside him, and he was bathed in a bright glare. He looked into it dumbly.

"What are you doing there?" a hard-edged voice demanded.

"Ever try takin' a leak with these coveralls on?" Rick said with an innocuous grin. "I'm with Commonwealth Edison. I had to go real bad and didn't figure anybody'd notice if I added just a little more pollution to this alley here." He lowered his head so they could see the insignia on the helmet. He continued to slip on the coveralls, which also had the company name stitched along the left breast area. Rick swallowed hard.

"Then get the fucking power turned back on," one of the cops said from the dark interior. The harsh light went out and he heard a guffaw of laughter from the squad car as it continued to creep down the alley. He breathed a sigh of relief and retrieved the knapsack. Tossing it on the seat, he started the truck and flipped on the lights. Rick drove down the alley in the same direction the squad car had gone. It had vanished into the shadows of the next alley.

Driving around the block, he hung a left on Wabash, then another left at Monroe. No other cop cars. He pulled into the alley again, but this time left the lights on. Halfway down he stopped. Shining his flashlight over the ground, he saw the grates and placed the yellow hard-hat on the dash with the Com Ed letters facing outward. After pulling his stocking cap back on, he shut off the truck but left the flashers going. Rick unfolded the thick hose that was connected to the pumping machine on the back of the truck and stretched it out to the grate. Then he took a pry-bar from the bed of the truck and jammed it between the edge of the metal and the cement. The grate rose as he bore down on the bar, and he grabbed the edge and lifted, pulling it over to the side. He shone his flashlight down the rectangular hole. There were four consecutive levels, each about six to eight feet high. He estimated that the lowest one would be about forty to fifty feet below street level. A detritus of sodden old newspapers, candy wrappers, and garbage lined the corners of each platform. The level that he wanted was the third. It was maybe thirty feet down.

Rick dropped the end of the hose down the hole, then set up some little orange pylons around the open area as a safety warning. Not that any self-respecting cop would take the time to get out of his car and actually go down there to check on him. He planned on hiding the ladder anyway.

Once he had everything set up—the hose, the pylons, and the little *Men At Work* sign—Rick started the portable generator for the pumping machine on the back of Henry's truck. It sputtered and squawked, but soon fell into the syncopated rhythm of a well-maintained engine. He slipped on his pack again, deciding to wear the coveralls down to at least the second level before taking them off, just in case. He unsnapped the aluminum extension ladder from the truck's bed and carried it to the edge of the hole. It was constructed so that there were overlapping platforms at each level, allowing someone to descend by merely re-positioning the ladder each time.

Rick set the thick metal rungs against the side and lowered it down to the first level. He pushed the hose down with it, then went down himself. The gaping maw of the first-level tunnel stretched out before him smelling wet and putrid. He picked up the ladder and lowered it down to the second level, glancing at his watch. One-forty-five. A little behind schedule. As he stepped on the rungs and started down he heard the chirping screeches and accompanying light-footed, quick movements. Rats, he thought. This place is probably loaded with them. The smell got worse the farther he went, but the furtive scurrying seemed to stop.

The Heist

★ ★ ★ ★ ★

Linc eased the washroom window down, then stepped over the glass on the floor. He shone his flashlight over the stalls and to the door. Silently, he moved to the door and opened it a crack. Nothing but more darkness, broken by the pale moonlight outlining a window on the hallway floor perhaps forty feet to his left. It wasn't much, but it was enough to give Linc his bearings.

Taking a few more minutes to check the hall, he pulled the door open and slid out. He moved swiftly, but cautiously, down toward the elevators. By the time he'd arrived, his movements had lost some of their stiffness and become more fluid. He slipped off the knapsack and swung it to the floor in front of him. With his mini-mag in his mouth, he searched through the pack and removed a long, thin screwdriver, a yellow plastic lantern, and more nylon rope. He was still wearing his Swiss-seat and D-ring.

Linc readjusted the knapsack on his back again and focused the beam of his flashlight over the surface of the elevator, centering on the round hole about five inches below the top of the right-hand door. He inserted the screwdriver blade into the hole, felt around for the spring-loaded safety catch that kept the door from being opened when the elevator car wasn't there, and twisted. The doors began to slide into the wall slots. Linc braced the door with his foot, preventing it from moving. He stuck the mini-mag between his teeth again and focused it on the lever mechanism inside. It was a flat steel beam that controlled the opening and closing of the doors. Looping the nylon rope around it several times and pulling it taut, Linc used a double square knot to secure the hitch. Then he grabbed the plastic lantern and twisted it on. The top extended to provide a lamp-like illumination. After securing it to the opposite end of the rope, he lay prone with his face over the edge and slowly lowered the lantern down the shaft. The area was actually rather large. More like a huge room with no walls. No floors either. Just lots of horizontal and vertical beams, within which the elevator cars were raised and lowered. Thick metal cables hung down at various intervals.

Initially, the luminescence of the lantern bounced off the square walls, showing the gray cement and oily metal I-beams. Then the illumination faded, and finally it looked like a small white dot as it came to rest on the bottom with a plunk. Linc bounced it several times to make sure, then, satisfied that he had plenty of rope left, lowered the excess coils downward. It would have been quicker to drop the rope, but there were several cross beams and he couldn't afford any tangles. As it was, he felt uncomfortable rappelling down the shaft in the dark. And it would be even darker after he let the doors slam shut. But it would be too slow to go down the stairs, and he would have his mini-mag. It would provide some brightness.

Linc stood up, and, after checking to make sure his knapsack was secure, slipped the rope through the D-ring once more. Then he backed over to the doors and tested the security of the knot. That was silly, he knew. He had to stop second-guessing things. He'd tied it; therefore it was secure.

I'd bet my life on it, he thought with a grim smile.

He stepped onto the little ridge of cement on which the track for the elevator doors was affixed, then, swinging his body inside the shaft, slowly let the doors slide closed. The darkness enveloped him suddenly, and he stood there, hugging the doors, letting his eyes adjust. When his night vision was as good as he figured it was going to get, he twisted on the mini-mag and scanned the shaft again.

The first crossbeam was about twenty feet down. There

was no cable in the center, which meant that the elevator had to be suspended above him. The shaft next to him had a thick cable hanging down. That car must be downstairs. Looks like I picked the right shaft, he thought, and started his rappel. Linc kept the miniature flashlight in his mouth, occasionally turning to gauge his descent, gliding downward at a slow, careful pace, walking several steps with his feet against the wall every so often. As he passed the doors for each floor, he paused to note the number. It took him several minutes to get to the single digits. Five, four, three . . . As he paused at the third floor he heard something and froze. It was a laugh. A woman's laugh.

Hanging there in the darkness, his mouth popped open and he dropped the flashlight. It made a series of awful bangs before ending with a splash. Linc remained in place, cursing himself silently.

"You hear something?" the woman's voice asked.

"Probably rats," said a masculine counterpart. "Now are we gonna do it, or what?" The voice was full of impatience.

"You think there are rats here?" Linc heard the woman say. Both the voices were husky whispers. They had to be close to the doors on the other side.

"Don't worry, baby. Any come around while we're doin' it, I'll shoot their asses."

Security guards, thought Linc. They had to be security guards. It made sense. No power. No alarms. The fucking building was probably crawling with them. He felt another surge of panic rush through him. He had to get to the tunnel and find Rick. If he could do that without getting caught, they could get away. To hell with the fucking box.

"Come on, baby, I got a hard-on all the way up to my chin."

"But what if Herman finds us?"

"I told you, he's sound asleep on the second floor, in Fielding's office, and there's no way he's gonna walk up two flights of stairs," the man said. "We got plenty of time." Their voices were getting distant, like they were walking away. "Now all we have to do is go up to that nice couch in the employees' lounge . . ." the voice trailed off. Linc stayed where he was, then slowly went down another floor. He couldn't see very well, so he "walked" down the wall until he got to the next set of doors.

He remembered Diane telling him about this hot-to-trot security girl who was supposedly "doing the do" with half the guards in the bank. That's probably who it was. Hopefully she and the guy would be occupied for a while. But they'd mentioned someone else. Herman. Linc knew Herman from the times he'd been in visiting Diane and checking the place out. Herman was this fat old German guy who looked like his mind was on the little genie in the Jack Daniel's bottle. Heavy, bulbous nose, mottled with busted veins, big gut, droopy eyes. No wonder the young lovers weren't worried about him climbing the flight of stairs to the third floor. They were probably right, he was most likely sleeping it off somewhere.

But Linc had to make sure. Regardless of what the lovers decided to do, he couldn't afford to assume any loose ends would be tied up for him. Suddenly he realized that he was again thinking as if they were going ahead with it. Hadn't he decided to abort the mission just a few moments ago? But why? If the two love-birds were so sure that Herman was sleeping it off, didn't it then follow that there were probably only the three of them in the building? "Them" meaning security; he smiled. It was starting to seem feasible again. There was a little risk, sure, but they knew that going in. He felt for a toe-hold by the second-floor doors and balanced himself. Then he moved his left hand along the top of the door until he found the safety-catch release. The doors to the second floor slid sideways into the walls.

Linc stepped into the hall and doubled up the rope, letting the doors close softly on the folds. He disconnected the D-ring and moved across the shadowy hallway to the recess of a closed office door. Slipping off the knapsack, he felt around for his spare mini-mag. That was one thing the Corps had taught him: always carry a back-up. His gloved fingers soon found the metallic cylinder and he withdrew it and scanned the hallway. A legend was on the wall opposite the elevators and Linc studied the white, block letters, which listed Mr. R. Fielding's office as Room 204.

The numbers had been painted on each frosty glass pane in gold, and outlined in black. Room 204 was down at the far end of the hall. Linc tested the knob. Locked. He squatted and pressed his ear against the glass. There was a faint, intermittent, buzzing sound. He pressed harder. The sound persisted with monotonous regularity. Then he recognized it: Snoring. The fat old fart was snoring. With a devilish grin, Linc backed off from the door and twisted the flashlight on. He dug through the pack and came up with what he was looking for: a small, wedge-shaped piece of wood. Linc took the screwdriver out and worked it in between the door and the jamb near the bottom, pressing the door inward. Then he quickly slipped the wedge in between the door and the frame and forced it up toward the latch as far as he could. Old Herman would have a helluva time opening the door now. The wedge would bind against the latch, making it damn near impossible to twist the knob.

Almost gleefully, Linc went back to the elevator doors and pushed them open. Now, as long as the dude upstairs didn't suffer from premature ejaculation, he and Rick would be in and out in no time. He held the flashlight tightly over his

watch-dial, illuminating the radium-coated numbers to luminescence. One-forty-five. Rick was probably already at the
tunnel waiting for him.

Wednesday, April 15, 1992, 1:55 A.M.

Rick had gone down to the third level of tunnels. He could
hear the rush of water in the one below him, the one that was
flooded. Flipping the catches on the ladder, he lowered the
extension, then placed it on its side, flat against the wall so
that it was braced in place. Glancing upward, he couldn't
even see the sky because of the alternating, overlapping platforms at each level. Nobody, he figured, would be able to see
the ladder even if they shone a light directly down the grate.
Plus he had pulled the grate back in place, more or less, before he had descended to the second platform.

He looped the end of the black nylon rappelling rope
around the side of the ladder and knotted the rope securely.
As he moved away, he let the line extend with him so it would
serve as a quick guide on the way back. Now all he had to do
was follow the tunnel to the bank entrance. He and Linc had
done that once before on one of their previous
reconnoiterings. He turned on his flashlight and moved
through the tunnel. The walls were cold cement, with heavy
angles that were squared off by rusted iron beams. The
ceiling was high, seven or eight feet in most places, descending in two arches that gave the tunnel an almost medi-
eval ambience. Rick felt like Errol Flynn in one of those old
movies, rushing through the castle to save Olivia de
Havilland. Suddenly the beam of light bounced over several
sets of gleaming, beadlike eyes. More rats. They danced away
from him as he advanced, emitting more of their high-pitched
screams. His feet sloshed through a few inches of dark,
scummy water. Condensation? As he paused to get his bear-

ings, he felt something under his feet. A strange vibration, like something roiling beneath him. Ignoring it, he moved on. He couldn't afford distractions. He had to press forward. The vibration seemed to fade.

The ceiling in this place was covered with metal boxes and pipes that probably contained some kind of wiring or phone lines. Rick followed these lines because he knew they led to the bank tunnel entrance. As he turned and followed the overhead lines, he noticed something else. Little geysers of water had begun sprouting about halfway up the walls in this section. Suddenly Rick realized what the vibration was, and he began a quick jog down the tunnel.

Linc continued his cautious rappel. As he got down past the first basement level, he noticed that the light from the lantern he had lowered seemed to be out. He stopped himself again, freed his left hand from the rope, and took the mini-mag out of his mouth, gripping it tightly, and held it down between his legs so it shone down the shaft. The lantern was floating in a pool of dirty-looking water. But it looked farther down than he had to go. He was almost at the second basement. That, according to his knowledge of the bank's subterranean floors, was the level where the freight tunnel entrance was.

A few more feet and the toes of his boots were resting on the edge of the elevator landing. He freed his left hand again and pressed down on the lever that worked the doors. It yielded easily and Linc's flashlight beam explored the dusty cement floor and walls. Carton after carton of cardboard boxes were stacked in symmetrical rows. Linc walked out onto the solid floor, then pulled up the rest of the rope. He'd had about twenty feet to spare. Pretty good estimate, he thought to himself. He cut off the rope and let the remainder of the line above him hang in the shaft. No way he could go back up to retrieve it, but he figured that once things got running right, the friction of the elevator would take care of it. The maintenance guys would probably find it, along with a lot of other shit, when they cleaned out the bottom of the shaft after the flood.

The lantern was useless. Supposed to be waterproof. Maybe I'll get my money back, he thought with a grin, shoving the lantern and what was left of the rope into his knapsack. He moved between the stacks of boxes, heading for the west wall of the building. When Diane had smuggled them inside before, they'd spent several hours checking each floor, including the three basements. The maintenance guy had finally found them and, after swallowing their claim to be lost electricians trying to check the burglar alarms, showed them the bulkhead that led to the freight tunnel. The old guy had been mighty cordial, especially after Linc presented him with a brown bag containing a half-pint of Old Turkey, and they spent a long twenty minutes "taking a break" and discussing what assholes their respective bosses were. During this time, Rick had been checking what kind of lock was on the bulkhead door.

It was one of those heavy-duty, hardened, chrome-covered security padlocks. That night, they'd promptly gone out and purchased several of them, then experimented to see what cut them the fastest. Nothing short of an acetylene torch seemed to have much effect. Even the longest bolt cutters barely made a scratch on the shackle, which was advertised as being able to withstand 6000 pounds of pressure. This pretty much deflated their plan until Diane calmly told them that all the keys had duplicates in the lock-box, to which she, owing to her position in the vault department, had occasional access. Rick told her the key should have *American* stamped on it and showed her pictures of what it should look like. The next opportunity she had, Diane merely picked up that key— it had been the only *American* in the box—and brought it home. Rick was able to make a duplicate, after which she replaced the original. Finally, Rick had sneaked in again, taking the elevator down to the archives with Diane, and checked the duplicate key in the heavy-duty lock. His uncle had taught him well. The big shackle popped open with a definitive click.

Now the beam of Linc's flashlight swept over the metal framework of the bulkhead. The metal door looked like something out of a submarine, or spaceship, all thick angular blocks of steel. The huge lock was laced through the circular hasp, securing the door. Linc felt in his pocket for the keys, took out the ring, and selected the duplicate that Rick had made. Inserting it in the lock, he gave a half-turn to the right. The lock popped open, and he slid the shackle out of its holder. The door swung outward with a resonant creak.

Rick leaned against the cement wall, his stocking hat rolled back on his head, his face covered with sweat.

"About goddamned time," he said. "This tunnel's crawling with rats."

Linc placed his gloved index finger in front of his pursed lips.

"We've got company upstairs," he said in a hoarse whisper.

They squatted between the caverns of cardboard boxes while they debated whether or not to abort the mission. Rick was all for getting out of there immediately and told Linc that there was no way he was going to spend the rest of his life in some prison. Linc managed to calm him with assurances. They were so close now, and the hardest part was already done. If they stuck to the plan, they'd be out of there in a flash. "With the cash," he added.

The plan called for them to get in and out without being noticed, so that, once it was done, nobody would even realize that they'd been there. Except Johnny "the Mink" Osmand, and he wasn't going to be telling anybody. Along with the key to the bulkhead lock, Diane had also given them the master passkey to the safety deposit boxes and the combination to the basement vault. With the time lock off, all they had to do was use the combination and twist the wheel to open it. The broken window, the dangling rope in the elevator shaft, the wedge in the Bank President's door . . . They were all minor things that wouldn't add up to squat. It couldn't have been more perfect. A dream come true. As long as it didn't turn into a nightmare.

With Rick convinced, they moved stealthily through the basement. The vault they wanted was up two stories. That was four flights. Linc used his mini-mag flashlight sparingly, because the batteries were starting to fade. But they dared not try to negotiate in the complete and utter darkness of the sub-basement for fear of making some noise that might alert one of the guards. Rick tugged at Linc's sleeve.

"You sure about there only being three?" he whispered.

Linc considered his answer.

"Yeah. I think they woulda mentioned it if they were worried about anybody else bein' in the building," he said. "The bitch was real worried old Herman would find 'em."

Rick heaved a sigh, but continued. At the stairwell they went up one at a time, the first man checking, then motioning if it was clear. Their ascent was silent, except for the squishing sound of Rick's sodden boots on the rough cement stairs. But that was barely noticeable.

For the first time since he'd gotten inside, Linc missed his weapon. They'd been trained to search and sweep with their rifles on their forearms, exposing as little of their bodies as possible. Now, they were like de-fanged tigers, acting stealthy, but with no real bite. But what would he do if he did have a weapon and one of the security guards confronted them? Shoot him? He'd done that to a few towelheads, but this wasn't the same, was it? That question he didn't choose to answer or even think about anymore. He just wanted to get on with it. To get it over with so that they could get the hell out of there.

Linc paused ever-so-slightly at the landing for the first sub-basement. Then he shone his light on the stairs and started up. At the middle landing, where the stairway turned in the opposite direction, he sneaked a quick look and then signaled for Rick by flashing the light twice. After creeping up the last few steps, Linc twisted the knob on the door and pulled it open a crack. He surveyed the interior of the basement room where the vault for the safety deposit boxes was located. It was fully furnished, unlike the two stark areas from which they'd come. Numerous tan drywall partitions had been erected across from the vault to allow for privacy after the safety deposit boxes had been checked out. Each one had a door that could be locked from the inside. After they got the vault open, Rick was to go inside, and Linc would close the big steel door behind him and keep watch from one of the dry-wall partitions.

Once inside, Rick would have to accomplish the final bit of trickery needed for the heist. He had to smoke a blank key, insert it, and make the final filing variations. Because he knew what type of key it was, and from making a duplicate of Diane's master, Rick didn't think this would take him too long. It would have been an impossible task during regular business hours, of course, but here in seclusion, he estimated that it wouldn't take him more than five to ten minutes. The blank was already partially filed. All he had to do was smoke it with the candle flame, insert it, and check where the impressions of the lever locations were.

Rick nodded and Linc pulled open the door and they crept swiftly down the long hallway, pausing at each juncture to check for the guards. Then, after crossing the final space that separated the offices and partitions from the waiting area and the vault, they were at the big steel door. Linc slipped off his knapsack as they both went to the floor. He unzipped the pocket at the back and withdrew the paper with the combination. After looking at Rick, he moved to the vault door and, with his partner on lookout, began spinning the dial.

Diane had painstakingly explained to him that he needed to turn the dial completely around once before stopping at the first number. There were no telltale clicks as he spun it either. It took him three tries before he finally got the hang of it. When he gripped the spoked wheel that operated the locking mechanism, and twisted it counter-clockwise, he encountered no resistance. The immense steel door swung open on its well-lubricated metallic hinges. Rick swallowed hard as he moved to the door.

"Don't turn the wheel back," he whispered. "Just push it closed so I can get out when I'm done."

"Hey, I just thought of something," said Linc. "What if the power comes back on all at once and you're still in there? It'll re-set the time lock, won't it? What'll I do?"

Rick frowned, then said, "Then we're fucked. But don't worry. They ain't gonna get it on again that fast, believe me. Besides, that's the least of our worries." He cut off the sentence abruptly, and Linc asked him what he meant.

"Never mind," he said, moving inside the vault.

The Heist

★ ★ ★ ★ ★

Rick gave himself a few seconds to adjust to closed-in space of the vault, breathing with steady deliberation.

I've been through worse, he told himself. A lot worse.

But in his heart, he knew that it wasn't the tightness of the walls that was bothering him. If anything would trip them up it would be the damn freight tunnel. The vibration under his feet that he'd felt earlier meant that the water had been rushing along under the floor of the tunnel he'd used. The erosion would eventually wear through, and when that happened, the incoming water would seek its own level, that of the lake or the river, flooding the next tunnel above. And from the feel of it, there had been a hell of a current at work beneath him.

Chapter 7

Wednesday, April 15, 1992

3:20 A.M.
It took Rick much longer to make the key than they'd figured. The smoking of the blank, even a partially-filed one like this one, was a tedious process that required constant reinsertion, extraction, and examination as to exactly where the lever locations had marked. Now he knew why they always drilled these things. Twice, Linc crept to the door and twisted the wheel to see if Rick was all right.

"I'd be a lot fucking better if you'd quit interrupting me," Rick's hoarse whisper rasped.

Linc slipped back to his hiding place in the adjacent viewing room. He'd picked one where he could watch both the vault and the stairway entrance from upstairs. As time drew on, he began to formulate a plan, should one of the guards come down to inspect the vault area. He'd just let him get nice and close, and then swing the door out and cold-cock the motherfucker. But he suddenly started playing the "what if" game. What if the guy doesn't come in range of the door? What if he goes to the vault and twists the wheel, finding it open? What if there was more than one of them? He closed off his mind to any more speculation. Christ, they were almost home free. The Corps had taught him to be cool, sit tight, even if it seems like the world's caving in on you, and your training and conditioning will pull you through.

That's all we have to do, he told himself. Just maintain our cool, and we'll be out of here in no time. That old fart Herman's probably still snoring up a storm, he thought. And that other guy's probably still getting his knob polished. He glanced at his watch. Three thirty-five. Christ, had they been in there that long? It didn't seem like it. The panic that he'd tried so hard to suppress came rushing back. Maybe it was better to just abort the fucking mission and get the hell out of there.

Then he heard the three metallic taps, each separated by two seconds. Rick's signal to come open the vault door. Was he done, or had he decided to abort, too? Linc surveyed the rest of the room through the slit in the door. It looked dark and quiet. He pushed open the flimsy door and moved silently to the vault. Grasping the spokes of the metallic wheel, he turned it slightly to the left and the huge steel door swung out toward him. Rick was standing there, his knapsack on his back.

"You got everything?" Linc whispered.

Rick nodded and moved quickly past him. Linc's eyes swept over the interior of the vault. Nothing to even indicate they'd been there. With a grin, he swung the massive door shut and twisted the wheel back to the right. Then he spun the dial on the combination lock. Exhaling slowly, he backed up two steps, then felt Rick tugging at his sleeve.

"Let's hurry," Rick said.

Linc just grinned and nodded. Then he leaned forward and whispered in his friend's ear, "Did you count it? Do it look like a lot?"

"Yeah, it did, but I just emptied everything in the box into my backpack," Rick whispered back. Then, more forcefully, "Now let's get the fuck outta here."

They moved with sly assurance down the hallway toward the basement stairwell, both knowing they had to be even more cautious going back because of the tendency to relax on the way out. Linc used his weakening flashlight to scan the stairwell, then held up his hand and motioned that he was going down. Again, their training had taught them to go one at a time, but Rick shouldered onto the stairway beside him.

"What you doing, man?" Linc said. "I'm going first."

"Ain't gonna matter at this point," Rick said. "We ain't got no weapons, and if one of us gets caught, the other's going down too."

Linc gave him a stern look.

"That kind of thinking get you killed, Marine," he said.

Rick compressed his lips and drew back, letting Linc descend the flight first. He knew his friend was right about the tactics, but his mind was racing back over that eerie feeling he'd had in the tunnel.

Linc flashed his light. The signal that it was clear. Rick went down to the curve on the first landing. Linc nodded and Rick took the next flight down, pausing at the bottom for his partner. Two more flights and they were at the second sub-basement. Beneath them they heard the slapping of water against the metal fire door.

"That basement just below us must be flooded," Linc said.

"Why the fuck do you think I was in a hurry?" Rick said. "Let's move it."

Using their flashlights they moved between the cardboard caverns. Linc jumped back with a grunt as several big rats scurried in front of him and vanished.

"What?" Rick asked.

"Motherfucking rats," Linc said. He swallowed hard.

"They're probably getting in through the tunnel. We gotta hurry."

He moved past Linc and headed for the door. They'd left the bulkhead door closed, the security padlock in place through the steel hasps, but unlocked. Now they would have to leave the door ajar, because there was no way either one of them could secure the lock without remaining behind in the room. They'd justified this part of their plan by figuring that the only person who'd come down here and discover the door unsecured would be the maintenance man, and it would be his ass if he reported it. So he probably would just lock it and figure one of the crew must have left it open. If things got straightened out with the flooding, and Diane went back to work, she could always sneak down and close it, saying that she had to look up some old records in the basement or something. Maybe even ask the maintenance guy to go down there with her to carry something up. That was the least of their worries, thought Rick. He shone his flashlight over the walls of the tunnel. They were wet with condensation. The floor still had the same few inches of standing water on the bottom. Beyond them groups of rats peered into the light, squealing with some sort of desperate-sounding anxiety.

Rick stooped to get through the low iron frame of the bulkhead door and stepped into the tunnel. No sense telling Linc about his fear of the water erosion, he thought. No need to panic him, since he never did learn to swim. Not that either of them would want to swim in the filth of this flood. He heard Linc's sloshing steps behind him. Rick picked up the rappelling line and passed it to Linc as they walked.

"Here, help me wind this up, will ya?" he said.

"What for?" Linc answered, smiling. "We playing Little Red Riding Hood, or something?"

"It's Hansel and Gretel," said Rick. "And who was

quoting chapter and verse to me a little while ago about not following procedures?"

Linc pursed his lips and began winding the rope into loose loops. They sloshed along, Rick using his light to follow the guiding line through the hundred yards or so of tunnel. Suddenly he heard Linc grunt.

"You feel something?" he asked. "Like something moving under our feet?"

Rick nodded. "Yeah. Let's keep moving. We should be all right." He was beginning to sweat again, and the weak feeling was starting to creep up his legs and into his belly. But they couldn't stop now. Not when they were so close. The beam of the flashlight swept over the curve of the tunnel wall, and, beyond it, about a hundred and fifty feet, were the landings.

"It's just up ahead," Rick said.

Linc nodded. He was breathing hard now. Real hard, Rick noticed.

Probably not from fatigue, either, he thought. It's gotta be because the confined area with so much water surrounding him. It's starting to get to him.

They rounded the curve, and he could see where the rope was attached to the ladder. There was a large flat cement platform, and Rick knew that was the way up and out as traces of ambient moonlight filtered its way down toward them.

He got there first and immediately grabbed the ladder and stuck it upright, bracing it for the climb. In a tangled heap were the Commonwealth Edison coveralls that he'd left there. Rick took them and tossed them up on to the next landing.

"Nice toss," Linc said. "For a white boy."

Rick was going to grin, but suddenly they both felt a shift underneath them. Then a roar a split second later, followed by a thundering rush, like a giant-sized toilet being flushed.

Rick began to scramble up the rungs and Linc started after him. Halfway up Rick saw the torrent sweeping toward them and managed to span the rest of the distance. He immediately pushed himself flat on the platform and reached out his hand for Linc, who grabbed for it, but missed. Rick felt their fingers touch, then saw Linc swept away in a cascade of foam and wetness. The ladder jerked from his grasp too. Rick slipped off his knapsack and threw it onto the platform above him, then got down on his belly again and, thrusting his face over the edge, surveyed the raging flow rushing beneath him. It had evened out slightly, leaving a gap of about three feet between water level and the ceiling of the tunnel. The ladder was braced diagonally against the walls of the tunnel. Rick swung his body down into the cold water and let the current sweep him against the rungs. Keeping his head above water, he groped for the line. It was taut. That meant that Linc still might have ahold of it.

"Hold on. I'm coming!" Rick shouted and went down under the horizontal ladder, surfacing on the other side, grabbing the rope and swimming, keeping his head in the air pocket next to the ceiling. He kept pulling on the line as he let the current sweep him along, hoping that by following the rope he'd find Linc.

The initial force of the water had knocked the wind out of him, and Linc felt his grip being torn from the aluminum rungs. He'd tried to remain calm as the rush snatched him, propelling him along through the opening to the next tunnel, slamming him against the concrete walls, scraping his face and chest, then turning him over so that his back smacked the next abutment. Spinning, he felt the knapsack being twisted off his shoulders, then rush away from him. Not knowing why, Linc grabbed for it but only felt it brush against his hands. He thudded against another wall, and he felt the sudden void of pitch darkness. But through it all he somehow managed to stay semi-conscious, the water trying to force itself into his mouth and down his throat.

It handled him roughly at first, then seemed almost gentle as it rotated him, in twirling fashion, along in the cold darkness. Linc's hands groped in the wet blackness, searching for something tangible, something solid to anchor himself. Something. Anything. Something brushed over his fingertips, and then dashed away. Startled, he swallowed a mouthful of water at the contact. More water flooded his mouth as he tried to cough, and Linc felt his consciousness slipping away as black dots coalesced, closing off the world.

The water lifted his head above the surface for a brief few seconds, shocking him back to life. He was exhaling when he was swept back under moments later, but as he went down his fingers made contact with something again. This time it flirted with him longer, whipping around over his wrist, before uncoiling again. Linc's arms worked downward instinctively, as his legs pumped, trying to run. The rope fluttered in front of him again, and this time he managed to snare it out of sheer chance. As he struggled for a grip, the current continued to tug at him, slicing into his hands, but he didn't dare to let go. He closed his fists tighter, and then felt his motion cease. Struggling to raise his head above the water, Linc opened his mouth, only to feel himself sinking farther down. Panicking, he released the rope with one hand and pawed at the water, but he was still sinking like a stone. The blackness was coming back again, washing over him like a warm breeze. He felt his fingers relax around the rope. It no longer seemed important. The only important thing was the warmth of the impending void.

The air hit his face like the smack on a fist. Sputtering,

Linc tried to breathe, but only expelled another mouthful of water. Rick's breath was bouncing off his cheek, and his friend was shaking him. He came to and suddenly realized it was dark, but not with the same kind of warm darkness that had been engulfing him. "Are you okay? Are you okay?" Rick was shouting at him. More water came out of Linc's mouth as he coughed and managed to snare snatches of a painful breath. He nodded.

"We gotta pull ourselves back along the line," Rick said. "Can you do it?"

Linc blinked and continued his struggle to gain his breath.

"Linc, can you *do* it?"

"Ain't we . . ." Linc sputtered, "done this before?"

Rick snorted a hoarse laugh.

"We only got about fifty feet or so," he said. "We gotta pull ourselves along underwater, hand-over-hand. We'll be going against the current, so it'll be hard, but it's our only chance. There's no way I can swim back towing you. Can you do it?"

"I'm a fucking Marine, ain't I?" Linc said.

Rick told him to go first. "You get in trouble, double your hand around the line and I'll try to kick us up to the air pocket."

Linc was still clearing his throat, his mouth tasting like the foul water. He managed to take a couple of normal breaths, coughed a few times, then managed a couple of deep ones. "I'm ready," he said.

Rick nodded.

"When we get to the ladder, we're home free," he said. "Twenty-five feet or so. You go first."

"I thought you told me fifty," Linc said, taking a deep breath and grasping the line. His hands sought out the line, and he began pulling himself along, his massive body suspended by the water. Soon he found a rhythm to it all. Suddenly, it was easy, almost fun, his great upper body strength moving him along with ease. It was almost like being able to swim, after all. Until his lungs started burning and screaming for air. He knew he dare not open his mouth, but he wanted to shout for Rick to help him. He started to double the rope over his hand when he felt Rick's arms encircling his chest, propelling him upward. Their faces broke the surface and they drank in the musty air.

"Figured you'd need a break," Rick said, holding Linc's head in the crook of his arm. "We should be almost there."

"Okay," said Linc.

"I got to teach you how to swim," Rick said.

"Yeah, but some other time, okay?"

They gripped the rope again and after going several more yards, Linc grasped a metal rung. He hung on, then Rick was beside him, grabbing his head and pushing him downward. Linc instantly felt panic as they submerged to go under the ladder, but then he felt them rising again, and the fear left him. Rick's kicking propelled them upward and Linc saw the flat surface of the water a second before his face broke through. His hands felt the solid assuredness of the cement platform a few scant feet above his head. Linc's fingers grasped the edge, and in one deft motion he pulled himself up and onto it. He managed to get to his knees and spent the next few minutes puking. When he'd finished and his breathing had returned to normal, he lay on his back.

"Oh, Lordy," he said. Suddenly he heard the chirping and saw scores of small, rodent eyes peering at him, maybe wondering if he was dead. He swore and kicked his legs, the movement sending them scattering.

"I'm going to dive down and set up the ladder," Rick said.

Rick's face disappeared beneath the surface. Linc waited, his breath coming in ragged rasps, as he lay curled-up on the cold cement. There was a splashing sound and Linc looked over the edge. Rick was there grasping the cement corner to keep himself afloat.

"Can't move it. It's wedged in place. Current's too strong," he said, gasping.

"Then fuck the ladder," Linc told him, stretching his hand downward. "I'll boost you up. You can stand on my shoulders."

"Then how're you gonna get up?" Rick said. Then added, "Wait," and disappeared under the water. Linc kept staring at the surface until he saw Rick's white face surfacing again. This time he held up his hand. Linc reached down and felt the rope. He pulled a few lengths of it onto the platform then held his arm down for Rick to grab. Their hands met, and Rick hoisted himself up, folding his upper body over the edge next to Linc. Once he was on the platform, he rolled over Linc's legs, anchoring him.

"All right, big man," Rick said. "Use your muscles and pull that fucker up."

Linc drew the line toward him, feeling the weight of the ladder ascending with it. The silver rungs broke the surface with a whoosh. They tugged and pulled on the rope until they finally managed to get a hold on the wet aluminum, pulling it to the next platform.

"Watch out for the puddle of vomit over there," Linc said as Rick began feeling around for something.

"Been there, done that," Rick said.

Then he stooped and picked up the knapsack from the corner and slipped it over his shoulders. Linc's face split open with a wide grin.

"Thought it got lost in the shuffle," he said, slapping Rick on the back. "Pretty soon you'll see. This whole thing was worthwhile."

★ ★ ★ ★ ★

4:37 A.M.

The disappointment came later, after they'd gotten back to Diane's place. They'd been stopped at several checkpoints, but the cops just took one look at them, both soaked to the skin and stinking like sewer water, and motioned them through. The knapsack had been stowed behind the seat, just in case one of the coppers decided to check the truck. At Diane's they took quick turns in the shower, and Linc gave Rick some of his clean clothes to wear. When they came out, Diane was already counting the money.

At first it looked like a lot more, but, as they counted it, they saw that it was mostly smaller bills. Fives, tens, and twenties. Not a fifty or hundred in the bunch. Basically, it was a flash-roll. It amounted to seven thousand dollars.

"Chump change," muttered Diane, who seemed to be devastated. She just sat there staring at the piles of cash. "Are you sure you got the right fucking box?"

"No doubt about it," Linc said. He picked up a VHS cassette tape in a white cardboard package. "Wonder what this is?"

"Probably a porno tape, or something," Rick said.

Diane snorted in disgust.

"All that planning, all the shit I went through, and for what?" she said. "Are you two positive you did the right one?"

Linc gave her a harsh glance.

"We almost got fuckin' killed in there," he said. "Drowned like motherfuckin' rats."

"We all took risks," she said. "You want a fucking medal? If it wasn't for me, you would've never even gotten close."

"Listen, 'hoe, we were the ones puttin' our asses on the line in there."

"What did you call me?"

118

"Hey," Rick interjected. "If we pool it, we still got enough to put down on a business or something."

"Shit. Chump change, that's all it is," Diane said dejectedly. She turned away from them. "We all still gonna be working for somebody else for as long as we can see."

"Hey, Rick's got a point," Linc said. "We can all chip in and—"

"Chip in, shit," she said. "I want my portion now, so I can at least *do* something worthwhile with it."

"Meaning what?" Linc said.

Before Diane could answer, Rick spoke quickly.

"Hey, could we all please cool it? It's almost five o'clock and we both gotta be at work in another two hours." He looked from Linc to Diane. "Diane, do you mind if I sack out on your couch for a little bit?"

"Go ahead, man," Linc said.

Diane was still glaring angrily at Linc when she answered.

"No, Rick, go right ahead," she said. "You can sleep on my couch, 'cause he's sleeping on the motherfucking floor!"

She moved to her bedroom door and slammed it shut. Linc stared at the door for a moment, then shook his head slowly.

"Hell, you can have the couch," Rick said. "I'll go out in the truck."

"Huh-uh," Linc said. "Just toss me one of them cushions." He walked over and stretched out on the floor beside the couch, then grinned up at Rick. "This ain't the first time."

6:30 A.M.

The door opened and suddenly the stark little six-by-ten windowless room in which Reginald Fox had spent an exhausting, sleepless night was bathed in light. Fox looked up from the curled, fetal position he'd managed to cram his long body into and stared at the source: an extremely powerful flashlight.

"Mr. Fox," a voice said from behind the beam. It was a deep, rich baritone, and the word "mister" had been drawn out with a glide over the first vowel, lending a slow, southern twinge to the sound. "It's time to rise and shine, sir."

Fox recognized the voice. It was that white-haired cracker asshole who'd shocked him with that crazy electronic stun gun. The lawyer rolled to his knees and stood up slowly. The anger and outrage had long since dissipated, and now he felt a searing terror begin to creep up along his bowels. Who were these people, and what did they intend to do with him? But his time in law school and in the courtroom had taught him to mask his emotions. Better not show them any fear, he thought.

"What the hell's going on?" he said in an almost demanding tone. "Where the hell am I? What fucking time is it?"

His fingers automatically traced over his barren left wrist.

"What time it is, will be up to you, sir," the southerner said. He became a back-lit silhouette as the door swung open all the way, revealing a lighted area behind him. "That is, it will be measured by the degree of your cooperation. All your questions will be answered in due time, of course, but now, I must ask you to accompany me."

He held out his hand, indicating that Fox should walk through the doorway.

"Do you know who I am?" Fox said, pointing all of his fingers on both hands back toward his chest as he walked toward the door. "I'm Reginald Fox, an attorney. And I do suggest that you let me get to a phone immediately, and let me get the hell out of here."

The Heist

The southerner smiled benignly as Fox moved through the hallway.

"I've got to hand it to you, Reggie," the man said. "For a Yankee lawyer, you're showing a lot of balls, even though you're probably really shitting in your drawers."

Fox stopped abruptly as he saw an immense form standing in front of him. He didn't have the Afro wig on, and his dark, shaved head glistened under the overhead fluorescent lights shining down from the ceiling. The huge black man held out a hand, palm upward, indicating that Fox should step into the open door on the left. The room inside held a small wooden table, two chairs, and a telephone that was sitting on the tabletop. It was one of those cellular models. The monster pointed to the chair farthest from the door. Fox went to it and sat down, trying his best to look as nonchalant as he could.

"Now," he said, trying to suppress the hint of a quiver in his voice, "would you mind telling me what this is all about?" He swallowed hard and looked from one impassive face to the other.

The southerner settled himself in the chair opposite Fox and leaned back, stretching out his legs. He was wearing ornate cowboy boots, Fox noticed. Black, with red and gold ornamentation along the sides.

"Mr. Fox," he said casually as he withdrew a package of long, thin cigars from inside his gray sport coat. "We have much to talk about, sir, and it will go along a lot smoother," he paused to look at Fox over the partially unwrapped cigar. "If you . . . cooperate."

"Cooperate?" Fox said. "How the hell can I cooperate if I don't have any idea what's going on? I don't know where I am, who you guys are, what you want . . ."

The southerner crumpled the cellophane and let it fall to

the floor. Then he took out a gold-plated, butane lighter and pressed down the button. A thin, bluish flame shot up and engulfed the end of the cigar.

"Mr. Fox," he began.

"Don't pull that syrupy, mint julep shit on me," Fox said, deciding that boldness might give him the initiative. Besides, he figured, if they wanted him dead, he wouldn't be sitting there. Better to act as if he were in control. Calling the shots. It worked in court, and what was court but a sidebar to life? "Either you tell me where I am," he held up a finger, "what this is all about," he held up another finger, "and let me call my office," the third finger, "or I'm not going to tell you shit."

The southerner puffed on his cigar, then licked his lips.

"I can see that this is not going as I had expected," he said. "I imagined that after spending the night in our commodious facilities, you would be more agreeable, Mr. Fox."

Fox just crossed his arms and legs and stared at the wall. The southerner took another long draw on his cigar and continued.

"It seems what we have here, is a communication failure," he said, withdrawing the cigar from his mouth. "What was that line in that old movie with Paul Newman? *Cool Hand Luke*? A failure to communicate." He paused to smile, then went on. "And in the interests of saving time and effort for all concerned, I do believe that some remedial education is in order. Gumbo."

Gumbo, Fox thought. He called him Gumbo.

The man who had been standing off to Fox's left reached out suddenly and grabbed the lawyer's thin wrists. Gumbo took a wrist in each hand and walked around behind Fox, stretching the lawyer's arms up over his head. The southerner slid the table up against Fox's chest, then the black giant leaned down, forcing the captive forearms down flat onto the tabletop.

"Do you recall elementary school, Mr. Fox?" the southerner said, hunching over so that he was eyeball to eyeball with the lawyer. "How your teacher would say something and you'd do it automatically, because you knew that you invariably had no choice. Because discipline was the fulcrum for learning."

Fox could feel the other man's breath on his face.

"Now we're going to return to those halcyon days of yore, Mr. Fox. To recover that discipline, that climate of cooperative question-and-response. And I'm going to use a little nursery rhyme to illustrate my point."

Gumbo's massive chest was pressing against Fox's shoulders, holding him down in the chair. The big black fingers of Gumbo's hand slowly slid down Fox's left arm, pressing the palm flat on the table. The southerner grabbed the lawyer's hand and straightened the index finger.

"This little piggy went to market." He released the index finger and peeled the middle finger out straight. "This little piggy stayed home." He grabbed Fox's ring finger next and forcibly extended it against the tabletop. "And this little piggy cried wee, wee, wee, all the way home." His lower lip twisted downward as he flicked the butane lighter and held the bluish flame against Fox's exposed flesh. The lawyer's high-pitched scream echoed in the tiny room.

Chapter 8

Wednesday, April 15, 1992

9:04 A.M.

Tina was both relieved and angry when Reginald Fox's call came into the office. Angry because, after flirting with her on the way out yesterday he hadn't even bothered to call her, and she'd ended up sitting by the phone all evening waiting for it to ring. But then she was a trifle bit relieved when he called in that morning saying he was sick, thinking that was, perhaps, the reason he hadn't called.

"I'm a bit under the weather," Fox said over the phone. "Started last night when I got home. Must be food poisoning or something. I'm going in to the doctor's this morning. Are there any messages for me?"

"No, Mr. Fox," Tina said, trying to sound professional, but leaving a hint of sympathy in her tone.

"Listen," he said. She suddenly got hopeful as he paused. "I need Dave to cover my cases in court this morning. Tell him to get continuances or something, okay?"

"Okay, Mr. Fox." The vestiges of sympathy fluttered away. At least he could have called to tell me he wasn't feeling good, she thought. Or maybe that we'd make it another time, or something.

"Oh, yeah," his voice said, sounding somewhat distant. "I need you to look up a client's home phone for me. Johnny Osmand's. You know the file number?"

124

"Yes, I do," she said, her tone becoming clipped. Of course she knew it. Did he think she was stupid, or something? She put him on hold without saying anything and left her desk to look up the file. The music that played on the hold button would let him know that she hadn't hung up. After retrieving the number she went back to her chair, settled herself, and picked up the receiver. "Mr. Fox, I have the number."

"Just a minute," he said, sounding nervous. Maybe he really was sick. He asked her for it and she repeated it.

"Thanks," he said. "Listen, if Mr. Osmand calls the office, just take a message. Don't mention that I called in sick, understand?"

"Yes."

"And just tell him that I've got to get ahold of him," Fox continued. "Tell him that something important's come up and it's imperative that we talk, okay? You got it, Tina?"

"Yes," she said. "I've got it."

"Good. Thanks. I'll call back later and check my messages."

He hung up. Tina looked at the phone briefly before slamming it down in its cradle. Asshole, she thought.

On the other end of the line, in the same small room that had earlier held his screams, a haggard, battered-looking Reginald Fox swallowed hard as he stared across the table at the southerner.

"That was real fine, Reggie," he said, his lips forming into a soft smile. He blew out a smoke ring. "Real fine."

9:35 A.M.

Diane hadn't even bothered to call the special number to see if there was any news about when the bank would be

125

opening again. She certainly didn't want to waste time wondering about it. She glanced at the stack of money bundled on her kitchen table. They'd left it there and gone off to work. Trusting souls, but then again, it really wasn't that much to worry about anyway. Certainly not the bundle she'd been counting on, hoping it would change her life. Now she knew that, despite the few grand or so she'd get from the heist, she'd still be in the same rut, getting up every day, taking the train downtown, punching in on that goddamn time clock, listening to her asshole supervisor ragging at her all the motherfucking time . . .

She went over and kicked the plastic garbage bag with Linc's and Rick's clothes in it. There was a note from Linc asking if she'd run over to their apartment and throw the stuff in the washer. Fuck him, she thought. What did he think she was, anyway? Some fucking maid, or something? She gave the bag another kick, which split the side open. The odor from the stinky clothes permeated the room, and she quickly carried the broken bag out to the porch. After slamming the door, she returned and looked at the money. She felt like taking the whole thing and going to Vegas or Atlantic City. Maybe she could win enough to set her up. But she knew next to nothing about card games or any other games of chance. She decided to hide the money before somebody got a glimpse of it through a window, or something.

The videocassette was sitting on the table next to the cash. After cramming the money into a brown paper bag and then sticking it in her hiding place under the stove, she picked up the video and slipped it out of the box. Walking over, she slid the cassette into the slot of the VCR and picked up the remote. The picture was black and white and centered on a long table at somebody's house. A group of white guys were all sitting around it, talking and telling jokes. She recognized

Johnny Osmand, a.k.a. Joe Orlando, only he looked a bit younger, his hair darker on top. Next to him was a greasy looking dago with some kind of dark mark on his right cheek. His hair was slicked back from his face, making it look fatter. But she could see from his look that he was "mean-fat." Nobody to mess with.

They continued to talk and her thumb pressed the fast-forward button. The figures did a jerky little dance as their heads and torsos bounced around. The fat guy with the birthmark got up and went to the front of the table. He began talking, using his hands a lot, like those Italian guys always do. The accelerated speed made the movements look comical. Fatso was pointing, then he went over and picked up a gym bag of some sort, with something long sticking out of it. A baseball bat. He took the bat and rested it on his shoulder, pointing again, like he was looking down the mound at a pitcher winding up with a fast ball. With a sudden jerk, the fat guy went around the table and, grabbing the bat with both hands, swung it at one of the sitting men. The guy's head went forward and hit the table. Several other men drew guns and pointed them at the guys sitting around the one that had gotten hit. The man next to him, a small guy with light hair, got up and started to run. Some big guy in a suit stepped in front of him and shoved him back. As the smaller man did a stutter-step backward, the guy with the bat smashed him across the lower part of the back. The small guy sank to his knees, and the fat man with the bat moved forward and raised it, like he was going to swing at a pitch.

Diane was so startled that she hit the stop button on the remote, instead of play, trying to slow the tape down to normal speed. After getting the picture back, she rewound it to where he picked up the bat and turned the volume up.

"So like I was tellin' youse," the man said, gripping the

baseball bat with both hands. "Bottom of the ninth, we're down by two, and the tying run's on third." He paused and pointed. "My fucking coach is tellin' me, 'go for a base hit, go for a base hit'." He raised the bat. "But I knew that sometimes you just gotta take the bat, and swing for the fucking fences."

He ran toward the table and swung the bat in a downward arc. The sound of the wood striking the seated man's head sounded like a pumpkin getting dropped. There were shouts and yells, the scuffling of chairs, and more urgent shouts. Some of the standing men pulled guns out of their pockets as the one guy at the table tried to bolt. When the big guy caught him and pushed him back, Fatso ran up and swung the bat into his back, with a whoomp. The man's grunt of pain could be heard, and he sank to his knees. The one with the bat raised it and muttered a profanity. Then he let it fly. Right to the kneeling man's right arm. There was a shriek of pain, groans, then another whack, this time to the other arm. The man on his knees stayed down, and the bat-man moved back to the table. He grabbed the hair of the first man he'd hit and lifted the bloody head. A dark gush spilled out of the mouth.

"Campo, you fucker," he said. "You ruined my friend Johnny's best fucking table cloth." There were hoots of laughter from some of the men.

Orlando, or Osmand, or whatever his name was, seemed to be laughing the loudest. "Oh, Vino, you're too much," he said.

The camera zoomed in on the bloody face, the eyes having that unfocused, glazed look of death. Vino dropped the head, letting it hit the table with a clunk, and went back over to the man he'd beaten before. He was still on his knees, all hunched over. The fat man circled him, leaning over, sneering.

"So, you son of a whore, whaddya got to say for yourself?"

"Uhhh, please, Vino," the man stammered.

Vino slapped him across the face.

"Shaddup, you fuck. You shoulda been thinking about this when you was planning on taking *me* out." He raised up the bat and swung it hard against the man's thigh, then slammed it down on his chest as he rolled over. He lifted the bat once more, and brought it down, again to the leg area. He paused and looked around. The picture was remarkably clear. Somebody had filmed this. Diane could see the sweat popping out on the fat cheeks. Fascinated, she continued to watch.

"I might as well take my time and enjoy this, huh, Pony?" the fat guy said. He brought the bat down again and again; each time there was a solid thunking sound. Shrieks of pain were replaced by low grunts as the sounds became more sodden, then the bat-man stopped.

"Game's over," he said, his breath coming in short gasps. "Clean this shit outta here."

"What about them?" one of the gunmen asked, gesturing to two men who were still being held at gunpoint.

"Them?" the fat guy said, walking over and gripping the face of one of them with his meaty hand. "If they'd been doin' their fuckin' jobs right, I'd be the one laying there bleedin', instead of Campo and Pony. So, like all good bodyguards, they should follow their bosses." He let the man's face go. One of the guys in the suits moved forward and cuffed the doomed bodyguard on the head several times with a sap. The man sagged, and the big guy did the same to the second prisoner.

"Give those guys the Hoffa-treatment," Vino said, still holding the bat at his waist. "But leave Campo and Volpone where they can be found. I wanna send a message with them two."

Diane let the tape run on, but when it degenerated into talking and jokes, she let it play out on the fast-forward mode. When it was done, she rewound it and carefully took it out. A double murder captured on video, and another two killings ordered. No wonder Osmand had kept this in his safety deposit box. It was probably some sort of blackmail insurance. And now she had it. Maybe, just maybe, when you have something that somebody else really wants, they'll pay to get it back. Perhaps they'd still be calling her Lady Di on some island somewhere after all.

10:00 A.M.

When Tony and Ray got to the booth in the restaurant, Kent Faulkner and Arlene already had their coffee cups half drained. A partially eaten English muffin sat on a dish in front of Faulkner. Ray smirked at it in disgust.

"At least you coulda waited till we got here," he said, straining to sound good-natured.

Faulkner, who had been leaning toward Arlene, moved back into his seat slightly and smiled, showing his rows of perfectly aligned teeth.

"Sorry, we drove in together," he said.

"Your car acting up again?" Tony asked Arlene.

"Oh, no, not really," she said. Then added with a smile, "You know how much I hate driving into the city."

Ray waited so Tony could slide in before him, then he took the outside seat.

"So what's the scoop?" Tony asked.

"Well, like I told you," Arlene said, "Fred okayed the deal, but he wants us to make sure that Osmand isn't just yanking our chains."

"So that means viewing the tape," Faulkner said.

"Is that what that means?" Ray said. He felt Tony's foot

nudge him under the table. The waitress came and refilled Arlene's and Faulkner's cups. Then she set new cups in front of Tony and Ray and flipped open her pad.

Tony just had coffee, but Ray ordered scrambled eggs, bacon, rye toast, and orange juice.

"That's a lot of cholesterol," Faulkner said. "You ought to watch it, Ray."

Ray stared at him over the rim of the coffee cup, then, as he lowered it, made a lips-only smile.

"I'm doing a lot of working out," he said.

"Well, you still got to watch it," Faulkner said. "That cholesterol's a silent killer. I did a paper on it when I was in the academy. I'll have to see if I can dig it out for you."

"Don't go to no special trouble," Ray said.

"It's no problem, Ray," Faulkner said, showing his perfect teeth again. "In fact, it was so good it was published in *The Law Enforcement Bulletin*. That's a magazine they publish out of Quantico."

Ray was about to make some smart-ass comment when Tony changed the subject.

"So how we gonna work this with the Mink?"

"Well, I left a message at Reggie's law firm this morning for him to call me," Arlene said. "As soon as he does, we can work out the details of how, when, and where we can view the tape." She leaned over and smiled at Tony. "Isn't it exciting to think about nailing Costelli? Especially for you, Tony, after all the time you've been after him."

"Yeah, it would be great," Tony said. "So you left a message? What time is Fox supposed to be in?"

"His secretary didn't say," she said.

"Maybe we'd better call again," Ray said. He started to get up, then stopped. "Say, Kent, maybe you should call."

Faulkner's brows knitted together slightly.

"I mean," Ray continued, "if *I* call they might think it's some asshole defendant, or something. But you, I mean, they'll probably think it's a judge."

Faulkner took a deep breath, then looked at Ray with a strained smile.

"All right," he said, getting up.

As he walked out of the room, Ray, who was watching him, snapped his fingers and said, "I shoulda asked him to check on that issue of *The Law Enforcement Bulletin* while he was going to the phone." He got up. "I gotta go to the head."

"I get the impression that Ray doesn't like Kent very much," Arlene said, a broad smile stretching across her face as they watched Ray's short, powerful body move across the room.

"It just takes him a while sometimes," Tony said. "I've known him a lotta years, and I know he wouldn't hesitate to lay down his life to save one of us."

She reached across and gave his hand a squeeze. It startled him. But before he could say anything, Faulkner was coming back. Arlene withdrew her hand quickly.

"Uh, I need the number," he said.

Arlene grabbed her purse and searched through it, finally withdrawing one of Fox's business cards. She handed it to Kent, and he went back towards the phones.

"How do you think we should handle this?" she asked.

"Well," Tony said, "we need to make sure that the Mink is ready to cooperate. If he can deliver this tape, and I don't think he would've mentioned it if he couldn't, then we've got to put him on ice till we're ready to move against Costelli. Because, make no mistake about it, once word leaks out that the Mink's gonna flip, Vino will order him taken out."

She shook her head. "And Osmand's one of his closest friends, isn't he?"

"These animals have no loyalty," Tony said. "Especially with their own necks in the noose. The two main things we've got to worry about are that the Mink's really sincere about testifying, and making sure that tape's as solid as he says it is."

"Like you said, it must be if he's offering it to us."

"Maybe," Tony said. "But all we got at this point is a lot of promises."

"That's still enough to feel confident, isn't it? I mean, what could go wrong now?"

"That's just what my partner said to me yesterday."

Faulkner came ambling back. As he slid into the booth, Ray appeared.

"Fox called in sick," Faulkner said. "But I left another message with his secretary."

"That's kind of odd," said Tony, leaning forward and steepling his hands. "Maybe we ought to order a surveillance team to keep tabs on his house."

"A surveillance team on a suspect's defense lawyer?" Faulkner said dubiously.

"Yeah," Ray said. "What's wrong with that? So he's a lawyer. What? You think their shit don't stink, or something?" Then, after flashing an ingratiating grin, "Oh, I forgot. You *are* a lawyer, ain't ya?"

"That's right, Lovisi," Faulkner said, his face reddening slightly. "I am, and I don't want to mess up this case."

"Kent's right, Ray," Arlene said. "We'd better run it by Fred first."

"Fine," said Tony.

"All right," Faulkner said. He got up again. "I'll go make the call now."

Arlene got up too, saying she had to pay a visit to the ladies' room.

When they both were gone, Ray said, "Did you hear that fucker? 'I am a lawyer.' " Then he leaned close to Tony and asked, "Well, did ya?"

"Did I what?"

"Did ya ask her out?"

Tony frowned and shook his head.

"Jesus Christ, Tony, what's the matter with you? What do you think I stepped out for? To leave you two alone for a few minutes."

"I told you, she's young enough to be—"

"Ah, shit," Ray interrupted. "I told you, that kind of stuff doesn't matter nowadays."

"It matters to me. Maybe I'm just old fashioned."

"Sometimes, if you don't take the bull by the horns, you lose out on a great opportunity."

"And sometimes if you do," Tony shot back, "he shakes you loose and sticks you right in your ass."

10:15 A.M.

When Henry got back to the dig site, the guys were taking a break. He noticed that the rest of the guys were acting very standoffish toward Linc and Rick. Even Dock, the assistant foreman who'd known Linc a long time, was silent. The meat wagon had pulled up and everyone had gotten their coffee and donuts and retired to take-five and eat. Linc and Rick were sitting by themselves on some empty wooden spools of cable. Taking a deep breath, Henry walked over to them.

"How you feeling today, Rick?" Henry asked.

"Fine, sir," Rick said, smiling.

Henry smiled back. Damn he liked this kid, in spite of everything, especially the way he laid that military-courtesy shit

on. It was always "yes, sir" and "no, sir." Too bad all his crew
didn't have those kinds of manners. Henry took off his hat
and wiped his brow.

"Where you been, Uncle Henry?" Linc asked, biting into
his donut and washing it down with some coffee.

"Some motherfuckers danced all over the roof of my
fucking truck last night," he said. "Found it this morning and
made out a police report, not that it's gonna make any difference, but I needed it for the insurance." He snorted and
looked around. "They probably gonna raise them premiums,
too, as if I don't pay enough already."

Linc and Rick exchanged solemn looks and Henry wondered if they might know something about the damage.

"I had to fire that Booker this morning," Henry continued. "So watch it. Some of the other guys may be pissed,
but, shit, the motherfucker showed up drunk. Again," he
added with emphasis. Then his eyes narrowed slightly as he
looked them over. "You sure you feeling okay? You both look
like the cat done walked all over you."

Linc grinned and said, "Woman trouble. Uncle Henry.
You know how that is."

Henry just gave a knowing cluck, accompanied by a big
smile. "Yeah," he said. "They sure gots a mind of their own,
don't they?"

11:00 A.M.

"Tina," Fox said over the phone, "have there been any
messages?"

"Mr. Fox?" she asked. "You sound terrible. Is everything
okay?"

Before he answered, Fox heard Germaine, who was sitting
across from him listening in on the extension, snap his fingers
sharply and point at him. Gumbo was right behind him.

"I told you this morning. I'm not feeling well," Fox said. "What about my court cases? Any problems?"

"Well, none that I'm aware of," she said. "Mr. Levitt said he would handle them when I told him you weren't feeling well. Did you make it to the doctor?"

"Not yet," he said quickly. "Has anyone called for me? Mr. Osmand?"

"Well, Kent Faulkner called earlier," Tina said. "You did have two calls from a woman, too."

"Who?"

"I'm not sure," she said hesitantly. "She must be a prospective client, because we have no listing of her in the files. A Ms. Jones."

"Oh?"

"Yeah, she gave the name Cleopatra Jones," Tina said with a snicker, then added, "she sounded black."

"Black?" Fox said, wondering who it could be. "Did she say what she wanted?"

"Well, it's kind of odd," Tina said. "I got this call asking to speak to you. When I said you weren't available, she asked when you'd be in. I asked who was calling and the person hung up. Then about thirty minutes later she called back. I'm sure it was the same woman; like I said, she sounded black. And this time she gave the name, and asked for you again."

"Did she say what it was regarding?" Fox asked rather impatiently.

"Let's see. Just a second . . ." said Tina. "Oh, okay, here it is. This is kind of weird. She said she had something you might be interested in. A tape belonging to a Mr. Orlando."

It took Fox a few seconds before he put it together; then he asked, "Did she leave a number?"

"She said she'd call back at eleven-thirty."

Fox closed his eyes and spoke slowly into the receiver.

"Tina, this is *very* important. As soon as she calls back, tell her I'm very interested in speaking with her. Get a number where she can be reached, and tell her I'll call her right back. Then call me on my portable phone immediately. Do y— understand?" He fumbled over his last words.

"Yes, sir," she said.

Fox hung up, and looked at the other man.

"Once I get you the tape. I'm out of it, right?" he asked.

The southerner set his phone down and smiled pleasantly.

"That's our deal, Reggie," he said. "Is that what that black gal wants to give you?"

"It has to be," Fox said. "Orlando is the name Johnny used for the safety-deposit box. Although how she got it, I can't imagine."

"Well, we'll just have to play this little ol' game out then," the southerner said. "Maybe we got more rabbits in the briar patch than we thought. We'll explore that a little bit later, but right now, you got another call to make." He nodded and Gumbo handed Fox the receiver again. He could feel the presence of the big man looming just behind him.

Chapter 9

Wednesday, April 15, 1992

11:45 A.M.

Diane had been insistent with the bitch on the telephone, saying that if Mr. Fox was so interested in talking to her, *he* could leave a number for her to call him back, not the other way around.

"I'm afraid that we aren't allowed to give out associates' personal phone numbers, ma'am," the secretary had said sarcastically.

"Well, can't you call him on another line, then?" Diane asked, just as sarcastically.

"Just a moment."

She heard the sound of music in the receiver and knew she'd been put on hold. Exhaling slowly, she ran over the plan again in her mind. Be firm, be plain, don't let yourself get bullied or trapped. The secretary came back on after a few moments.

"Hello, Ms. Jones?"

"Yes," Diane said.

"Mr. Fox says you can reach him at the following number." She read it off. Diane didn't even say thank you before she hung up. She reached into her purse for some more change, but bowed her head slightly as she deposited it. The number rang twice before someone answered.

"Mr. Fox?" she asked.

138

"Yes," a voice said. "Who is this please?"

"Jones," Diane said, trying her best to sound as cool and calm as she could. "Cleopatra Jones. You got my message earlier?"

"I did," said Fox slowly. "You have the item that you mentioned?"

"I do."

"How did you get it?"

"That's none of your business."

"Well," Fox said, "I do have to be sure you really have it, don't I?"

"It's a VHS tape in a plain white box," Diane said with precision. "The picture is in black and white and it shows a party, a man with a baseball bat, and Mr. Osmand. You want me to go on?"

She heard Fox clear his throat.

"I think that will suffice," he said. "What exactly do you want?"

"My offer is simple. I want a million dollars or the tape will go to the police. Hundreds in unmarked bills will be fine," she said like she'd heard them say on TV.

"A million dollars," Fox snorted. "Ah . . . where are you?"

"Never mind where I am," Diane snapped. "Do you want to deal or not?"

"Well, a million dollars is a lot."

"Oh, come on. What's a million to you people?"

"I mean, it's going to take some time to raise that kind of money." He was pausing between his words. "Do you have a number where I can call you back?"

"No, Mr. Fox," Diane said. "I'll call *you* back. Now do we have a deal, or not?"

"I'm sure we will." His voice sounded hesitant. "But I'll need to run this by a few people."

"No," she said. "I won't deal with anyone but you. I have to see you make the drop; then I call you and tell you where the tape is."

"Okay." He paused again and she began to wonder if someone else was there, advising him how to answer. "Why don't you call me back in forty minutes or so? I have to make a couple of calls."

"All right," Diane said. As she hung up, she breathed a sigh of relief. Everything was going according to her plan. The phone rang as she turned away and she picked it up without thinking. Probably the operator wanting more money.

"Hello," she said. There was no response, so she hung up. Going back over to the counter, she sat on the stool again. The waitress came and refilled her coffee cup. Diane smiled a thank-you and glanced at her watch. She had forty minutes to go over the plan again in her mind before calling them back.

Germaine, who had been listening in on the extension right across from Fox, scribbling and passing handwritten notes across the tabletop, smiled and asked, "So did you figure out just who this little gal is, Reggie?" He collected the notes he'd passed, arranged them in a neat little stack, and unwrapped another one of those thin cigars that were making Fox feel even sicker.

"She has to be the girl from the bank," he said. "That's the only thing I can think of. She sounds black, and that chick who was working the safe deposit boxes the day Osmand took me down there was black too. She must have remembered my name. Though how she got the tape, I still can't figure."

"Does what she said about the tape sound accurate?" Germaine asked.

"I guess so," Fox said. "I've never seen it. I just saw the

box that day he showed it to me and told me what it was."

Germaine considered this as he wrinkled the cellophane and dropped it on the tabletop. He looked up as Bobby Mallory came in carrying a heavy twenty- by twelve-inch paperbound book with a blue cover. Mallory grinned as he set the book on the tabletop in front of Germaine.

"Okay," Mallory said. "The automatic-callback number that printed out on the LDS screen comes back to a pay phone at this address here." He traced his thumbnail across the fine print on the multi-columned page. "Wagner's Restaurant on a Hundred-and-Eleventh and Michigan."

Germaine looked at the address on the page and then back up to Mallory.

"Is that far from here?" he asked.

"It's in Roseland," Mallory said. He shrugged. "About twenty or thirty minutes."

"Good, then if we leave now—"

Mallory cut him off with a laugh.

"Hold on. It ain't that easy. That's a shine neighborhood." He glanced warily at Gumbo, who was still standing behind Fox, his arms crossed, his face impassive. "What I mean is, us white guys would kinda stick out, if you know what I'm saying."

Germaine smiled as he blew a puff of smoke out from between his teeth.

"I appreciate your candor, Bobby." He took a long draw on the cigar, then said, "I guess you and that other boy— what's his name? Del Bianco?—will have to take my associate, Mr. Queen, over there and kind of show him a little bit of Chi-town."

Mallory looked at Gumbo, who hadn't moved at all since the last time, and smiled.

"Be glad to," he said.

141

★ ★ ★ ★ ★

12:30 A.M.

The restaurant was starting to fill up with the lunchtime crowd, but they were mostly on the other side where the tables were. Diane kept her seat at the counter, near the pay phones. She drank another cup of coffee, ordered some soup, and went to the ladies' room. So far, so good, she thought.

When she came back to her seat, the waitress was setting the soup down. As Diane sat down, she noticed that she still had this section practically to herself, except for this huge guy with an immense Afro sitting two stools down from her. Diane smiled to herself. Didn't he know those hairstyles weren't even in style anymore?

She paid the girl for the cream of broccoli soup and took a sip. After a few more spoonfuls she glanced at her watch. It was almost time. She took a deep breath, going over the plan once more on just how she wanted Fox to take a taxi to Water Tower Place to meet her. She'd take the money, which would be in a small handbag, and then give him a key to the locker where she'd put the tape. They would make this last exchange once she was in her own cab and he was standing outside on foot. It felt like a good plan. Like one she'd seen on a TV movie-of-the-week. She'd even taken the name Cleopatra Jones from one of those black heroines in an old seventies movie. She could change cabs a couple of times to make sure she wasn't followed, then just head on out to the airport and fly away to someplace warm. Maybe she'd take Linc along, but maybe not. After the way he'd talked to her, calling her a 'hoe, and all.

Diane got up and went to the phone, sorting out her change. She dropped the coins into the slot and dialed. The phone rang twice before Fox answered it. He sounded nervous.

"Mr. Fox, this is Cleopatra Jones," Diane said.

"Okay, I've talked to my people and they're interested," he said. "But we have to be very sure that we get the tape if we're going to pay out all that money."

"I've got that all figured out, Mr. Fox," Diane said. She heard a beeper going off behind her, and glanced around. The big brother's shoulders were rolling as he looked at the pager on his belt. He got up and moved toward the phone next to her. Diane turned her back and lowered her voice, so she could have more privacy.

"First, I want you to put it in a blue handbag," Diane said. "Then—" She felt a big hand crowd over her mouth and something nudge against her, and, with a shudder, her whole body went numb. Her lungs expelled almost all their air, then she tried desperately to inhale, but she couldn't. The hand was gripping her mouth so hard. She felt another shock and then black dots swarmed in front of her eyes.

"Hey, baby what's wrong?" Gumbo said as he caught her limp form slinking to the floor. He snatched the receiver and said, "Hey."

"You got her?" Germaine's voice asked.

"Yeah," Gumbo said.

He hung up the phone and squatted slightly to swing his arm under Diane's legs. Then, lifting her like she weighed next to nothing, he carried her toward the front doors.

"Hey, what's goin' on?" the waitress said.

"Nothing," Gumbo answered. "She need her medicine, is all."

"Well, you want me to call the ambulance or something?"

"Naw, she's my lady," he said, pulling the door open. "I'll take her."

* * * * *

Diane was vaguely conscious of being carried, then placed inside a van. The slamming of the door seemed to rouse her slightly, but by that time, she felt the cold hard metal of the vehicle's floor under her. Blinking several times, she tried to move, but couldn't. Her eyes focused on the massive black figure that was sitting on the fender well, hovering over her. But the Afro was gone. His scalp looked slick now. Craning her head, she saw there was another guy sitting across from him. Slowly, he started to come into focus. He was a white guy, young and skinny, wearing glasses and a hat. His eyes were glued on her.

"Funny," the honkey said with a grin. "She don't look like Tamara Dobson, does she?"

2:26 P.M.

With another day of no court because the Federal Building was still closed, like most of the other buildings in that ten-square-block area, Tony and Ray decided to take off early and hit the Armory for a workout. On the way the car phone rang and Ray, even though he was driving, snatched it up.

"Lovisi," he said. "Yeah, he's here. Just a minute."

He handed the phone to Tony, who answered, "Cardoff."

"Tony?" the familiar voice asked. "This is Nate Wells."

"Yeah, how you doing?"

"Not so good," Nate said. "You guys busy?"

"Not really," Tony said. "Still waiting for our offices to open up. Why? You got something going?"

"I need a favor, man. We over here at the projects sitting and waiting for some bad asses who done a drive-by, and one of my snitches beeps me. You remember that guy I was telling you about at the gym?"

"Yeah, sort of," Tony said.

"Not a bad guy," Nate continued. "Out on parole now for burglary. Got him a shoplifting beef he's working off for me, and now he done got busted again."

"Where's he at?"

"He's over in District Five. Sounds like just some nothing bust, but I was trying to squeeze him for a line on the dude that's been supplying the GD's with their firepower."

The GD's, which stood for Gangster Disciples, were one of the major street gangs coming into prominence now that the El Rukins had been effectively shut down.

"What do you want us to do, Nate?" Tony asked.

"Just run over there and see what kind of shit he's talkin'. If it looks good, maybe you can get him to make a buy from the gunrunner-dude, and we'll have a reason to take him down."

"Sounds good," said Tony. "What's this snitch's name?"

"Cole," Nate said. "Booker Cole. You might have to buy him a half-pint to keep him happy."

Ray kept driving south on the Dan Ryan until he got to the cut-off for the Calumet Expressway. They were at 111th Street inside of fifteen minutes and driving through the historic Pullman section of Chicago. The District Five station house, which also housed Area Two, was a brand new brick building laid out with the same sweeping architecture of the more recently-constructed district stations. Its brick front had a large glass picture window by an expansive foyer. Directly inside the front doors, there were pictures of Mayor Daley, the brand new Police Superintendent, Matt Rodriguez, and the various other higher-ups in the Police Department, descending to the Fifth District Commander. Tony and Ray passed by the front section and went immediately to the island-like counter where several uniformed coppers sat. A female was seated at a radio console; a heavyset sergeant was hunched over a typewriter, swearing as he lifted his glasses to inspect what he had typed. The third officer, a young guy with a crisp light-blue shirt on, stepped up to greet them. His nametag said O'Shay.

"Whatever it is, we don't want any," he said with a grin.

"Cardoff, Organized Crime Division," Tony said, flipping open his badge case, thinking that O'Shay looked more Hispanic than Irish. He nodded at Ray. "My partner Ray Lovisi."

"Glad to meet you," O'Shay said, shaking each of their hands. "What can I do you out of?" The grin returned.

"An officer from Gang Crimes called us," Tony said. "Apparently you're holding one of his snitches and we're here to play let's-make-a-deal."

O'Shay pursed his lips as he considered this, then went for a clipboard on the sergeant's desk. The Sarge only glanced at him peripherally and went back to his typewriter. O'Shay returned to the counter and asked Tony what the guy's name was.

"Booker Cole," Tony replied.

After running his finger down the list of names, O'Shay stopped and nodded.

"Yeah, we picked him up from a liquor store in Roseland," O'Shay said. "There's a note to flag him from a Detective Wells. That your buddy in Gang Crimes?"

"That's him," Ray said. "Can you bring the asshole into one of the interview rooms?"

"Coming right up, Sarge," O'Shay said.

They started down the hallway, but Ray suddenly stopped.

"You got a cigarette machine here?" he yelled to O'Shay.

"Down in the break room," O'Shay called back.

When Tony looked at him quizzically, Ray said, "You ever

seen one of these dogs give up anything without getting a couple of Kools?"

After getting the cigarettes, they went back to the interview room. Booker Cole sat hunched over a simulated-wood table, his head in his hands. He looked up at them as they entered.

"How you doin', Booker?" Ray said, moving over and kicking out the chair opposite the black man. "I'm Detective Lovisi, and this is my partner Detective Cardoff."

"We're friends of Nate Wells," Tony added.

This introduction seemed to satisfy Booker, who nodded, straightened up, and asked if either one of them had a cigarette.

"Sure," Ray said, taking out the pack of Kools and shaking one out for him. He snapped the safety match on the striking pad and lit it for Booker, who leaned forward, canting his head. After he drew in on the cigarette, he slumped back, ready to talk.

"So how ol' Nate doin'?" he asked.

"He's a little busy right now," Ray said. "So he sent us instead. Nate told us you might be able to help us out a little bit."

"With what?"

"With the guy who's been supplying guns to the GD's," Tony said.

Booker contemplated this for a moment, taking a long hit on the cigarette. Then he leaned forward and blew the smoke out of his nose.

"Lookie here," he said, his voice barely above a whisper. "You get me outta here on an I-Bond, and I'll see what I can dig up, okay?"

An I-Bond was short for Individual Recognizance Bond, which meant that Booker would be free on his signature until his court date instead of posting the specified amount of money required by statute.

"Yeah, right," Ray said. "Don't try to run a game on us, man. We been doing this shit too long."

"You want that I-Bond, you're gonna have to do more than that," Tony said.

"What I gots to do?"

"Make an introduction for us," Ray said.

"To two white guys?" Booker said, smiling incredulously. "You outta your minds? This dude ain't about to sell to no white boys, and you guys got cop written all over you."

"Who does he sell to, Booker?" Ray asked.

"He sell the D's mostly," Booker said, finishing up his cigarette and stubbing it out in the ashtray. "Sometimes people from the neighborhood."

"What kind of shit he sell?" Ray asked.

"What kind you want?" Booker shot back. He held his fingers to his lips, mimicking a request for another cigarette. Ray gave him one.

"Automatic weapons?" Tony asked.

Booker nodded.

"Where's he deal out of?" Tony asked.

"Outta his car mostly," Booker said, the embers of the cigarette glowing brightly between his fingers. "A dark blue Malibu."

"What's this cat's name?" asked Ray.

"Jem Dandy."

"What's his real name?" Ray said.

Booker answered with a quick shrug, accompanied by a shake of his head.

"How about this?" Ray said, leaning forward. He had to squint slightly because of the cigarette smoke. "You make a phone call for us, setting up a deal for an Uzi or Mac-Ten.

Once it's set up, we get you outta here, you make the buy, and turn the gun over to us. Then we'll take care of this bullshit shoplifting-beef."

"Shit, man, you ain't gonna arrest him tonight, is you?"

"Nah," Ray said. "We just get the fuckin' gun, then that gives us an in for a warrant later."

"He won't even know you were part of it, when it finally comes down," Tony said. "You got our word on it."

Booker frowned for a moment, then licked his lips.

"You get me outta here on an I-Bond tonight?" he asked, bringing the cigarette to his lips.

"And, we might just throw in a half-pint," Tony said.

"Okay," Booker said after a moment, "I guess we got a deal."

It took about fifteen more minutes to set the deal up. They checked the station records for arrests and information on anyone known as "Jem Dandy," but found nothing. "But we might've arrested him on another name. This could be a new street name," O'Shay offered. After getting Booker's property, and letting him dig the number out of his little address book, he made the call on one of the special phones in the interview room. The conversation started off rather smoothly, with Booker saying how he got himself fired, and wanted to pick up on a little action.

"What you lookin' fo'," the voice on the other end of the phone asked him. "A baby-nine, or something?" Tony was listening in on an extension. Booker made the motion with his fingertips on his lips again. Ray gave him another cigarette.

"I don't wanna mess with no little pussy-guns," Booker said. "Man, I'm looking to get me something big."

"Big? Like how big?"

"You get me a Uzi?" Booker asked, almost coyly.

"What you want with a gun that big and nasty?" Jem Dandy asked.

"Hey, man, do I ask you about yo' business?" Booker said with just the right mixture of outrage and propriety.

"That kind of firepower don't come cheap, man," Jem Dandy said, suspicion edging into this voice. "I mean, I got it, but I also gots to wonder how you can come up with the bread for it, brother."

The tone seemed to worry Booker, who glanced nervously at Tony. Tony, his hand covering the phone, mouthed: *Tell him you'll go for the nine*. Booker's brow furrowed in incomprehension, the look in his eyes of incipient panic. Ray drew a nine on the paper and tapped it. Booker glanced at it and seemed to immediately recapture his composure.

"Okay, I'll tell you what," he said. "I always like to check out my merchandise a little anyway. How much that baby-nine goin' fo'?"

"I could let it go fo' say, three yards," Jem Dandy said.

"Shit, two-fifty and you got a deal," Booker said.

"All right, but you better have the cash, man. No fucking food stamps or dope or pussy or nothing. Just cold, hard cash, understand?"

"That's cool," Booker said. "I'll be callin' you in a bit. You still gonna be at the same place?"

"Yeah," the voice said. "I'll be waitin'. You call me and then maybe we meet at that same place as last time."

"You got it." The connection broke.

"Well, that's that," Booker said, slapping his hands together with exaggerated motions. "Are we outta here, or what?"

"Not so fast," Ray said. "Give us the address where this thing's going down."

"Plus, we need time to get the buy money," Tony added.

"You mean I got to set in jail all that time?" Booker said mournfully.

"We'll be back in no time," Ray said, pushing the paper and pen across the table. "The address." He punctuated it with a peck of his index finger.

As Booker scrawled the numbers on the piece of paper, he looked up with a smile. "You gonna check this out, huh?" he said. "See if I'm bulljivin' you or not. Well, that's okay, 'cause I'm not, but how about leavin' me the rest of them squares while I waits?"

Ray frowned and shook out three more cigarettes.

"This should hold you," he said.

Chapter 10

Wednesday, April 15, 1992

4:10 P.M.

Linc was glad when they broke work off early, because he figured it would give him a chance to shoot over to Diane's and fix things up. He had Rick stop his Eagle Talon at a flower shop on the way so he could get a dozen long-stemmed roses. When he didn't have enough, he came running back out to the car to borrow a ten from Rick.

"You could probably get carnations instead," Rick said, plucking the bill from his wallet.

"You don't use carnations for a long-stem-roses job," Linc said with a grin.

That line came back to him when he waved as Rick drove away after dropping him off in front of Diane's. He chuckled softly, then turned toward the house, hoping to himself that the flowers would turn the trick and make her forget what an idiot he'd been. Why had he disrespected her, calling her a 'hoe? It was just that he'd been so tired, and she didn't realize what they'd been through. She was always being so damn critical. Sometimes she didn't understand nothing, he thought.

The house had belonged to Diane's grandmother, and the elderly lady, who was now in a nursing home, let Di stay there. It was an old wooden-frame two-story house badly in need of a paint job. The dilapidated garage looked pretty shabby too. Linc thought absently that maybe he'd get some paint when the weather got better and slap a coat on. He walked down the narrow strip of sidewalk toward the back door. No sense giving her a fit by trying to go in the front with his muddy work boots on. The rusty metal gate listed so badly it couldn't even be secured. He'd have to see about fixing that too, he thought as he switched the roses to his left hand to get out his key. One of the thorns pricked his finger. Damn, those things were sharp. Like razors. Swearing under his breath, he managed to get the keys out, and slipped the right one in. The knob turned and the door gave, meaning the deadbolt wasn't on. Good, that meant she was probably home.

"Hey, baby," he called out, entering the kitchen.

No answer.

Maybe she ran out to the store for a second; he knew she wouldn't leave for long without doing up the deadbolt.

Linc thought of the pretty glass vase in the living room that would look great with the roses set inside and headed through the archway that separated the two rooms. Suddenly an arm closed over his throat, cutting off his wind. A voice said, "Don't move, motherfucker."

Another form appeared before him, arms outstretched. This one Linc could see, was a white guy.

Reacting out of instinct and training, he swatted back at primary threat: the person cutting off his air. The man grunted as the thorns of the roses raked over the left side of his face. The grip around his neck relaxed and Linc shifted his weight and fired off a snapping front kick at the honkey in front. His boot caught the guy in the balls, and the guy sagged to the floor. Raking the flowers again, he felt the other assailant's grip slacken even more.

He ducked down, at the same time pushing upward on the encircling arm. Immediately after slipping out of the guy's grip, he pushed the man's side hard, sending him toward the wall. Linc saw that this second guy was big and black. The man turned, regaining his balance with an uncanny precision, like a fullback keeping from going down after being hit. Linc threw the roses at the man's shiny head. A Michael Jordan wannabe look: almost shaved-slick. But he kept coming, and Linc suddenly noticed just how large this cat was.

Bigger than me, that's for sure, he thought, moving back into the kitchen. His instinct was to fight these fuckers, but he didn't know if they had guns, or something. He figured them for burglars. Probably crackheads looking to make a score. One of them being white kind of threw him. But there might be more of them, too, he figured, so he decided escape was the best course of action.

The big man was almost on top of him when Linc, using his quickness, lashed out with a left. But the guy blocked it and countered, sending Linc back against the kitchen counter. Damn, this fucker was strong. Like a motherfucking buffalo. He swung up his right leg and kicked the man's left knee, then followed up with a glancing right off the slick head.

But he shook it off and lunged at Linc again, this time getting in close enough to grab him. Linc knew that with the bigger man's superior weight he'd get taken to the floor, which wouldn't be good, especially with the honkey already getting up from his knees. Instead of trying to meet the force of the man's body head-on, Linc pivoted and, grasping the other man's left arm, managed to flip him over with a hip-throw. He landed on his side and was already rolling to his feet when the white guy came rushing at Linc. This one was young, but skinny, so Linc merely swatted him away with a mean right lead. The white guy reeled against the refrigerator, causing the brother to stall for a second getting to his feet.

That was all the time Linc needed to grab the nearest thing to him, a toaster oven, and swing it in an arc against the big man's face. He bellowed like an enraged bull. Linc shot for the back door and twisted the knob. He was down the steps and approaching the garage when the first shot smacked into the old wooden structure. Shit, they were shooting at him. Linc vaulted over the fence and bolted forward, keeping the cover of the garage between himself and the shooters. After rushing down the alley a few more feet, he turned left, pushed open a rickety old gate, and ran through the yard toward the next street. Another shot sounded.

Running up the yard, Linc glanced quickly over his shoulder. Seeing no one, he pushed through the front gate and shoved it closed behind him. They had guns, and he had nothing. He needed to hide, but where? Then he spotted the porch of the adjacent house. It was one of those old extended wooden structures with the pillars that ran the height of the front of the house. Lattice-panels had been fitted in place on the sides by metal pins. But the area under the steps was open. Glancing again, seeing nothing, Linc made a quick two-step over to the next yard. He flattened out and did a low crawl under the steps, hoping there wouldn't be a rat's nest or something under there. It was dark and moist. The resident had apparently been using the space to store his old laths and storm windows, and Linc's left knee knocked into the corner of one. Fighting to suppress the pain, he scurried in close to the house, then pulled some of the filthy old windows on top of him. The cinder blocks of the foundation felt cold against his back. He forcibly shortened his breathing to controlled gasps through his open mouth. Then he heard the scuffling of footsteps.

"Shit," a voice said. "Where the fuck he go?"

It was the white guy.

"We gotta get that tape," another, deeper voice said. "He must be the boyfriend."

Tape? Linc thought. What the hell were they talking about?

"Yeah, well, we still got the bitch, don't we?" It was the white guy again. "Uh-oh, sounds like we got something else, too. Hear that?"

Linc strained to listen, then he heard it: the echo of sirens.

"I told you not to shoot," the black voice said. "I coulda chased him down."

"Yeah, right. Come on, we gotta get outta here. I'll call Bobby to pick us up."

"Not without the tape."

"We ain't gonna be able to get it if we're in fuckin' jail, man. We'll squeeze the bitch again. Make her tell us exactly . . ." the voice trailed off. Linc stayed where he was, waiting and wondering who these guys were, what they were after, and, most importantly, if the woman they had was Diane.

Linc waited in the darkness underneath the porch for a good ten minutes before pushing off the storm windows and moving to the edge of the lattice. Peering through the holes, he surveyed the street. A few kids were playing a couple of yards down. There were cars parked along the curb, but he didn't even know what kind of car these dudes had. Deciding he'd be better off trying to get back to the house and calling the police, he crawled over to the pillars by the steps and pushed through the slanted opening. Standing, he brushed himself off, then saw the fucking shorties watching him. He walked back the way he'd come, but warily. As he approached the alley, he veered off to the adjacent yard and began peering around the garage toward Diane's house.

Suddenly he heard a voice say, "Freeze, police."

It was a woman's voice. He started to look around, but the voice said, "I said freeze, motherfucker. That means don't move." Out of the corner of his eye he saw a uniformed black woman approaching him from the left, her gun stretched out in front of her. "Put your hands on that wall," she said. Linc complied, actually feeling sort of relaxed that it was the police, and not the other two guys, who had found him.

"I got shot at by two guys," Linc started to say.

"Just keep your fucking hands on that wall," the cop said, moving forward and running her hands over his body.

"Look," Linc said, "that's my girlfriend's house. I been stayin' there. I come home and find these two guys breaking in."

"How'd you get so dirty?" the cop asked.

"I work construction," he said, feeling her hands tug at his wallet. "And then I hid under a porch when they started chasing me."

He heard some huffing sounds and saw another cop, a white guy, come running up.

"You got him, Julia?" this cop asked.

"No, she doesn't," Linc said.

"Shut the fuck up," Julia, the female cop said. "It says here you live in Beverly. What you doin' in this neighborhood?"

"Look, I *do* live in Beverly," Linc said, desperation creeping into his voice. "I told you I stay next door with my girlfriend, too. Her name's Diane Cassidy." He repeated the address and phone number. "I got keys to her house in my pocket."

"Come on," the male cop said, grabbing him by the arm. "Let's check it out."

Linc was going to tell him to keep his hands off him, but decided it would be best to have a police escort going into the house. They went up through the yard and across to Diane's.

There were more police standing at the side of the house. One of the patrolmen was busily writing on a clipboard. He looked up as they approached.

"The inside's been tossed," he said. "Who's this?"

"Says it's his girlfriend's house," Julia said. "Found him creeping around the yard next door."

"Can the neighbors verify that you live here?" the male cop backing up Julia asked.

"I guess so," Linc told him. "But like I said, I got the keys right inside my pocket here."

After verifying with the elderly woman who lived across the street that Linc did in fact stay there periodically, they all went inside. Linc saw the roses trampled and scattered over the kitchen floor. His mind was racing, trying to figure out just what was going on, and how much, if anything, he should tell the cops.

The officer with the clipboard came up to him and asked what happened. He recounted the events, leaving out the words he had heard while underneath the porch.

"You ever seen these guys before?" the cop asked. "Around the neighborhood, or anything?"

"Huh-uh," Linc said slowly.

"Where's your girlfriend at?"

"I don't know," Linc said. "I figured she'd be home now. She works downtown, but she been off since the flood."

"Yeah, that's a trip, ain't it?" the cop said. He continued to write on his clip pad. "Can you tell if anything's missing?"

Linc looked around at the living room, which had a couple of chairs overturned. A large garbage bag sat in the middle of the floor in front of the television. Inside it were all of Diane's VHS tapes. Aside from the scattered roses, the kitchen looked pretty normal.

"I really don't know," he said quietly, reaching down to pick up a rose.

"Looks like they were getting ready to rip off your VCR. Well, I'll tell you what," the cop said. "We've ordered an evidence tech to stop by, but we're a little backed up right now. You can wait here for him, and then get with your girl-friend when she comes back and make a list of what's been taken. The investigator will be getting in contact with you."

"Sounds good," Linc said. "Okay to use the phone?"

"Yeah, I'll be finished with this in a couple of minutes."

Linc dialed his uncle's number and asked him to come over to Diane's as soon as possible. Henry picked up on the urgency in Linc's voice and said he'd be right there. It took him about ten minutes to arrive, and the last of the police were just leaving.

"What's the cops doin' here?" Henry asked, his eyes narrowing as he looked at Linc.

"Two guys broke in here and took a couple of shots at me," Linc said, watching the squad car pull away. Then he turned and went back through the house to the kitchen. Henry followed.

"Two guys *what?*" he asked. "Who were they? What'd they want?"

Linc was down on all fours now in front of the stove. He was busily unscrewing the dust catcher on the bottom.

"I don't know who they were, Uncle Henry," he said. He had one side unscrewed and moved over to the other.

"What you doin' on the floor?" Henry demanded.

"Diane has her special hiding places that she thinks nobody'll find," Linc said, taking the long cover off the bottom of the stove. This was the place she always hid important things, like money, jewelry, and hopefully . . . Linc stretched his arm under the stove and felt around. Lots of dust motes, the gas line, then he found it. A cigar box. He pulled it out and opened it. The stack of cash had been rubber-banded and compressed into the box. It still looked like a lot more than it was. Henry's eyes widened when he saw it.

"Where's all that from?" he asked suspiciously.

"You got your light with you?" Linc said, ignoring his question.

Henry felt his pockets and shook his head. Linc peered under the stove again, then got up quickly and went across the room and grabbed the broom. He knelt and racked the end of the handle under the stove several times. Another cigar box came out. This one had the rest of the money, jewelry, papers, and a bank book in it. He peered under the stove again, then, after racking the broom handle a few more times, he stood up and angrily flung it across the kitchen. His uncle was staring at him, eyes narrowed almost to slits, with a side-long-type look. Finally, he said, "You wanna tell me just what the fuck you is into?"

Linc looked at the floor. His mind was racing, trying to figure out where Diane could have hidden that tape.

"I asked you a question, boy," Henry said, his voice raising to a brassy rumble. "What kinda shit you into? Drugs? Cause if it is, I'm gonna kick your fuckin' ass, ex-Marine or not." The veins were starting to stand out on his expansive forehead. Linc looked at him for a moment, then put an arm on his shoulder.

"Uncle Henry," he said slowly. "I'm sorry. I can't tell you everything right now, not because I don't want to—"

"Bullshit," Henry said, grabbing the front of Linc's shirt with his big hands. "You tell me right now. I got a right to know."

Linc just stared at him, then said, "Yeah, you do. It ain't drugs. But I can't tell you everything because there's things I don't know myself." He gently tried to remove his uncle's hands, but the fists drew him in tighter. "I'm gonna need your help, that's why I called you, but I also need you to trust me on this. Right now I have to do two things: call Rick, and search this house. Will you help me?"

He stared into Uncle Henry's loam-colored eyes, then felt the tension on his shirt front go slack.

Linc walked over and sat down in one of the kitchen chairs. He took a deep breath, and then let it out slowly.

Better get it over with, he thought.

Looking up at his uncle he began, "You see, it all started with Diane seeing this dude at the bank."

6:15 P.M.

When Tony and Ray got back to District Five they had the buy money, a beat-up old car from the narcotics division, and a black officer from Gang Crimes South. Ray also had a half-pint of Seagram's Seven in his jacket pocket. After pulling Booker out, they prepared the I-Bond and Ray gave him a cigarette while he signed the bond slip and began putting on his jewelry.

"Before you do that . . ." Tony said as Booker was bending forward to put in his shoelaces.

Booker looked up, then grinned. He stood and kicked off his shoes.

"I gotta strip, right?" he asked.

Tony nodded. It was standard procedure when an informant made a buy to have him strip down prior to conducting the transaction. The reason had to do with courtroom testimony, so some smart-ass defense attorney couldn't grill you by asking, "Officer, isn't it possible that this informant could have had the contraband concealed on his person before he made this so-called buy?"

Booker stripped off his pants and shirt. His underwear had that dingy, unwashed look. The T-shirt was a sallow color. "You wants me to drop my drawers too?" he asked.

"Just take 'em down to your knees," Ray said.

He did, then, without being asked, turned around, bent over at the waist, and spread the cheeks of his buttocks with his hands. This guy had been in the joint before, that was for sure. He lit up another cigarette while he was getting dressed. When he was finished, they went over the plan with him briefly. Booker licked his lips.

"You gonna let me drive, or what?" he said.

"I'm driving," the black undercover cop said.

Ray pulled out the half-pint and handed it to Booker, who nodded a thank-you, and unscrewed the lid. He raised the bottle to his lips and drained about a quarter of it.

"You gonna give me a little tip for this, ain't ya?" he asked, a warm grin spreading over his face.

"First we gotta get it done," Tony said. He'd been against giving Booker a drink before the buy, but Ray said it would make him seem more natural. Booker made the call, and Jem Dandy told him to meet him in the abandoned parking garage behind the old Gately's People's Store in ten minutes. Tony and Ray left immediately to find a place to set up a surveillance. Booker and the undercover officer, whose name was Jerome Terry, went out to the beaten up old Chevy and got in.

"You sure he don't know this car?" Booker asked nervously. "I mean, this cat smell a rat, he shoot you first and say he sorry later."

"Relax, brother," Jerome said. "I don't even work 'round here."

The Heist

★ ★ ★ ★ ★

They took 111th Street down to Michigan and turned left. The block was starting to buzz with the usual evening traffic. Various small shops had already flipped on their lights, anticipating the darkness that was just beginning to descend. Crowds of people milled about in front of the liquor stores, and a group was listening to a boom-box in front of the twenty-four-hour currency exchange. All had their hats cocked ominously to the left, signifying gang affiliation. Jerome glanced over at them momentarily.

"This next street up here," Booker said, unscrewing the lid of the half-pint and taking another quick sip.

"I know where it is," Jerome said.

They went down a sloping hill and Booker pointed to the alleyway. An overhang was suspended between the front building and the immense parking garage that once provided parking for the entire business district, due to the narrow width of the side streets. The People's Store had gone out of business, and for a while, the massive building sat empty. Then, with the resurgence of small businesses in the area, mostly clothing, jewelry, and wig shops owned by enterprising Koreans, the avenue had come to life again. But instead of one large department store, the old Gately's had been subdivided into several smaller shops. The second floor was still empty, as was the parking garage. The only exception was a furniture outlet that did periodic business in one side of the structure.

Jerome hung a right and went slowly down the block. The tan brick wall had been defaced numerous times by graffiti artists, who sought to advertise their gang's dominance. But one of the drawings depicted the figure of a man in a red, black, and green shirt. The caption alongside it read: RED BLOOD, BLACK PEOPLE, GREEN EARTH.

As they passed the parking garage, which bore a No Trespassing sign on the front, the inside seemed dark and foreboding.

"Go down to the corner and make another right," Booker told him.

"You sure he's in there?" Jerome asked. "I didn't see nobody when we drove past."

"He in there," Booker said with a smile. "We got to pull around and come by the back way."

Jerome turned right at the corner and right again at the mouth of the alley. The houses to his left were all set up higher than usual because of the slope. It gave the alley a cavernous appearance. Dodging a big metal Dumpster, he let the car creep slowly down toward the overhang. When they finally were parallel to the beginning of the parking garage, they saw a guy in an old OD field jacket leaning against the wall smoking a cigarette. He wore a black " 'do-rag" over his hair, and had tight black-leather driving gloves on. Booker said, "That's him."

Jerome stopped and cut his lights off. Booker was already out of the car and walking up to Jem Dandy. The other man's stare went from Booker, to the car, to Jerome, and then back to Booker.

"Who's that?" he said, nodding at Jerome.

"A friend of mine," Booker said. "Gave me a ride."

Jerome came up and grinned at Jem Dandy. "You can call me Jay," he said, extending his hand.

Jem Dandy ignored the outstretched hand.

"I don't call you nothing if I don't know you," he said. Then, to Booker, "What the fuck, man, you know I don't deal with people I don't know."

"He cool, homey," Booker said. "Besides, I'm the one you's dealing with."

Jem Dandy looked coldly at Jerome for a moment more, then said to Booker, "You got the bread?"

"Sure do," said Booker. "You wanna see?" He took the roll of bills that Tony had given him and flashed it flamboyantly.

"Cut that shit out, man," Jem Dandy said, grabbing Booker's arm. "You want everybody in the fucking world to see?" For a second Booker thought it was all going to unravel, but then the other man seemed to relax a little. Maybe he smell the booze on my breath, Booker thought.

"Come on." Jem Dandy stepped through the opening into the darkened garage. He looked at Jerome. "You can wait there." Booker followed him into the shadows. The structure was multi-tiered and without lights, so the first level was almost totally dark a few feet beyond the edge. Jerome got back inside the car and started it up.

Booker trailed along behind Jem Dandy until they got to the stairwell. The metal stairs had once been painted green, but most of the paint had long since peeled off. Jem Dandy went up the stairs and made the turn. He paused on the second landing and withdrew a small silver gun from the lower left pocket of his field jacket. Booker moved up beside him and stared down at it.

"That the baby-nine?"

Jem Dandy nodded, locked back the slide, and handed it to Booker. "It's an H&K. Holds seven-and-one. Sweet shooting little thing. Lemme count the bread while you looking."

Booker handed him the roll of bills and held the gun up. He stretched out his arm and pretended to fire at some imaginary opponents. Jem Dandy smirked as he busily counted.

"Where you know that dude from?" he asked.

"Who, Jay?" Booker said, still practicing his aim. "He cool. I been knowing him for a long time."

"He from the 'hood?" Jem Dandy asked.

"He been cribbin' with some chick over on the West Side," Booker said. "Least that's what he told me."

"Heard you got busted," Jem Dandy said. He pocketed the bills and Booker suddenly realized he didn't have any magazine or bullets for the nine. But he was sure that Jem Dandy had some for his.

"Aaa, yeah," Booker said. "Got me an I-Bond courtesy of the sheriff. Met up with Jay when I was down at the county. You gonna give me some bullets for this motherfucker?"

"Oh, yeah," Jem Dandy said, reaching into his pocket again. He withdrew a magazine and seven bullets. Booker held out his hand.

"So who you dealin' with now?" Booker asked. "People or Folks?"

"People, Folks, it don't matter to me none, as long as they got the green." Jem Dandy smiled as he patted the pocket with the money. "Say, I wanted to ask you something," he said, before giving him the ammunition. "You know Henry Bartwell, right? That big dude that runs that construction company over on State."

"Yeah, I know him," Booker said. He shook out a cigarette from the pack and lighted it. "Why you asking?"

"Is he cool?"

"What you mean?"

Jem Dandy handed him the magazine and the bullets.

"He called me a little while ago," Jem Dandy said. "Him and his nephew bought a Glock from me." He started to say something else, but held back.

Booker raised his eyebrows.

Jem Dandy continued: "I been knowing Henry for a long

time from the neighborhood, and all. Sold him a .38 snub some time back. But his nephew I ain't seen around much. He okay too?"

Booker grinned as he fitted the bullets into the magazine. This was going to work out better than he'd thought.

"They bought a Glock, huh?" he said. "That's one of them German guns, ain't it?"

"Austrian."

"Yeah, they cool. What they want a gun for?"

"I don't know," Jem Dandy said. "But they want some specialized stuff in a hurry. That's why I asked you about 'em."

Booker took the half-pint from his jacket pocket and unscrewed the top. "Here's to good deals," he said, and took a sip. He held the bottle out to Jem Dandy, who took it and raised it to his lips. He smiled and handed it back to Booker.

"What you mean by specialized?" Booker asked. "I don't want to go over there messing with them."

Jem Dandy laughed.

"They want me to get them an H&K Mac-Ten or an M-16. Something fully au-to-ma-tic," he said, intentionally hitting each syllable of the word.

Booker gave a low whistle. "You can get that kind of shit?"

"Fuck yeah," Jem Dandy said. Booker offered him another swig, but shrugged and pocketed the half-pint when the other man shook his head.

"The nephew just got out of the Marines, or something," Booker said. They started back down the stairs. "He been working for Big Henry, but he cool, as far as I know."

This seemed to satisfy Jem Dandy, who, when they reached the first level, slapped Booker on the back. "My ride's that way," he said, nodding toward the street. They did the "brother handshake," and Jem Dandy turned and walked toward the front of the structure. "Catch you later." Booker stood alone in the shadows grinning, knowing he had the baby-nine in his right pocket, the half-pint in his left, and the knowledge that was gonna stick it right up that mother-fucking Linc's tight, black ass.

Chapter 11

Wednesday, April 15, 1992

7:08 P.M.

Linc sat heavily in one of the kitchen chairs and put his head in his hands, feeling the frustration burning in his gut. Uncle Henry sat across from him looking equally haggard, and Rick leaned against the wall near the doorframe. After Rick had gotten to Diane's, Linc and Henry had gone out and purchased the Glock. When they'd returned, the three of them made a systematic search of the entire house, but failed to turn up the tape. Henry, whose reaction to hearing the whole story had been the old shake of the head and accompanying disgusted frown, told Linc to go over it again in his mind.

"Where would Diane hide something like that?" he asked.

"I can't figure it," Linc said. "She always kept things under the stove. That was her hiding place. Her special safety deposit box, she called it."

"Then we must've missed something," Rick said. He went back to the stove and knelt down again, shining the flashlight under it. Finding nothing, he went to the cigar boxes that Linc had found under there earlier. One held the money, the other an assortment of jewelry and papers.

"The real important stuff she kept in her lock box at the bank," Linc said. When he mentioned the bank, he caught Henry's baleful stare and looked away. Rick started sorting through the papers again.

"Hey, look at this," he said. He held up a single flat key with a number on it. "This looks almost like a safety-deposit-box key, but it's not. More like a locker key of some sort."

Linc leaned forward and took it. It wasn't familiar at all, but that didn't really mean anything. But, somehow, the more he looked at it, the more it reminded him of something. He held it out to his uncle, who took the key in his massive fingers.

"Looks like it's from that rent-a-box place over on 113th," he said. The three of them looked at each other, then Linc started to get up. "No, you stay here," Henry said. "I'll go over there and check. Nobody be looking for me."

"Be careful, Uncle Henry," Linc said.

Henry just smiled and patted his ample gut, where the butt of a .38 snubnose was sticking out from his pants. He slipped on his jacket to cover the gun.

His uncle hadn't been gone more than five minutes when the phone rang. Linc grabbed it quickly.

"Linc?" It was Diane's voice. She sounded scared.

"Baby, are you all right?"

Rick went for the extension phone in the living room.

"I'm okay. Linc," she said hesitantly. "Listen, I need you to go pick something up for me, okay?"

"Yeah," he said, letting his voice sort of hang there.

"It's in box fourteen twelve at that rental place on a Hundred-and-Thirteenth," she said.

Linc nodded to Rick to see if he'd gotten that.

"Where are you, baby?" Linc said.

"I'm . . ." her voice trailed off. Then, her tone reflecting some kind of pain or pressure, she said, "Never mind that now. I need you to get this for me right away. The key is—"

"I know where the key is," Linc said, cutting her off. "In

fact, we already got the tape, so let me talk to the mother-fucker that's holding you right now."

There was silence on the line, then some obvious scuffling, and it sounded as if a hand was slipped over the receiver.

"I'm waiting," Linc said.

"Hello, Linc," a strange voice said over the phone. It sounded like some cracker.

"You one of the motherfuckers that was here this afternoon?" Linc demanded.

"No," the voice said. "But I am the person who's sitting next to your lady-love here."

Linc said nothing. He just waited. Finally the voice continued.

"I understand that you have something that we're interested in."

"The tape?" Linc said, trying to cover his nervousness with bravado. "Yeah, I got it. You let Diane go and we'll talk about you getting it back."

The voice chuckled softly, then said, "I think we both know that's not how it works."

"That's the only way it's gonna work," Linc shot back. "You let her go, or else."

"Or else what, Linc? You going to run to the cops and tell them you broke into a bank vault and stole a tape and an unspecified amount of cash?" He laughed again. "Get serious, son. That's what your girlfriend tried before, and look how that turned out."

Frustrated, Linc told him again to let Diane go and arrangements could be made to give him the tape. "Otherwise it's no deal."

"Linc," the voice said, seeming slightly strained this time. "I am a very busy man and have several things on my agenda.

I'm going to expedite this conversation with a little demonstration. Are you listening?"

Linc heard Diane's voice on the line saying, "What are you doing?" Then suddenly her tone shifted to a high shriek of pain that lasted for a full five seconds, her voice going up the scale so high that it became no more than a husky shell of a scream.

"All right, all right, stop it!" Linc shouted.

The screaming abruptly trickled to a low moaning sound.

Germaine came back on the line. "Linc, that was just a sample, a sample of the pain this poor girl is going to have to endure unless I receive assurance of your full cooperation. Am I making myself clear?"

"Yeah," Linc said haltingly. "Just don't hurt her again." His voice was quieter now. Devoid of the false bravado, and imbued instead with an overwhelming helplessness.

"That's good," Germaine said. "Now, do you have the tape?"

"Not with me," Linc said. "I got it hid."

"Do I have to provide you with another little demonstration to end your annoying coyness?" He heard Diane's moan become more audible again, rising to another high-pitched scream.

"Okay, okay, it's at my apartment," Linc said rapidly, trying to buy himself some time. The scream stopped again.

"All right. Linc. This is what I want you to do. Go get the tape and wait at your apartment. I'll call you there at," he paused, "ten o'clock."

Linc said, "Okay, but let me talk to—" The phone went dead. He stared over at Rick, then hung up the receiver. Rick walked over to him and put a hand on his shoulder. There was something in the guy on the phone's voice. An eerie calmness, even when Diane was screaming. He was like ice water.

Like her pain didn't mean nothing to him. Linc knew they had to get the rest of those weapons fast, and they had to get a plan to deal with this situation. But most of all, he knew that he was going to have to kill that motherfucker on the other end of the phone.

Germaine hung up and glanced at Diane, who was now shivering in the corner, holding the bloody welt on her arm where the pliers had pinched her flesh, and sobbing softly. He looked at her momentarily, then said to Gumbo, "See, another amateur."

"He didn't move like no amateur," Gumbo said, rubbing his fingers over the cuts on the side of his face. "I'm gonna enjoy taking him out."

Germaine inhaled loudly and held up his index finger.

"Regrettably, I don't think that's wise. I can't waste you on taking out some small fry like him," he said. "Remember, we're on a very delicate timetable here. I'm gonna need you with me tonight when we proceed with phase two. Del Bianco can get a couple of his local boys and take out this Linc. Tommy saw him at the house, right?"

Gumbo nodded, his eyes impassive.

"Good," Germaine said. "Let them do that, and we'll concentrate on the more complicated matter." He motioned at Diane. "Secure her and bring me Mr. Fox, so he can make his phone call."

8:15 P.M.

Johnny Osmand ruminated over the events of the last few days as he drove his Lincoln Continental north on the Tri-State Tollway. Every few minutes he glanced in his rearview mirror to check the traffic behind him. If a car even looked like it was following, he would slow down or pull off onto the shoulder. No sense relaxing until this thing was over, but then, why would the Feds be tailing him now, since it was all but certain that he was going to play ball? But what about Vino? If word had gotten back to him . . . But hell, there's no way that could happen this soon. Christ, not with all the precautions he'd taken.

That's why Fox's call had taken him a little bit by surprise. The lawyer sounded nervous, telling him that they had to have an emergency meeting. Something else had come up that needed to be discussed in person. And in private. The Mink had gone through enough court trials to know that nothing was ever simple to these damn lawyers. Probably some minor clause in the deal that Fox wanted to check on. The guy was thorough, he had to give him that. Probably more than a little upset that he was going to be losing out on the big bucks and notoriety that a federal trial would generate, but that was just too goddamned bad. Hell, it wasn't his ass on the line.

He checked the mirror again, then speeded up, zigzagging through some of the slower traffic. No other cars did likewise. Maybe right before the deal was sealed he'd go back to the safety deposit box and put some more money in it as a bonus for Fox. But not much more. He grinned, thinking about how he'd gone back there last Friday afternoon and taken most of the large bills out of the "Orlando Box," as he called it. After showing it to Fox last week, and seeing the venal gleam in his eye when he asked, "How much you got in there?" the Mink knew he had to adjust things. With the lawyer on the list as co-renter, nothing would stop him from going into the box and removing the cash himself, if he wanted to make a score. So Johnny went back there after court and cleaned it out, leaving only about seven grand in the box, even though it looked like a lot more.

The Heist

He glanced at the sign that said the Hinsdale Oasis was a mile away. Not a bad place for a meet, he thought. It was a little bit farther for Fox to come, since he lived north in Skokie, but it was essentially a midway point. With Fox parking on the southbound side, and Johnny parking on the northbound, they could meet in the middle restaurant part without drawing any undue attention to themselves. Maybe he'd get something to eat, too. He was starting to get hungry. Johnny slowed down and suddenly veered right to make the exit abruptly. At the top of the entrance ramp he stopped and swung around to check which cars came up after him. When a minute passed and no other cars entered the oasis, he felt safe. He parked the Lincoln and walked slowly toward the brightness of the restaurant area, lighting a cigar as he went.

Inside the doors there were circular stands of pay phones, a small gift shop area, and several video games. Beyond that were the Wendy's restaurant and a smaller snack stand. The eating area was no more than a quarter full, but there were several people standing in the ordering line. The Mink decided to see if Fox was there first, before getting in line. He puffed copiously on his cigar as he went through this middle section and onto the area beyond it, which was a mirror image of the other entrance, with the small shop, video games, and phones. He did see a couple of guys on the phones, but they looked pretty innocuous, except for that big black mother.

Christ, Johnny thought, as he passed by the huge man. That guy's big enough to be King Kong's grandson. He smirked to himself at his joke and pushed through the doors. Standing just under the overhang, he surveyed the parking lot and saw it. Fox's silver-gray sports car was sitting about fifty yards away, looking sleek and shiny under the lights. He squinted and noticed the movement in it. Fox was talking on one of those cellular phones, the dumb son-of-a-bitch.

175

Didn't he know that those things could be intercepted and recorded? Johnny stormed over to the Jaguar and tapped on the lightly tinted window. It lowered electronically and the Mink saw that this wasn't Fox after all, but some white-haired guy.

"Oh, sorry," Johnny grunted, "I thought you was somebody else."

"That's perfectly all right," the guy in the car said.

Johnny turned to go back and saw the big black guy standing almost immediately behind him. A van pulled up, blocking the view of the restaurant, and King Kong's Grandson reached out and stuck something against Johnny's side. He heard a zapping sound, and his teeth snapped shut. All his breath seemed to go out of him. He couldn't move. Like his whole body had gone to sleep. The side door of the van slid open and Johnny felt himself being hoisted inside as if he weighed no more than a rag doll.

Oh, fuck, he thought, as the door slammed shut and the van took off. That son-of-a-bitch Fox set me up.

Chapter 12

Wednesday, April 15, 1992

9:45 P.M.

Tony and Ray sat in their dark green, unmarked Chevy across the street in the Metra lot, four houses south of the apartment building on 114th and Hale. It was one of those three-story, block-like structures of brown brick that extended up to the crenulated roof. The names by the doorbells had listed Weaver/Jackson next to apartment Two-A. By what he termed "shrewd police work," ringing the doorbell of apartment One-A and listening for the sound, Ray had deduced that Two-A was on the north side of the building. After receiving no response at any bell, they went around the back and checked the rear door. As city apartments went, this one was pretty nice. Well maintained, clean, and functional, locked security doors.

After deciding to wait it out and see if Linc returned, they made a quick trip to the McDonald's at 119th and Western. Tony bought a salad and coffee. Ray got the works, which included a Big Mac, fries, and a Coke. Once they were ensconced down the block, they settled in to wait as darkness crept over the area. Soon, the lights in the other apartments in the building came on, but Two-A remained dark. Tony picked at his salad, then glanced at Ray as he took a bite of his hamburger.

"You know what I been thinking, Tony?" Ray asked, his

cheek bulging from the food as he chewed.

"What?"

"How much I enjoyed doing what we did today," Ray said. "You and me driving around the South Side, working on a case."

Tony nodded, eating a bit more of his salad.

"I mean," Ray continued, "it sure beats the hell out of sitting around the goddamn Federal Building waiting for Faulkner and Arlene to criticize our every proposal, don't it?" He shook his head. "Lawyers and Feds."

"They're just doing their job," Tony said. "You know as well as I do, all the investigation in the world doesn't mean squat if the case isn't winnable in court."

"That's exactly my point. They're lawyers, we're street cops." He shoved a handful of fries into his mouth, chewed briefly, then said, "You know, I just might transfer out of this unit once you retire. Maybe I'll get back into Gang Crimes, or something."

"Better hold off on that," Tony said. "The way Rodriguez is talking, they might be transferring a lot of the guys from Gang Crimes into the Organized Crime Division."

"Oh yeah? What do you think?"

"You want to know what I think?" Tony asked with a grin. Ray nodded, his mouth full again. "I think you keep eating shit like that, you're never gonna get down to one hundred sixty-five pounds."

Ray smirked, then said, "I been thinking about entering in the light-heavy division anyway."

"You're too short for light-heavy," Tony quipped.

"Too short, huh?" Ray said defensively. "You apparently didn't see how bad I was punishing that tall guy yesterday at the gym. Or did you forget? I forgot you're getting on in years."

"I'm serious," Tony said. "You ought to start taking better care of yourself. Getting more roughage in your diet."

"What's that got to do with me supposedly being too short to be a light-heavy?"

"They're two distinct facts, both related because, as a boxer, you need to be in top physical shape, and secondly, a good big man will almost always beat a good little man."

"What did you put in that coffee, anyway?" Ray said. "Those two statements aren't even slightly related. And as for that bullshit about a good little man, what about Rocky Marciano?"

"What about him?"

"He wasn't that much bigger than me, and he won the heavyweight championship."

"Apples and oranges," Tony said. "Marciano was short, but built like a brick shithouse. But he did have trouble with bigger guys. And he didn't fight anybody the size of today's heavyweights."

"Sure wish I coulda seen him in action," Ray said.

"I did," Tony said. "When he fought Charles in fifty-four."

"No shit? He knocked him out, didn't he?"

"That was their second fight," Tony said. "Same year, different month."

"Remember that Calumet City copper who was fightin' a few years back? What'd he call himself?"

"The Choirboy. He wasn't bad, either."

"Yeah, I know," Ray said. He washed down the last of his hamburger with some Coke. "How come you never turned pro, Tony? All those boxing trophies from when you was in the Navy."

Tony blew out a slow breath before he answered.

"I guess all I ever wanted to be was a cop," he said.

★ ★ ★ ★ ★

9:50 P.M.

When the phone rang Vino left his grandson's party and took it in his private study. The few remaining guests, including the youngest Costelli daughter, her husband, and their ten-year-old son, Salvatore, were getting ready to leave. Vino stepped into the darkened room, went to the huge oak desk, and picked up the receiver.

"Yeah," he grunted. "Go ahead."

"Yes, sir, Mr. Costelli," the voice on the other end on the line said. "Just wanted to let you know that we got that special order in that you requested."

The voice had a southern twang to it and Vino knew who it was.

"Good, good," Vino said, smiling. The door creaked open and his daughter stuck her head in.

"Daddy?" she said tentatively.

"Yeah, sweetie," he said, covering the mouthpiece.

"I just wanted to tell you we're leaving." A small boy rushed through between his mother's side and the doorframe. He ran to Vino, arms outstretched, and gave the older man a hug.

"Grandpa, why you sitting in the dark?" the boy asked.

"I'm just on the phone," Vino said. "Now gimme a kiss before you leave."

The boy dutifully planted a kiss on his grandfather's cheek.

"Now be sure to thank Mommy for letting you stay up so late on a school night," Vino said, his hand still over the mouthpiece.

"We don't got no school tomorrow, Grandpa. It's Easter vacation."

"Well, you be good or the Easter bunny won't bring you

no candy," Vino said. Then to his daughter, "What kinda way is that for a kid to talk? 'Don't got no school.' What kinda place they running over there?"

His daughter smiled as she moved toward him, grabbed her son's hand, and gave her father a peck on the cheek.

"He's only ten, Daddy," she said as they moved back toward the door.

"Yeah, well, just the same," Vino said after them. He spoke into the phone again. "Just put it on ice and I'll be by to take a look at it later."

"Roger, willco, sir," the voice said.

9:54 P.M.

Rick drove his Eagle Talon slowly down the block. Linc was crouched down in the passenger seat, his knees on the floor. He looked up at Rick and asked if he saw anything.

"Yeah, just passing two guys in a dark Chevy," he said.

"One of them a big, black motherfucker?" Linc asked.

"Huh-uh. Both white."

"Go around by the alley," Linc said. "Drop me off, then pull around to the front and go in that way. Once you're inside, I'll come up the back and help you sweep the building."

"Let me do that alone," Rick said. "They won't be expecting a white guy."

"We don't know that for sure," Linc said, then added grimly, "we don't know what Diane's told them about us."

"All right," said Rick, "but hang back for a minute or so. If I spot trouble, I'll try to get out. If not, you be my back-up."

"Got you," Linc said, wishing they didn't even have to go in. But they had to be there by ten to receive the call from Diane's abductors. He felt the car turn right, slow down, then turn right again. Straightening up, he adjusted the plastic garbage bag with the M-16 inside. They'd chosen the 16 over the

H&K due to both his and Rick's familiarity with the weapon. He pulled back the charging handle and got out a few garages down from the rear of their apartment building as Rick slowed down to a stop.

"Catch you inside," he whispered as the Eagle sped away. Now, he thought, comes the tricky part.

Rick pulled around and went down the block. He saw an open spot in front of an adjacent building and took it. As he got out, he glanced at the dark Chevy. The two guys were still sitting in it, but seemed to pay him little attention. His gaze transferred to the buildings on either side of his, then to the shrubbery, which consisted of several large evergreen bushes near the entranceway. Everything looked normal. The lights in their apartment were still off, and would stay that way. They intended on using their mini-mags for light until they got the call; then they would retreat to a hotel and plan out their next move.

Rick took out his key and opened the front door, resisting the temptation to check their mailbox. Probably just full of junk mail anyway, he thought as he moved toward the stairway, wondering if Linc was at the back door yet.

Linc used his flashlight to sweep the area by the Dumpsters and in-between and under the cars that were parked in the rear of the building. There was no way he was going to walk blindly into an ambush. There had to be a reason that the asshole on the phone wanted him to be in his apartment at ten o'clock. Chances were that they were planning something. But they had no choice, under the circumstances, as long as the motherfuckers had Diane.

He moved up to the rear door and stuck the butt of the rifle, still concealed in the garbage bag, up under his arm.

Transferring his keys to his left hand, so he could keep his right free, he softly sorted through them and selected the door key. Then he placed an ear to the solid-wood door. Everything sounded quiet inside. Squatting, he looked under the door for telltale shadows of people standing on the other side. Nothing. He began to feel better as he rose, using the beam of his flashlight to guide the insertion of the key into the lock. Then he saw it: a fresh scratch in the wood near the jamb. A closer inspection revealed two tapering pry-marks, as if someone had inserted something between the door and the frame. Sticking the key inside, he twisted it, feeling the lock release. The door opened silently and Linc stripped the garbage bag off of the M-16 and swiveled the switch from safe to auto.

Even though the front hallway was deserted, Rick felt it would be prudent to check out the laundry room on the first floor before going up. He walked down the hallway, making no sound on the carpeting. The door of the room was usually closed this time of night, unless there was somebody in there doing laundry. He paused at the door and removed the Glock from his belt. Holding it down by his leg, he turned as he opened the door. The room was dark, and Rick switched on the light while still outside in the hall. The machines sat in peaceful tranquility. Checking behind the door by looking through the crack before entering, Rick stepped inside and moved quickly to the back wall, the big auto-pistol leveled in front of him.

After realizing that the room was clear, he reinserted the pistol in his belt and covered it with his jacket again; then he moved back to the stairwell and began to go up. The rear entrance was located on the east side of the building, and it was impossible to get to the back hallway from the front, unless you cut through one of the apartments. If he cleared all the front landings, and Linc did the back, the only other place they had to worry about would be the inside of the apartment itself. And if they saw no signs of forced entry, they would feel pretty secure. They only had to wait for the call, then they would be out of there. And the bad guys wouldn't have a clue where they'd gone.

Rick moved quickly, but cautiously up to the second landing, his hand inside his jacket gripping the Glock. The hallway looked clear. He stood momentarily on the second level taking in the sounds of the building. The noise of a television filtered out from one of the rooms on the third floor, but theirs was silent. Rick proceeded up to the third landing and paused there also. More sounds: a woman talking, a phone ringing. Nothing out of the ordinary. He went back down to his apartment, wondering about Linc. As he got to the door, he heard the phone start to ring. Hurriedly, he stuck the key in the lock, realizing a second later that he'd let his guard down a little too soon.

From inside the darkened apartment a muffled voice growled, "Step in and close the door, motherfucker, or I'll blow your fucking head off."

Linc was certain that the pricks were in the building, but he didn't know where. He'd cautiously advanced up to the second floor and was heading up the stairwell toward the third when he heard the voice. It had come from inside their apartment. Going back down, he strained his ears to try and hear more. There was definite movement inside now, and he heard Rick's voice loudly say, "Who the hell are you?"

The space under the door showed that it was still dark inside the apartment. Linc swiftly put his key in the doorknob lock and twisted. The door didn't swing open, and he realized that the deadbolt must be fastened also. Hoping no one inside had heard him, he withdrew the key and re-inserted it in the deadbolt slot. He knew it would make a noticeable scraping sound when he turned it, so he adjusted his footing so that he could bring up the rifle barrel as he swung the door open. The only thing he'd have to worry about was not catching Rick in his field of fire, if things got hot.

Rick reached over and flipped on the wall switch as soon as he stepped into the room, figuring that the light would temporarily blind them as well as let him immediately know who and how many he was dealing with. As he did this, his right hand was pulling the Glock out of his waistband. He saw three men inside, the closest being a slender-looking white guy with dark, slicked-back hair. That one was holding a .45.

Diving forward toward the center of the living room, Rick rolled as he went. The round exploded past him as he hit the floor and he brought the Glock up and squeezed the trigger. The .45 exploded again, followed by the Glock. Rick heard a window shatter behind him, and the skinny dark-haired guy slumped forward. Another hood leveled a gun at him, but suddenly this guy was falling forward, the blood spurting out of his mouth. The third guy did a jerky two-step, clutching his chest, as the pop-pop-pop of the M-16 reverberated through the apartment like rolling thunder, shattering the front picture windows. Through it all the phone continued to ring.

Ray was crumpling up his bag of McDonald's papers into a little ball when he saw the lights go on in the apartment. He nudged Tony.

"Looks like our pigeon's come home to roost," he said.

"Yeah," Tony said. "He must've come in the back. Too

bad we didn't see him carrying something that could be construed as a weapon."

"We didn't?" Ray said, grinning.

Tony grinned back, but shook his head.

"You been hanging around Arlene and that fucker, Faulkner, too long," Ray said. "Well, you want to go roust him anyway?" Suddenly the unmistakable sound of gunshots erupted, followed by the rat-tat-tat of a fully automatic weapon and the tinkling of exploding glass. They looked quickly at each other.

"Christ, that sounded like a machine gun," Tony said.

"Yeah, we better call for a back-up," Ray said, unsnapping his holster and taking out his .38 snubnose.

Tony took out his gun too, then picked up the mike and reported the incident and their location to the base. He finished with, "Ten-one, officer needs assistance. Shots fired, possible automatic weapons." Then he was out of the car and running to catch up with Ray who was already moving across the street in a crouch. Getting up to the front of the building, they could see that the front picture windows for the second-floor apartment were spider-webbed with bullet holes. Ray tried the front door. Locked. He buzzed one of the doorbells and yelled, "Police!" several times into the speaker. The front door buzzed open. He went inside, aiming his .38 snubnose upward as he approached the staircase. Tony was at his side.

"Let's be smart and wait for the back-ups," he said.

"But then whoever's up there might get away," Ray protested.

"Fat lot of good these will do against a fucking machine gun," Tony said, nodding his head at his revolver. Then he said, "Oh, what the hell. Cover me."

Tony crept up the stairs, his gun outstretched, to the mid-floor landing. Pausing and crouching behind the banister, he directed his aim toward the second-floor apartment. Ray quickly went up, going all the way to the wall; then he assumed the ready position and proceeded up to the next landing. Tony followed, pausing at the top of the stairs. Ray crept over to apartment Two-A and listened. All was quiet, except for the sound of a continuously ringing phone. He tried the knob. Locked, he mouthed to Tony, who nodded and moved up beside Ray.

Ray stepped in front of the door, lifted his foot, and sent a powerful kick just below the doorknob. The solid wood buckled slightly. Ray kicked it again, but it still held. He gave it another kick, and this time the door swung inward with such suddenness that it smacked against the wall and came flying back at them.

Ray's shoulder took the impact of the swinging door, as he crouched low against the shattered doorframe, his gun outstretched as his eyes swept the apartment. Furniture seemed to be in place, except for an overturned chair in the living room. Besides the front picture window being shattered, the wall next to it was pockmarked with several bullet holes. The lights were still on. Moving past him, Tony entered, and saw the feet of the first body.

It was lying face down between the living room and the kitchen. Blue dress pants and fancy black shoes. He went to the hallway, which was dark, and took a cover position. Ray followed, carefully moving over the dead man's legs so as not to step in any blood. Tony flipped on a light switch in the hall, and Ray went down to the first doorway. It was a bathroom. After it was cleared, Tony went to the next room, a bedroom. Empty too. And so they went, methodically clearing the rest of the apartment, the ringing phone punctuating their every move. There were three dead bodies all situated between the kitchen area and the living room. A single set of bloody footprints went through the kitchen and out the back door, which was standing open. They followed the fading red imprints down the stairs until they disappeared.

Sirens sounded, and Ray went to the front door and took out his badge. He met the uniformed coppers as they were ascending the stairs.

"Looks like a triple homicide," he said. "Better call it in, then seal off the back."

The young uniform cop nodded and went back down the stairs. His partner followed Ray upstairs.

"We already cleared the place," Ray told him. "Guard the crime scene here." He pointed to the open front door, then went inside. "Put out a city-wide that we're looking for a male black, possibly armed with an automatic weapon," he said.

"Pretty vague," the patrolman muttered.

"Yeah, well that's all we got right now," Ray said angrily. Tony was leaning over one of the bodies.

"Look at this guy, Ray. Don't he look familiar?"

Ray cocked his head and stared at the face, which Tony was gripping by the hair. A trickle of blood seeped from the lifeless lips. It was a white male in his early thirties, a bit on the slender side. The black hair had been combed back unctuously.

"Yeah, he does, sort of," Ray said. "Looks real dead, too."

The phone still kept ringing.

"I do know this guy," Tony said. "Gimme a minute and it'll come to me."

"Fine," said Ray. "In the meantime. I'm gonna answer that fucking phone."

He went toward the nearest extension, despite Tony's protestations, and picked it up carefully by the cord and the other end.

"Yeah," he said into the receiver, trying to imitate a black voice.

"Linc?" the voice on the other end asked. It was a calm, almost southern-sounding voice.

"Yeah," Ray said. "Who's this?"

"No, this isn't Linc," the voice said slowly. "Is Tommy there?"

"Tommy's indisposed," Ray said, still mimicking the black inflection. "Who this?" Ray paused, then added, "What can I do for you?"

There was silence at the other end, then the line went dead.

Ray hung up too, carefully placing the phone down and wiping it where he'd touched it.

"That was smart," Tony said. "Now what if the murderer used that phone and you just destroyed his prints?"

"Relax, Dick Tracy," Ray said. "The guy on the other end asked for our buddy Linc by name."

"Who else did he ask for?"

"Somebody named Tommy."

Tony bit his lower lip, then snapped his fingers.

"Tommy Del Bianco," he said, pointing down at the corpse. "He's one of Vino Costelli's boys."

"Vino," Ray said quizzically. "What the hell's *he* doing mixed up in this?"

Tony shook his head.

"Of course you know that you probably wouldn't have put the face with the name if I hadn't answered that phone like I did."

Tony looked at him, rolled his eyes, and shook his head again.

Germaine terminated the call on the cellular phone, set it down on the table, and leaned back in his chair. The room was small and barren, except for the card table, the three chairs, and the phone. He appeared pensive for a moment, then turned to Gumbo and said, "Looks like Tommy and company failed to accomplish their end of it."

"Shit," Gumbo said, his massive bulk hovering over the tabletop. "That no-good, honkey motherfucker." He used a sharp gesticulation to punctuate every other syllable. "The only thing he was good at was walking around pretending he was bad."

Germaine sighed heavily and rested his chin on his hands.

"I knew that Linc would be tough," Gumbo continued, "something about the way the motherfucker moved." He paused, as if recalling the earlier confrontation. "I wish I woulda handled that one myself."

"Relax," Germaine said. "We still have his lady friend. And she's our leverage. All we have to do now is figure out a new way to contact him. Put him where we want him."

"That ain't gonna be easy now. He gonna be real suspicious."

"This regulation is proving interesting. And what would life be without a few challenges? Come on." Germaine got up from the table. "Let's go get things set up so old Vino can have his fun."

Chapter 13

Thursday, April 16, 1992

1:10 A.M.

Linc set the Exacto knife down and massaged the bridge of his nose with his fingers, as he tried to sort out their next move. The smell of Hoppe's Solution was pungent, and he looked at Rick, who was reassembling the M-16 after cleaning it. He was wiping each part with a rag before insertion. They'd managed to get away quickly after escaping down the back stairs. Linc had gone down the alley, hiding in one of the recesses of a nearby garage until Rick, who'd gone calmly around to the front of their apartment and got the car, had driven down the alley to pick Linc up.

All the way to the motel Linc had stayed crouched on the floor, figuring the police would be more than likely looking for a black man than a lone, white driver. Once they were safely inside the room, they turned on the television and waited for the re-broadcast of the ten o'clock news. Most of the telecast was still devoted to the flood, day three, but they did cut to an on-scene reporter covering a "breaking story on the South Side." The mini-cam showed a quick shot of their apartment building, lighted by the camera crew's floodlights, and the reporter did a voice-over, talking about police investigating a shooting on the second floor, but giving no details, other than to say that it was possibly "gang related."

"Well, that's good news, ain't it?" asked Linc. "They don't know shit."

Rick only grunted and continued wiping down each part of the rifle.

"You do the Glock that way too?" Linc asked.

"Yeah," Rick said.

"So you got any ideas?"

Rick just sighed and shook his head. "You're not gonna like them," he said. He slipped the cotter pin into the carrier assembly, securing the firing pin, then tapped it on his palm, checking the fit.

"Try me," Linc said, picking up the Exacto knife and the cardboard videocassette box again. He was sitting on one of the twin beds, hunching over so that his elbows rested steadily on his knees.

"I think we're in over our heads," Rick said. "This thing tonight showed that."

"What you talking about, we kicked their asses," Linc said.

"Yeah, and now we got the cops on ours."

"Man, you heard the newscast. They think it's gang-bangers."

"Linc, use your head," Rick said. "It happened in our apartment." He paused, giving his words more effect. "It's only a matter of time before they put two and two together."

"So what you saying?"

"I'm saying that maybe if we go to them—"

"No way, man," Linc said. "No way."

"Why?"

"What we gonna tell 'em? That the fucking Mafia's after us 'cause we broke into a bank vault and stole a motherfucking tape?" He held up the empty box. Rick said nothing. "And what about Diane? You just gonna leave her, too?"

"She's one of the reasons I think we should go to the authorities," Rick said. "We're gonna need back-up to take these guys on. Plus, we're running low on ammo. Tonight we were lucky, and we don't even know if they'll contact us again, after what happened."

"Oh, they'll be a callin'," Linc grinned. He held up the empty box and wiggled it. "As long as we have what they looking for, they gonna find a way to get ahold of us."

Rick shook his head again.

Linc grabbed a precisely-cut slice of the heavy-grade sandpaper and fitted it into the cassette box again, so that it rested snugly in the rectangular end. He stuck another similarly-cut piece of sandpaper in the other end, then slipped the plastic VHS cassette back into the box.

"You think the fucking cops are gonna give two shits about Diane, Rick? You think they gonna be extra careful so she don't get popped?" He snorted derisively and slid the cassette tape out of the box.

"Look, all I'm saying is, maybe we better think about what we're up against."

"Uncle Henry said he'd back us up."

"Christ, Linc. He's no kinda back-up."

"The fuck he's not," Linc said. "You ever hear of the Blackstone Rangers? The P-Stone Nation? Uncle Henry grew up with those guys. They were the baddest dudes around, even before they became the El Rukins. And he spent his time in the service, too."

"Yeah, building roads in the Army Corps of Engineers," Rick said. "He wasn't even in the infantry, for Christ's sake. And we've practically used up all of the money buying these weapons."

"That the bottom line for you?" Linc asked. "The money?"

"Of course not," Rick said. "But we're running short of resources all the way around."

Linc was securing two sets of old fashioned, wooden kitchen matches to the bottom of the VHS cassette with electrical tape. He slit the ends of the box, inserted the cassette, and then re-secured the ends with more tape. Rick watched as he quickly pulled the cassette out of the box and the matches suddenly burst into bright flame. Linc blew them out.

"Once this baby is filled with black flash powder," he said, watching the smoke curl up from the extinguished match-heads, "we'll have another nice little surprise for them."

"Smoke and mirrors ain't gonna help us get Diane back," Rick said.

"If that's the way you feel, man, then don't help. Don't go with me. It's your choice. All I know is, these motherfuckers got my lady, and they been trying to get us. We go to the cops, we dead meat. We don't meet these fuckers and get them first, we dead then, too." He tossed the still-smoldering cassette down on the bed and stood up. "What's it gonna be, Rick? I gotta know right now. You with me all the way, or what?"

"There's no way I can convince you to go to the cops, huh?"

Linc shook his head.

Rick stared silently for a moment. "Then I guess I'm in," he said finally.

Linc grinned and held out his hand. Rick reached across and they shook.

Semper Fi, " Linc said.

The Heist

★ ★ ★ ★ ★

1:37 A.M.

Germaine walked alongside of Vino down the narrow, long corridor inside the meat-packing plant. There were numerous solid-steel doors, all closed, and a series of fluorescent lights above that gave the corridor a harsh, yellow cast. Behind them the massive figure of Gumbo lumbered nimbly.

"He know what's going on?" Vino asked.

"If he doesn't by now," Germaine said with a smile, "he must have a pretty damn good idea."

Vino gave out a staccato-like laugh. He was carrying a black and navy-blue canvas gym bag in his right hand. It made a hollow sounding thump as it banged against the cinder block wall.

"Good. Let him stew a little bit," Vino said. "I was at a party for my grandson. His tenth birthday."

"An important event in any young man's life," Germaine said. They turned and went into the large, open factory area. It was dark, except for a few firelights, and composed of various machines and steel tables. Several freezers sat along the back portion, and across from them were a series of walls that formed rooms without any fronts. Vino paused and flipped on some light switches that caused a flickering, delayed reaction along the ceiling of the immense room.

"Where's he at?" Vino asked.

"Room five, just as you instructed," Germaine said.

Vino smiled and started forward, then abruptly stopped.

"What about the tape?" he asked.

"There's been a slight delay in procuring that. I had hoped to present it to you tonight, but we've run into some unforeseen circumstances."

"Huh? What's that mean?"

"We are certain that, with the proper assistance from your

195

people, we can get it tomorrow," Germaine said. He punctuated his sentence with his expansive smile.

Vino's nostrils flared.

"Without the fucking tape, this whole thing could blow wide open," he said. "What the fuck, I was told you was the best. The Regulator, they call you. Didn't I explain to you how fucking important that tape is?"

"Try not to distress yourself, Mr. Costelli," Germaine said calmly. "I made a slight miscalculation tonight and, unfortunately, could not attend to the matter myself. But, as I said, I'm quite confident that this situation will be rectified shortly."

Vino stared at him for a moment. "It better be."

"Well, that's one of the reasons we're holding Mr. Fox in abeyance," Germaine said. "He's our insurance to making sure we get the tape."

"Who? Ab-what? Speak in English, for Christ's sake."

"Mr. Fox. Mr. Osmand's attorney."

At the mention of the Mink, Vino smiled again. What the hell, I ain't gonna let nothing spoil this moment, he thought, as he glanced into the depths of the factory and then looked back to Germaine.

"Okay, make sure you get it tomorrow," he said. "Now, if you'll excuse me." He grinned malevolently.

"Certainly, sir," said Germaine. "Ah . . . do you want this disposed of in a covert fashion?" He pointed toward the room.

"There you go again, using them big fucking words, Germaine. I told ya, speak in English."

"Do you want us to stick around and help you get rid of . . ."

"Oh, nah, my boys can handle that," Vino said. "I want this motherfucker found so it'll send a message: Nobody snitches on me. Nobody."

His lower lip pulled up tightly over his upper and he stared upward into Germaine's eyes.

"We'll leave you to your pleasures then," the tall southerner said. He turned and walked back toward the corridor. Gumbo stared momentarily at the short man holding the gym bag before following Germaine. After they'd disappeared, Vino went slowly down to room five. It was one of the open-ended rooms across from the freezers. A series of parallel steel cables were suspended just below the ceiling, and hanging from one of them, his arms stretched above him, his feet barely resting on the floor, was Johnny "the Mink" Osmand. His blue sports shirt was caked with sweat, despite the cool temperature inside the factory. His hands had been manacled and looped over the wire, which bent considerably under his weight. Vino paused to watch him for a moment, then moved forward and grabbed a handful of his thick hair.

"Hello, Mink," he said.

"Vino?" Osmand said, his voice sounding filled with equal parts of fear and desperation. "You the one that grabbed me? What's going on?"

"You know goddamn well what's going on, you motherfucker." He released the hank of hair with a sudden push, then spit in the other man's face. "After all I done for you, you're ready to sell me out like some fucking piece of meat."

"I don't know what you're talking about," Osmand said. "I wasn't gonna—"

"The fuck you weren't. Don't fucking lie to me," Vino said, pointing his finger now, his voice a husky whisper.

"But I wasn't. Honest."

"You denying you met with the fucking Feds making a deal to sell me out?"

"Well, I . . ." Osmand swallowed hard before continuing.

"I was meeting with 'em, sure, for Christ's sake. But I was stringing them along. Whaddya want? They had a case going against me."

"And you couldn't wait to spread the cheeks of your ass, could ya?" Vino moved forward, using his finger to punctuate his words. "You couldn't take it like a man, could ya? Could ya?"

His last words elevated to a shout, and he slapped Osmand's face.

The hanging man writhed in pain as the manacles cut into his wrists. He mumbled something unintelligible.

"What was that?" Vino demanded. "What were the words to come out of that fucking Judas mouth of yours?"

"It wasn't me, Vino," Osmand said, raising up on his tiptoes again to ease the pressure on his wrists. "Honest. It wasn't me."

"Bullshit. I told you, don't fucking lie to me." Vino went to the gym case, unzipped it, and withdrew the Louisville Slugger that had previously adorned his wall. "Remember this, Johnny?" he asked with a grin.

"Hey, Vino, please . . ."

"Save it."

"No wait, look," Osmand said, the desperation suffusing every word. "I got something on you. Something bad, and if anything happens to me, people got copies that'll be sent straight to the cops."

"Oh," said Vino, adjusting his grip on the taped handle of the bat. "And what might that be?"

"It's a tape," Osmand said. He licked his lips. "Of you whacking Campo and Volpone."

"Oh yeah?" Vino said calmly, taking a practice swing, knowing the whoosh would fill Osmand with incipient terror.

"Is this the part where I'm supposed to ask," Vino took another swing, "how many copies you got? And who's got 'em?"

"I got a couple," Osmand said quickly. "And all kinds of people got 'em."

Vino moved forward and delivered a low swing to Osmand's left foot. The hanging figure's whole body seemed to jerk upward with a shriek, then slump down. The wire made a rasping sound.

"Wrong answer, Johnny," Vino said. "And for your information, I already know about the fucking tape. Have known about it for some time, and I'm already making plans to get it."

Osmand seemed to consider this for a moment, then said softly, "Vino."

"Yeah?" he answered, stepping closer.

Osmand mustered enough saliva to spit in the other man's face as he leaned close. Vino immediately jumped back and pawed at his cheek with his palm.

"Fuck you then," Osmand said.

That made Vino smile. He gripped the bat once more and stepped slowly around in back of the dangling figure.

"You think you can make me mad so I'll do you quick, huh, Mink?" he said. He whirled suddenly and smacked the bat against Osmand's lower right leg. When the screaming had subsided, Vino leaned in close, from the side this time, and gripped the Mink's thick gray mane again.

"This is only the first inning, motherfucker, and I ain't even gonna *start* swinging for the fences till the bottom of the ninth."

Chapter 14

Thursday, April 16, 1992

8:35 A.M.

"You guys look terrible," Arlene said, placing a hand on Tony's shoulder as he slumped forward at the desk, which was covered with handwritten and typewritten reports, open mug books, and various bulletins and Teletypes. Several Styrofoam coffee cups also sat in various stages of fullness over his desk and Ray's.

"Isn't it great to have our office open again?" Kent Faulkner said, coming into the room a few steps behind Arlene. She was wearing a dark blue skirt with matching jacket. The blouse under it was a pale tan silk. Faulkner put his hands on his hips, spreading open his gray, double-breasted suit. "What the hell, you guys come in early or something?"

"Or something," Ray said.

"Tony, what's going on?" Arlene asked. "Are you okay?"

"I'm fine," Tony said, managing a weak smile. "Just not as young as I used to be. These things tire out an old man like me."

"Old man, my ass," Ray chimed in. "You been running me ragged all night."

"You mean you've been at this all night?" Arlene asked.

"Yeah, we got involved in a triple homicide last night on the South Side," Ray said.

"Homicide?" Faulkner said. "I saw something about one on the news."

"So you've been here all night?" Arlene asked.

"Not here," Tony said. "It happened over on 114th and Hale."

"That's the one I saw on the news, all right," Faulkner said.

Ignoring him, Tony continued. "We spent most of the time over at District Twenty-Two. We just came by here to follow up on something."

"You said that was a triple, Ray?" Faulkner asked.

"Yeah, you shoulda seen Tony run up them stairs," he said. "Two of 'em were offed with a machine gun."

"Oh my God," Arlene said.

"A machine gun," Faulkner said. "No kidding."

"Tony, you should have been more careful," Arlene said. "You could have been killed."

"A machine gun," Faulkner repeated. "That's wild. I haven't fired one of those since Quantico."

"Come on, Mr. FBI," said Ray, getting up suddenly. "I'll let you buy me another cup of coffee and I'll tell you all about it."

Faulkner looked somewhat perplexed as Ray slapped him on the back affectionately and steered him out of the room. As he did so, Ray turned and winked several times at Tony, then cocked his head fractionally toward Arlene.

"I thought Ray didn't like Kent," she said, watching the uneven pair amble away.

"Ray's just being Ray," Tony said with a smile.

"So tell me what happened," she said.

He recounted the events briefly, telling her about the call from Nate Wells, the controlled buy, and the information about an automatic weapon sale that led them to the Beverly neighborhood.

"We were staking the place out, waiting for this Linc guy to come home so we could roust him," Tony said, "when some kind of shoot-out started in the apartment."

"So you really did run up the stairs like Ray said?"

"Well," he said slowly, "the shooter was gone by the time we got up there."

Arlene shook her head.

"I really wish you'd be more careful," she said.

"Why, you afraid this old man'll get hurt?"

"Yes, I'm afraid you'll get hurt. And don't go calling yourself an old man, either. You're not that old, and you're still very handsome."

This raised Tony's eyebrows. Could all of Ray's teasing be right? Did Arlene really find him attractive? He cleared his throat.

"Well, Ray and I have handled a lot of hot situations in our time," he said. "We were pretty careful covering each other."

"Wouldn't it have been more sensible to wait for back-ups?"

"Well, yeah," he said slowly, "but we figured that if we did, the suspect would get away and some innocent person might be injured or killed."

He noticed that Arlene was staring at him, her head canted to the left, an admiring look on her face.

"Anyway," he continued, the excitement creeping back into his voice, "one of the guys who was killed was Tommy Del Bianco. He's one of Vino Costelli's boys. After we finished up the reports at Twenty-Two, we grabbed breakfast and shot down here to review the info we had on file concerning Del Bianco and Costelli. Then we tried to find the other two in the mug books, but boy, all these punks start to look alike after a while."

"You're so dedicated," Arlene said. "So different from other cops I've known."

"I don't know about that," Tony said, self-effacingly. "So what's the latest on the Mink deal? Fox ever call you back?"

"No," Arlene said. "I put a call into his secretary yesterday afternoon, but she said he was ill. Out with the flu. I'll try again today."

"Probably just sick over the thought that this great trial opportunity is about to go down the drain," Tony said. "This trial could have made him, if he'd played his cards right."

"You look so tired," she said. "Why don't you go home and get some sleep?"

"I'll be okay. Ray and I are going to follow up on one more lead on this shooting suspect first."

"I sure admire your dedication," Arlene said.

"Just doing our jobs," he replied. "The first twenty-four hours of a homicide investigation are crucial."

"Isn't Violent Crimes doing the follow-up?"

"Well, yeah, but we figured to give them a hand on this one," he said. "I'd sure like to get something good on old Vino before I retire. Something that I'm sure is gonna stick."

"If the Mink has that tape, like he says, we shouldn't have much to worry about," Arlene said. "Right?"

"There's always something to worry about when you're dealing with these types," Tony said grimly.

Arlene was sitting in front of him, staring with her head cocked to the left again. "I'd like to ask you something," she said.

"What?" Tony managed a grin.

"Do you have any plans for this Saturday?" she asked somewhat tentatively.

Tony was stunned.

"Ah, no," he said.

"Then would you consider coming over to my place Saturday evening for dinner?" Arlene asked.

"I . . ." Not knowing what to say, he hesitated, then said, "I'd be delighted."

"Great. How's seven o'clock sound?"

"It sounds fine," he said.

The phone rang and Tony reached forward and grabbed it.

"Cardoff," he said.

"Yeah, Tony it's Bob O'Neil from Violent Crimes. Got some more info on that triple from last night."

"Great, Bob," Tony said, searching through the mess on his desk for a pad and pencil. Arlene, who had apparently figured out what he was looking for, gave him one off her desk.

"One of our uniforms, a Julia Edwards in Ten, was getting briefed in roll call this morning about the possible machine gun being out on the street and she remembered the address. It seems she responded to a shots-fired call over on 113th and Wentworth and stopped this guy Lincoln Jackson. He claimed to be the boyfriend of one Diane Cassidy, who lives at the Roseland address. This was verified by the neighbors. Seems this guy Jackson walked in on a burglary in progress and the suspects took a couple shots at him. The ETs dug one of the slugs out of the garage."

"She sure it's the same Lincoln Jackson?" Tony asked.

"Yeah," O'Neil said. "She ran his D.L. and questioned him as to why he was in Roseland when his license had a Beverly address."

"She sounds like a sharp kid," Tony said. "Give me what you got on Jackson."

O'Neil rattled off Linc's full name, date of birth, and driver's license number.

"No criminal history through us," he said.

"I'll check through my end up here," Tony said. "Meanwhile, you gonna check with this Cassidy gal?"

"Shit, when I get a fucking chance," O'Neil said. "We just had three more sunrise bodies."

It was an old Chicago Police saying that when the sun came up, so did the dead bodies.

"Well, Ray and I can do that," Tony said. "We'll get back to you later."

"Great. I'd appreciate it. I'm waiting on calls from the patrolman who took the report and from the ET," O'Neil said. "Maybe they got something more in their notes."

"Give me that Cassidy woman's address," Tony said.

There was a rustle of papers, then O'Neil read him the address.

"Okay, give me a holler if you get anything more," Tony said. He gave O'Neil his car phone and beeper numbers.

Just as he was finishing, Ray and Faulkner came back. Tony briefed Ray as he was downing the last of his coffee. He finished with, "We got to find out how Vino Costelli ties into all this."

"I guess we better hop on out to Roseland then," Ray said.

Tony nodded, got up, started slipping on his sport jacket, and suddenly realized he'd been on the go since yesterday and needed a shower.

"You guys mind if I tag along?" Faulkner asked.

"Yes," Ray said harshly. "This is Chicago P.D. business."

"Kent," Tony said, "Ray and I can handle that end of it. We're familiar with that neighborhood anyway. What you *can* do for us is to use your FBI contacts to check out this Lincoln Jackson guy. He checks out negative through the city, but that just means we haven't arrested him. He may have a record in another state or in the suburbs."

Faulkner pursed his lips and nodded.

"Yeah, I can do that," he said, giving Ray a sideways glance.

"Besides, if Fox calls back and wants a meet, we don't want Arlene to have to go by herself, do we?" Tony added, smiling benignly.

"I reckon not," Faulkner said.

Tony gave him an affectionate slap/squeeze on the shoulder and winked at Arlene. Then he and Ray left.

As they rode the elevator down, Tony asked Ray why he'd done that.

"Done what?" Ray asked.

"Acted so rude to Kent," Tony said. "The poor guy was only trying to help."

"Kent?" Ray said, raising his eyebrows in exaggeration. "Since when did you start calling that shitbird Kent?"

"Come on. He ain't so bad."

The elevator doors opened at the main level of the Federal Building just as Ray loudly blurted out, "Fuck him. He's a fucking Fed, ain't he?"

They curtailed their conversation until they got to the underground garage; then after getting in the car, Tony resumed.

"You know," he said, "maybe you should take a couple of days off or something."

"Huh? Why?"

"You're sounding pretty stressed out."

"Me?" Ray said. "How do you figure?"

"Just the way you're acting toward Kent. You really ought to try to get along, you know."

"There you go with that 'Kent' bullshit again," Ray said. He wheeled the car out of the underground parking garage and headed west on Adams toward the expressway. "That

206

guy's a dickhead-and-a-half. Where's he from? Virginia, or someplace?"

"You could do worse for a partner once I leave," Tony said.

"I already told you. I'm transferring back to Gang Crimes once you retire."

"Like hell," Tony said. "You're gonna stay in Organized Crime till you make sergeant."

"Horseshit," said Ray. "What's got you so wound up about this Faulkner guy, anyway? I thought you hated the fucker."

Tony just stared impassively out the window. They were heading down Halsted toward the Ryan entrance ramps.

"Come on, Tony. Don't try to bullshit me. Something's bugging you and I bet I know what, too." Ray glanced at him with a sly smile. "I bet you're kicking yourself in the ass 'cause I gave you the perfect opportunity to be alone with Arlene and you didn't ask her out, right?"

"Wrong," said Tony. "She asked me over to dinner."

"No shit," Ray said. He grinned again and gave Tony a quick punch on the arm. "See? What did I tell you?"

"I just don't know," Tony said, shaking his head. "We're not even in the same generation."

"So what? Look at Clint Eastwood. He's no spring chicken anymore either, and the girls are always going ga-ga over him."

Tony sighed. The car phone rang, saving him further comment. It was O'Neil. Tony put it on speaker so they both could hear.

"Yeah, Tony, I talked to the patrolman who took the report," O'Neil said. "He remembered that this Linc guy called his uncle to come house-sit with him while they waited for the girlfriend to return home. The uncle's name is Henry Bartwell." He spelled it. "Checked him out and he shows a couple of arrests for minor shit way back in the late sixties. Back when Jeff Fort was just forming the Blackstone Rangers, for Christsake."

"Anything recent?" Tony asked.

"Huh-uh," O'Neil said. "I made a quick call over to five. It seems the uncle's gone legit, at least as far as anyone can tell. Had some kind of construction business over on State in Roseland for quite a few years."

"Give me the address," Tony said. "We'll check that out too."

As soon as O'Neil had hung up, Kent Faulkner called. Tony winked at Ray as he spoke.

"Yeah, Kent. That was quick."

"Well, you know us *federalies*," Kent said. "We can move pretty fast when we have to."

Ray rolled his eyes, but said nothing.

"First of all, there's no arrest record for Lincoln Jackson," Faulkner said. "But I did find something else. He's an ex-Marine. Was in for seven-and-a-half years, and was in the invasion of Panama and the Gulf War. His MOS was advanced recon. Won a bronze star in Panama and a silver star in the Gulf for calling in an artillery strike on his own position when the Iraqis stormed into Khafji."

"Sounds like a real American hero," Tony said. "Any word on why he got out of the Marines?"

"He got riffed," Faulkner said. "Reduction In Force. Guess they decided they had enough guys in his MOS and that was that."

Tony thanked Faulkner and told him to keep him posted on any new developments with Fox or the Mink. When he pressed the button to terminate the call, he noticed a worried look on Ray's face.

"Now what's wrong?" he asked.

"I was just thinking," Ray said. "I sure hope this ain't a case of a gyrene gone bad."

"Oh yeah, that's right," said Tony. "You're an ex-Marine yourself."

"There's no such thing as an ex-Marine," Ray said.

"Once a jarhead, always a jarhead, eh?"

"Fuckin' A," said Ray. *Semper Fi.*"

"Ray Lovisi, USMC," said Tony. "That does have a ring to it. Reminds me of that other famous Marine. In fact, you look a little like him."

"Who? Chesty Puller?"

"No, Gomer Pyle."

9:05 A.M.

Henry Bartwell had been out to the construction site at seven, and not seeing either Linc or Rick, left the job in the charge of Dock, his sometimes foreman. He then went back to his office under the guise of doing some paperwork but really just wanted to try and sort things out. After grabbing a cup of coffee and a couple of cinnamon donuts from the neighborhood shop, he went back to the trailer. He'd only been there mulling things over for about ten minutes when the phone rang. Thinking it might be Linc, Henry grabbed it just after the first ring.

"Is Linc there?" a woman's voice asked. It was imbued with desperation.

"Who is this?" Henry demanded. Then it came to him. "Diane?"

"Henry, I need to get ahold of Linc," she said. "Do you know where he is?"

"Diane, are you all right?" he asked. "Where is you at, girl? We been worried sick about you."

"I can't go into that now," she said. He could tell by the

strained tone that something wasn't right. "I need to get a hold of Linc right away."

"He ain't here," Henry said, wondering now whether someone was listening in on the conversation. "He didn't show up for work this morning, and I ain't heard from him."

He heard her rapid breathing coming over the line. Then she said, "When you do, tell him to call me at this number."

"Wait a minute. Let me get a pencil."

His big hands rifled through the mess of papers on his cluttered desk until he found a blank four-by-five tablet. He gripped the pencil hard and told her, "Okay, go ahead."

She read off a phone number and asked him if he had it.

"Yeah, I got it," Henry said. "Now, tell me, are you all right?"

"I can't talk anymore. Good-bye."

The line went dead.

Henry looked at the phone number that he'd written down on the tablet. Being in business as long as he had, he knew the number for Illinois Bell crisscross information by heart. He dialed it and read off the number that Diane had given him.

"I'm sorry, sir," the operator said. "That's a mobile number."

"Can you tell me who it comes back to?"

"I'm sorry, that's all the information we have," the operator said.

Henry let out a slow sigh and hung the phone back up. He set the tablet down on top of the clutter of papers and picked up his coffee, which had gotten cold and bitter-tasting. A sharp knock on the trailer door startled him, and he rose and opened it. Two white guys stood outside, one taller and older looking, the other short and young, but he knew immediately that they were cops.

"Mr. Bartwell," the older one said, holding up his Chicago

Police star. "I'm Detective Cardoff and this is my partner, Detective Lovisi." The short cop held up his badge. "Can we come in and talk to you, sir?"

"Well, I was just getting ready to go out," Henry said.

"It'll only take a couple of minutes," Lovisi said. "It's about your nephew, sir."

Henry felt a lump in his throat. Had something happened to Linc? Was that why he hadn't heard from him? "Come in," he said, stepping back from the door. Lovisi and Cardoff went up the cement block steps. Henry stood by the desk and nervously grabbed the cup of cold coffee, debating what and how much to say. He decided to let them make the first move.

"Sorry I don't have any coffee to offer you gentlemen," he said, "but I runs things on kind of a shoestring budget."

"That's all right," Cardoff said.

They continued standing in the narrow confines of the trailer's office. Henry, not wanting to sit and have them towering over him, leaned on the edge of the desk. Remembering Diane's call and the phone number, he quickly shot a glance at the tablet before looking at both of them and smiling pleasantly.

"You know a Lincoln Jackson, Mr. Bartwell?" Cardoff asked.

"Yeah, he's my sister Emma's boy," Henry said. "Why? Is he all right?"

"Why would you think he wasn't?" Lovisi asked.

"Well," Henry said, quickly searching for words, "when the polices comes around, usually there's something wrong. He ain't been in no accident or nothing, has he?"

"Not that we know of," Cardoff said. "When was the last time you saw him?"

Henry considered this before answering. No telling what

they knew, or didn't know, but he decided to stick to the facts as much as possible.

"Yesterday afternoon," he said.

"And about what time was that?"

"Look, maybe you'd better tell me why you is asking me all these questions," Henry said. "I gotta right to know if my nephew's hurt or in some kind of . . . in something, don't I?"

"We'll get to that, sir," said Cardoff. "You were telling us about where and when you saw him yesterday."

Henry blew out a slow breath. Stick to the facts, he told himself.

"It was about five-thirty or six," he said. "He called me and told me his girlfriend's place had got broken into. I went over and sat with him while we waited for the police. Brought some wood over to fix up the back door."

Lovisi read off Diane's address and asked if that was the place.

"Yeah, that's it."

"What happened after that?"

"Nothing, really," Henry said. He took another sip of his coffee. "The police came and went, and I went home. I guess Linc did the same."

"Where does Linc live?" Cardoff asked.

"He live in Beverly," Henry said. "Over on Hale."

"He works for you?" Lovisi asked.

"Yeah, when he come home from the Marines I give him and his friend jobs," Henry said. "They was supposed to show up this morning, and didn't even call in. Put me in a helluva bind. Got me a minority-business contract for part of the deep tunnel dig." He offered up a proud smile.

Cardoff took out one of his cards and handed it to Henry, who took it gingerly, holding it only by the lower right corner.

"If Lincoln does get in touch with you, Mr. Bartwell, I'd appreciate it if you'd give this to him and tell him to give me a call."

"Sure will," Henry said, placing the card down on the desk.

"Here, let us give you our beeper numbers," Lovisi said, reaching for the four-by-five tablet on the desktop. Henry's hand shot out to quickly grab the tablet and he ended up knocking over the coffee cup. The brown liquid spilled all over the papers on his desk, including the cop's card. "Shit," Henry said, grabbing the tablet, ripping the page with the phone number on it, before handing the tablet to Lovisi. He took some of the paper napkins out of the Dunkin' Donuts bag and began sopping up the spilled coffee.

"Oops, that's my home number," Lovisi said, tearing off the sheet he'd been writing on. "Here's our beeper numbers," he said, and handed it over. Henry scratched the dark coils of hair around his ears as he looked at it, then ran his palm over the smooth expanse on top of his head.

"What's Linc's friend's name?" Cardoff asked matter-of-factly.

Henry glanced up from the paper, then figuring that they probably knew already, said, "Weaver. Rick Weaver."

Cardoff wrote that down.

"Where's he live?" Lovisi asked.

"Ah, he live with Linc," Henry said slowly. "They shares the apartment on Hale."

Cardoff nodded absently, scribbling some more notes on his pad.

"But they both young, good-looking studs," Henry added quickly. "Probably cribbin' with some chicks, or something."

Cardoff nodded again, still writing. Then he looked up.

Damn, this dude's eyes were piercing, Henry thought.

"Mr. Bartwell, I've spent my whole career involved in the kind of shit that your nephew appears to be involved in."

"Look," Henry said, cutting him off, "I don't know nothing about that."

"Let him finish," Lovisi said. "This is important."

Cardoff continued, "We're not after him. If he does call, tell him that. This is a lot bigger than him, and if he doesn't get our help, he's gonna get swallowed up by it."

Henry stared back at Cardoff, and, saying nothing, nodded fractionally.

The flimsy trailer door slammed shut behind them as they left, walking the thirty feet or so back to their car. Inside the vehicle, Ray immediately asked Tony if he had a pencil. Tony offered him his pen, but Ray just frowned.

"No, I need a pencil," he said, frantically opening the glove compartment and rummaging through it.

"For what?"

"Godamnit, all the fucking bullshit in here but what you need," Ray muttered. "Ha," he said, holding up a yellow-colored pencil. He grabbed Tony's notebook, flattened out the four-by-five sheet of paper he'd taken from Henry's tablet, and began a light, zigzag-shading motion over the surface with the conical edge of the pencil.

"What you got?" asked Tony.

"Saw this in an old Charlie Chan movie," Ray said, still shading with the pencil. "Did you get a look at that guy's desk?"

"Yeah, it was a real shit pile," said Tony. "Kinda reminded me of yours."

Ray shot him a frown. "Yeah, it was," he said. "And it's an old Lovisi proverb that when you're looking at a shit pile, the turd on top is always the freshest. Wa-la." He held up the paper, which now showed the white impression of a phone number inside the gray shading. "Did you see the way that guy was hawking this number when we were talking to him? Like he wanted to grab it real quick so we wouldn't see it, or something."

"Call information and see if you can find out who it's registered to," Tony said.

Ray grabbed the car phone, dialed the number, and read it off to the operator.

"Shit," he said, hanging up the phone a moment later. "It's a mobile number."

"Well let's call Faulkner and see if he can find out who it belongs to," Tony said. "Maybe it's this Lincoln guy's phone."

"Oh, are we back to calling him Faulkner now?" Ray said sarcastically.

"Just make the fucking call, would you?" Tony said with a grin. As Ray was punching in the number Tony added, "That was good work, Ray."

"Thanks."

"No, I mean it. It was."

Ray shrugged.

"You know," said Tony, "you're even starting to look a little like Warner Oland."

"Who?"

"The guy who played Charlie Chan."

"Yeah," grinned Ray, cradling the car phone against his ear, "but you're too damn old to be my number-one son."

9:20 A.M.

Linc returned from his trip to the front counter to get a newspaper just as the waitress was at the table refilling Rick's coffee cup. "You want some more, too, honey?" she asked

Linc. He smiled and nodded. After he'd slid into the booth, Rick's inquisitive gaze asked the unspoken question.

Linc shook his head.

"Everything looks cool," he said, picking up his coffee cup and spreading the paper out on the table. Most of the news still centered on the massive efforts to repair the damage from the flood and get the Loop back to a functioning level. Several pages showed diagrams of the tunnel systems, maps of the areas without power, and various pictures of the endless series of heavy-duty hoses pumping water from the basements of the flooded buildings. Linc found a small blurb about the shootout buried in the *Metro News* section. After reading it, he pushed it across the table, his index finger on top of the heading.

Rick turned the paper over and began to read it. Linc got up and said he was going to check in with Uncle Henry.

"You sure that's wise?" Rick asked.

"Why?"

"I mean, you sure you want to drag him into all this?"

Linc considered his answer, then said, "He'll understand, he's family. Besides, we gonna need another ride soon, or at least a place to stash yours."

"Yeah," Rick said reaching in his pocket and taking out his prescription medication. "Good thing I had these on me, or they'd probably be looking to nail me when I went in for a refill."

Linc just nodded as he got up. He knew that the cops probably had Rick's name if they'd searched the apartment, and he was certain they had his by now. But he also knew that he had to keep Rick cool, at least till the action was over. He was going to need him to get Diane back. He was going to need Henry, too, and a lot of luck. Once she was free, he'd figure how to get them all out of it. Take the blame himself, if need be. He wasn't exactly sure he could, but didn't want to worry about all the details just yet. He had to concentrate on the task at hand: freeing Diane. Then he'd figure out the rest of it. There had to be a way. He wasn't exactly sure just how, but there just had to be a way, and he knew the key to it all was that tape.

He moved toward the double set of pay phones in the vestibule, got some change for his dollar at the register, and dropped the coins in the slot. Henry answered immediately after the first ring.

"What's happening?"

"Linc? That you?"

"Yeah."

"Boy, I been worried clean outta my mind 'bout you," Henry said. "Why didn't you call me? Everything okay?"

"We're doing all right," Linc said. "Sorry about not calling, but we ran into a little problem over at the apartment last night." He told him about the firefight.

"That was your place?" Henry asked incredulously. "I heard about it on the news, but they said some shit about gangs, or something."

"They just blowing smoke."

"Well they blowing it pretty damn close, 'cause two cops was just here."

"What did you tell 'em?"

"I didn't tell 'em shit," Henry said. "What you think I am?"

"Sorry, Uncle Henry, but I'm kinda on edge. Didn't mean nothing by it."

"Oh, hell, I know that. But say, that ain't all. Diane called."

"She did," Linc said. "What she say? She okay?"

"If you let me finish, goddamnit, I'll tell you," Henry said.

"She left a number for you to call her. I checked it out and it's one of them mobile phone units, so we can't find out who it belongs to. And she didn't sound right."

"What you mean, like she was hurt, or something?"

"Uh-uh," Henry said. "Like she was scared. Real scared." Linc wrote down the number, then asked Henry if he had time to meet them with his Oldsmobile Ninety-Eight.

"Yeah," he said. "But the Caddie's running better."

"The ninety-eight's best," Linc said. It was one of those older, gas-guzzler models with a big trunk, and just enough rust spots to make it look like the "typical ghetto ride" to any inquisitive cops. "I want to stash Rick's Talon till we need it."

"That ain't no problem," Henry said. "I can put it in my garage."

"What about the plates?" Linc asked. "If they been snooping around, they might see you driving it."

"Yeah, I never thought of that."

"Can you stop by the currency exchange on the way?" Linc said. "Tell 'em your plates was stolen and get one of those stickers for the back windshield. We'll take the plates off here and you can drive it back to your place."

"Okay," Henry said. "I'm leaving now."

Linc hung up and stared at the number his uncle had given him. After exhaling a sigh, he fed more coins into the slot and punched in the digits. It rang twice before the guy with the southern-sounding voice said hello.

"Lemme speak to Diane," Linc said.

"Oh, Linc, my man," the guy said. "She can't come to the phone right now."

"Listen, motherfucker—"

"Linc, that kind of verbiage is counter-productive."

"All right, motherfucker. What you want me to call you?"

After a pause, the guy said, "Germaine. Now let me just assure you that your lady is all right, and all her needs are being cared for with the utmost attention."

"Yeah, right," Linc said. "Just like you tried to take care of *my* needs last night." He almost said "our needs," but he caught himself. It was better not to let this guy know that he wasn't alone in this.

"Linc, that was a most unfortunate incident," Germaine said. "And let me assure you that those men last night were acting without my sanction or approval, and without authority."

"Is that so?"

"It is, Linc. And not only that, their actions were diametrically opposed to the way I wanted to handle this endeavor. Regrettably, I was tied up on another matter and couldn't attend to it personally."

"I still need to talk to Diane," Linc said.

"You will, son, you will. But first we have a little matter that we have to work out."

Linc said nothing. Germaine continued.

"You still have that item that I'm interested in?"

"Yeah, I got it."

"Good," Germaine said. "Now I've been authorized to make amends for the unfortunate beginning by including a . . . finder's fee for you. Say, one hundred thousand dollars in exchange for the tape."

Linc said nothing for a few seconds, then finally, "All right, but Diane goes free now, or it's no deal."

"I'm afraid it can't work that way, Linc."

"Then it's no deal. Let her go now or . . ."

"Or what, Linc? You'll destroy the tape? You'll turn it over to the cops?" Germaine's tone was laced with derision. "Now, we both know none of those is a viable option."

"Let her go now, man. I'm telling you. You let her go now, then we deal."

"Linc," Germaine said, his voice as cool as dry ice, "call me back when you want to talk sense." He terminated the call. Linc stared at the phone, fighting the urge to grab more coins and redial the number. But no, that would be playing right into their hands. The only chance Diane had, the only chance they all had, was for him to set it up right. Think it through, and set it up right. And it had to be good the first time, because he knew he wouldn't be getting any second chance.

"What if he don't call back?" Gumbo asked Germaine, who was removing the cellophane from one of his special cigars. Germaine smiled as he placed the thin, brown cylinder between his lips and lighted it.

"He has to," he said. "As I told him, he's out of options." He puffed to get the cigar going, then gestured toward the door of the small room where they were keeping Diane. "We have his lady-love, and he knows we can and will hurt her, slowly if we prefer, until he acquiesces. And besides, without us he essentially has nothing of value anyway. He can't turn the tape in, because it's the only ticket to getting Diane back. And he can't go to the police, because there'd be too many questions he'd have to answer, and that wouldn't get her back either."

Gumbo nodded slowly. "So we the only game in town, then."

"Exactly," Germaine said. He blew out a cloud of smoke.

"So what we do now?"

"We wait for him to call back, then set up the meet."

"And?"

"And," Germaine said, exhaling another cloudy breath, "we get the tape, and then we kill him."

Gumbo's heavy lips stretched over his huge teeth, all the way back to his incisors.

"Good," he said in a low, guttural voice.

11:35 A.M.

The ringing of the car phone snapped Tony into consciousness. He blinked his eyes several times, not realizing immediately that he'd been asleep. They'd been parked on Wentworth, a few houses down from Diane's house, waiting and hoping for someone to come home. Ray already had the car phone to his ear and was talking into it.

"Yeah, Kent, that's great. Real fast. Uh-huh, hold on, lemme put you on the speaker." He pressed the button then set the car phone back in its cradle. "Go ahead," he said.

"Hi, Tony," Faulkner's voice said. "I was telling Ray that I got the lowdown on that mobile phone number, and you'll never guess who it comes back to."

"Who?"

"Reginald J. Fox," Faulkner said. "It's his personal line."

Ray and Tony exchanged glances.

"Well we gotta get a tap on it right away," Ray said. "If Fox is tied into this shooting thing, with Costelli's boys, this could be big."

"I don't know," Faulkner said. "I have some real reservations about going before a judge and asking that the opposing counsel's phone be tapped."

"Goddamn, Kent, we're really on to something here," Ray said.

"Well, you and I know that because we're looking at it from a cop's perspective," Faulkner said. "But a judge might not see it that way."

"Well, see what you can do, Kent," Tony said. "We've got to unravel this thing quickly, or we'll be left at the gate."

"Okay," Faulkner said, the sigh that preceded it coming over very clearly. "I'll see if I can get an appointment to see somebody in the morning."

"In the morning," Ray said angrily. "Christ, it's only eleven-thirty."

"Ray, I'm gonna have to research the case law on this first, so I don't wind up looking like an idiot," Faulkner said, anger creeping into his tone, too.

"Fat chance of that not happening," Ray muttered.

"What?" Faulkner said.

"He said do the best you can, Kent," Tony quickly interjected. "But make sure that nobody on our end calls that number. No sense letting them know we have it."

"Yeah, good point," Faulkner answered. "Oh, say, Tony, Arlene wants to talk to you."

Tony snatched the phone out of its cradle and put it to his ear as Ray pointed his finger and grinned with exaggerated lasciviousness.

"Tony?" Arlene said. "Where are you?"

"We're staking out that guy Jackson's girlfriend's place, hoping he'll drop by so we can talk to him."

"Oh my God, you must be exhausted," she said.

"Yeah, well, to tell you the truth, we were just about to rein it in." When Ray heard him say this, he went into some more exaggerated expressions and finger-pointing. Ignoring his partner's pantomime, Tony asked her what she wanted.

"Ah . . . anything else going on?"

He heard her sigh. "We got another report a little while ago. The Mink's wife called the Palos Heights Police this morning. He's missing. Didn't come home last night."

"Where was he supposed to have gone?"

"She said he told her that he had a special meeting with his attorney."

"That sounds bad," Tony said. "Either he's taking it on the lam, which I doubt, or they got him. You get ahold of Fox to see if he actually met with him?"

"Well, that's another strange thing," she said. "His office doesn't know anything about it. Reggie's been off sick the past two days. I left another message for him to contact me as soon as possible."

Tony considered this for a moment. He didn't like the sound of any of it.

"Oh, I almost forgot," Arlene said, "I was just wondering about Saturday."

Here it comes, Tony thought, she's come to her senses and is calling it off. Strangely, he felt crushed, yet flooded with relief at the same time.

"Yeah?" he said. "Bad timing? It's no problem if you can't . . ."

"Oh, no," she said. "I just wondered if you wouldn't mind making it tomorrow night instead. Unless you're busy, or something."

"No, I'm not busy," he gulped. Further words failed him.

"Good," she said. "I'll expect you at seven then? Or is that too early?"

"No, it's fine," he said. "Keep me posted on the other stuff."

After hanging up, Tony briefed Ray on the latest developments.

"Shit," said Ray, plopping the car into gear. "We might as well get outta here."

"Where we going?" Tony asked.

"I'm going to take you home, so you can get some sleep," Ray said. "Then I'm going to go see my brother-in-law."

"Your brother-in-law?"

"Yeah," Ray said glancing over at Tony with a grin stretched across his face. "He works for Ameritech. A technician. He'll get me a tap on this fucking number."

"Hey, we don't want to mess things up," Tony said. "Let Kent handle it."

"Fuck Kent," Ray said. "The son-of-a-bitch moves so fucking slow that the whole thing'll be over before he finishes looking through his law books. Did ya hear that prick?" He lapsed into an exaggerated southern twang to mimic Faulkner's Virginia accent: " 'We're looking at things from a cop's perspective.' Shit. That fucker wouldn't make a pimple on a real cop's ass."

"Yeah, but just the same, we gotta make sure everything's nice and legal. There's no sense getting evidence that'll be tossed out when the case gets to court."

"Well, I'm just trying to give us the edge, that's all," Ray said. "And I'll take any edge I can get, even if it's nice and *illegal*. What did Arlene want?"

"Oh, nothing," Tony said.

"She cancel your date, or something?"

"It's not a date," Tony said petulantly, "it's just dinner, and no, she didn't cancel it."

"Sure sounded that way," Ray said. "Look, Tony, don't feel bad."

"She didn't cancel. She just moved it up to tomorrow night instead," Tony said. A second later he was sorry he did, because Ray's grin was positively rakish.

"Now knock that shit off," Tony said.

"What shit?" Ray said, shaking his head. "But ya gotta admit, it works every time."

"What?"

"Sunrise bodies," Ray said.

"Huh?"

"Dead bodies start popping up, these women start plopping themselves down. It makes them feel . . ." he paused, obviously searching for the right euphemism, "romantic."

"Oh, you're so full of shit."

"No, it's true," Ray said. "I know for a fact. Used to go out with this chick from the Medical Examiner's Office. I knew that she'd be in the mood every time I picked her up at the morgue."

"Knowing you," Tony said with a wry smile, "she was probably a permanent resident there."

Chapter 15

Thursday, April 16, 1992

12:50 P.M.

Linc saw Henry's beige-colored Olds Ninety-Eight coming down Western toward him. He'd told his uncle to take a circuitous route and to stop several times to make sure no one was following him. Linc waved and the car swung over to the curb. Henry lowered the passenger's-side window electronically, and Linc leaned over, his forearms crisscrossed on the door.

"Thanks for coming," he said. "Pull into the parking lot." He gestured toward the adjacent restaurant. Henry nodded and Linc pushed off the vehicle and made a show of stretching while he surreptitiously looked up and down the street for cop cars. Satisfied, he turned and walked back toward the rear of the lot. Rick, who was standing in the vestibule pretending to be on the pay phone, made eye contact with Linc, put the phone back in its cradle, and went out to meet him. They walked toward Henry's car, which was now parked in the back of the lot next to Rick's black Eagle Talon.

Linc got into the front passenger seat of the ninety-eight and grinned at his uncle. Rick slipped into the left rear and hunched down.

"I see you got the sticker," Linc said, glancing toward the back windshield.

"Yeah, got one for Rick's car too," Henry said. "Figured they'd be looking for his plates."

"How'd you do that without the title, Henry?" Rick asked.

"You can't be black and stay in business as long as I have without learning some shortcuts." Henry held the license-applied-for sticker over his shoulder.

"I'll go take off my plates," Rick said, getting out.

"What's the plan?" Henry asked Linc.

"First, I'd like you to drive Rick's car over to your garage, or someplace safe, where we can stash it temporarily. We'll take the Olds."

Henry nodded.

"Then I got to figure out the rest of it," Linc said.

"You call that number?"

"Yeah. They got Diane, all right, and they want to trade her for the tape." Linc frowned. "At least that's what they saying they gonna do."

"What you think?"

"I think I gotta take these motherfuckers out before they take me out." He looked at his uncle. "I'm gonna need some help."

"You got it."

"Uncle Henry, are you sure? I mean, this shit's gonna get real nasty, and I can understand if you . . ."

"Shit, boy, you trying to tell *me* something? I was on the streets killing motherfuckers since before you was even born."

Linc grinned at his uncle's hyperbole.

"It's you, me, and Rick then," Linc said. "You still got your twelve-gauge?"

Henry nodded.

"Good. Get some extra shells. Deer slugs. All I got to do now is figure out a place where we can pull this off."

"What kind of place you looking for?" Henry asked.

"Someplace big, but isolated enough that we can take care of business and not arouse suspicion. And it's got to have a back way out so we can scoot when it's over and not look back till we safe."

Henry considered this for a moment, then said, "I think I know where."

2:20 P.M.

The eastern section of buildings had held up better than the ones farther west but, despite its dilapidated state, the property still impressively took up eight city blocks. Henry cruised by slowly, letting Linc and Rick survey the massive corrugated sides, which extended up three full stories. The gray metal showed streaks of black where dirty snow had melted down the sides, and sections of the blue sky were obliquely visible through the roof. The big red letters were intact on the east building, but attrition had worn off the ones on the west structure:

V I S C O V S I N   S T   W O   S

Still, the dark outlines of the missing letters could partially be seen against the gunmetal-colored sidewall.

Two neatly painted white signs with block letters were posted with two-by-four braces in front of each gate advising of the Wisconsin Steel Works Environmental Cleanup and prohibiting any trespassing. Smaller, secondary signs advised that the property was now owned by the U.S. Government. The seven-foot cyclone fence with the three strands of barbed wire along the top looked ineffective. Perhaps fifty feet inside the fence, next to the small wooden shack labeled Gate Six-A, the remains of a huge crane sat abandoned. The brightly painted metal of the cab had given way to extensive rust. The segmented, angular metal arm of the crane reposed about twenty feet away in the middle of the expansive cement driveway that once allowed access to the middle section of the facility. Beyond that, the empty frame of a large overhead door extended into the cavernous darkness of the front of the west building, its blackness like the open maw of some great, dead beast.

"I worked a lot of hours in them mills," Henry said, negotiating the bridge over the Calumet River on 106th street. "At one time they was a way of life for a man in this city, long as you was willin' to do the work."

He turned right at the base of the drawbridge and went along the entranceway to another steel mill, this one still operational, that sat on the opposite side of the river from the old mill. Henry swung the car to the left along the drive and into an alley that ran parallel to the railroad tracks. He pointed out the passenger's-side window.

"That's the back of the place," he said. "This plant here ain't even operating on three shifts anymore, I don't think. After the sun goes down, this whole area's like a no-man's land."

"This looks pretty good," said Linc. "But we gotta section it out into zones. Uncle Henry, can you take us back to that tunnel we saw along the road?"

Henry nodded and proceeded down the alley, then made a left. He drove back to 106th, then went west to Torrence. Turning again at the intersection, he drove south. The railroad tracks on this side of the river ran parallel to the street. They started out level at the intersection, then gradually rose along an elevated grade. About a hundred yards east the grade was about thirty feet high, and a huge reinforced culvert sat along the east side of the street. Henry slowed, surveyed the mirrors, then made a quick left onto the gravel road inside the culvert. They were in darkness for about ten seconds, then passed into the open again, on the other side of the elevation. Perhaps fifty feet beyond them was the river. The road they were on now was macadamized and twisted its way along the shore of the Calumet River toward the abandoned grounds of Wisconsin Steel.

"This lead all the way back to the mill?" Linc asked, pointing toward the distant superstructure.

"It used to," Henry said. As they got nearer, the road angled off to the right and ran almost directly along the river bank. It twisted back, heading toward the large expanse of open field adjacent to the first buildings of the mill.

"Can we leave the car here and go check this place out?" Linc asked.

"I guess so," Henry said. He put the Olds in park and shut off the engine. The three men got out and headed on foot across the field.

"This is too open," Rick said. "No cover."

Linc nodded, agreeing with that assessment.

"We'd be better off using this as our escape route," he said. He stamped his feet. "This ground's pretty hard. We should be able to park one of the cars over in there, by one of those buildings. That way, when we hit 'em and take Diane, we can regroup here, take the car, and get back on the street through that tunnel."

"The Talon should get over this with no problem," Rick said.

"Right," Linc said. "Uncle Henry, that'll be your job. You get Diane and head back outta here through the tunnel."

The older man nodded, his eyes scanning the other two.

"And you, Rick," said Linc. "We can leave you off at the bridge so you can work your way in from the other side. If we can, let's try to draw them into that building there," he pointed to the west plant. "That way you can use that outside stairway to take the high ground advantage."

"Where you gonna be?" Rick asked.

"I gotta stay in the middle where they can see me; otherwise, they'll never fall for it." Linc shrugged. "They'll be looking for me and hopefully think I'm alone. I'll hand 'em the fake tape, and when it explodes, that's when you two can hit 'em from the sides. I'll take out whoever's left in the middle. But wait till I've got Diane clear before you start firing."

"You're putting yourself right out there in the open?" Rick said. "That's suicide."

"I'll have to hope that they won't shoot till they get their hands on the tape," Linc said. "But what other choice do we have?"

Rick said nothing.

"Come on," Linc said. "Let's go in and scout it, and make some diagrams to get familiar with the terrain. This area here is gonna be section A." He moved his hand out in a small circling gesture. Rick got out his pen and paper and began making rough sketches of the roads and terrain.

"I gotta question," Henry said. "How you gonna get the motherfuckers to come here? I mean, what if they refuse, or want to name their own place?"

"I guess I'm gonna have to do some fast talking," Linc said, trying to sound more optimistic than he felt.

4:55 P.M.

Linc slipped the quarter into the pay phone and punched in the number. The money dropped through and the computerized operator requested "fifty-five cents, please, for the first three minutes." Linc redeposited and waited for the ringing. The sweat was dripping down his sides underneath his shirt.

Negotiate from a position of strength, he told himself. The southern guy, Germaine, answered on the third ring.

"Yeah, G," Linc said. "It's me, and I'm ready to talk turkey."

"Excellent, Linc," he said. "Now here's what I propose—"

"Fuck what you propose," Linc said. "This is how it's gonna be. You be in Hegewisch tonight at eleven-forty-five, and I'll call your little mobile phone and tell you where to meet me."

"Hegewisch?"

"Yeah, right. You know where it's at, don't you?"

"Of course," Germaine said.

But Linc got the impression that he really didn't.

"But I don't think that sounds very satisfactory."

"I don't give a fuck what you think. That's the only way we gonna play."

"Listen, son." His voice exuded calmness. "I'm not stupid enough to walk into an ambush, and that's exactly what this sounds like."

"That's real funny, considering the changes you put me through last night," Linc said.

Germaine sighed heavily.

"Linc, I thought I explained that to you before. Those men were renegades, acting without authority."

My ass, Linc wanted to say. Instead he said, "Look, the place I got in mind is big, deserted, and abandoned. And besides, how the fuck am *I* gonna try anything? You think I'm stupid enough to try and go up against someone like you?"

"I would certainly hope not."

"I won't," Linc said. "I know who I'm dealin' with. I just want my lady back, man. That's all I want."

"And the money, Linc," Germaine said. "Don't forget about the money. A hundred thousand. It's all yours for the tape."

"No tricks?"

"No tricks," Germaine said. "You have my word on it."

"Right," Linc said. "Now let me talk to Diane."

"I'm afraid she's not in the immediate area here."

"Bullshit," Linc said. "You put her on now, or else it's no deal." His voice softened slightly as he added, "I got to know she's okay."

Germaine was silent for a moment, then said, "Call me back in exactly ten minutes." He hung up.

Linc put the pay phone back in its cradle and glanced at his watch.

"Oh, baby, baby, is it really you?" Diane's voice asked over the phone.

"It's me, baby," Linc said. "You okay?"

"I'm all right, Linc," she said, but her voice sounded quavery. "I really am. They been treating me better since you been being cool. And they already told me they gonna let us go, once you give 'em the tape, baby. They gonna give us some money, too. Lots of money. They showed it to me. Just don't try nothing, baby. Please."

"I ain't gonna try nothing," he said calmly. "I just want to get you back, is all."

"Promise me, baby," she said. "Promise me you not gonna do nothing stupid, baby. Please."

"I promise," he said, trying to choke back his tears. "I promise . . ." Not to do anything as stupid as you tried, he thought. "Just don't worry, baby, everything's gonna be all right. I'll be comin' for you tonight, okay? Now put that guy back on."

"I'm here, Linc," Germaine's voice said.

"Be there tonight," Linc said. "Eleven forty-five." This time it was his turn to hang up.

The jangling of the phone snapped Tony awake for the second time that day. This time he'd dozed off in the easy-chair in his living room with the TV blaring on some news channel about the efforts to stem a seeming resurgence of the flood water in the Loop basements. The phone kept on ringing as he rolled out of the chair and stepped over to the table.

"Tony?" Ray's excited voice leaped out of the receiver at him before he'd even had a chance to say hello.

"No, it's Richard J. Daley," Tony said. "Who the hell did you think it was? You called me, didn't you?"

"Christ, what side of the bed you get up on?" Ray said. "Listen, remember I told you about my brother-in-law? Well, guess what? We finally got that little scanner/receiver working, and I just intercepted a call."

"You what? Are you fucking nuts? You know what Kent said."

"Hey, fuck Kent," Ray said disdainfully. "Now listen to me, if we wait on this, we're gonna miss it. It's going down to-night."

"What? When?"

"Eleven-forty-five," Ray said. "That's all I got so far. It sounds like they're holding this guy Linc's girlfriend, and want to exchange her for some videotape. It's got to be the one the Mink was talking about."

"The tape," Tony said incredulously. "How the hell would he get it?"

"Shit if I know, but that's what they said. Now what have you got to say?"

"Lovisi, you're a fucking genius."

"Don't I know it?" Ray said. "But it is nice to hear from my peers. Now, are you up for it tonight?"

"You better believe it," Tony said. "Where's it going down at?"

There were a few moments of silence before Ray answered.

"Well, we sorta didn't get that part yet."

"Huh?"

"Well, Christ, we just got the fucking thing working a little while ago," Ray said defensively. "Anyway, I figured if you and me got in the unmarked with the scanner and just waited, maybe they'd say something else and we could figure it out. Unless you want to go lean on the uncle some more."

Tony sighed. He was bone-weary, but he knew if he didn't go with him, Ray would be out there in the car alone.

"No, we better not do that just yet," Tony said. "Come by at about nine-thirty or ten. I want to try and get some more sleep."

"Okay, great," Ray said. "I will. And dig out your vest, too."

"Already done," said Tony, but he was thinking that a bulletproof vest wasn't going to stop a round from an M-16.

Chapter 16

Thursday, April 16, 1992

8:50 P.M.

Linc set his half-eaten hamburger down on the motel table and looked at his watch again. His stomach was too queasy for him to try to eat any more, and they'd gone over the plan so many times now that he was beginning to doubt it. And doubt himself. There were too many intangibles. But when hadn't there been intangibles? There sure had been some in Panama, and in the Gulf too. Plenty. But this time was different. This time it was just them. Nobody else. And then, there was Diane.

Henry shifted on the bed and sighed heavily.

"What's up?" Linc asked.

"I was just thinking, maybe it's a good thing that I got no woman to answer to, being gone all this time," Henry said. "But I am worried about setting things up for tomorrow on the job. You sure it wouldn't be all right for me to run home just for a little while?"

"Can't do it, Uncle Henry," Linc said. "They may be watching for you. I'm just glad we got Rick's Talon outta there with no problem."

"Maybe I better call Dock," Henry said, reaching for the phone. "I know they ain't gonna stop sending me bills just 'cause you guys are in shit up to your knees."

"Wait till Rick gets back, okay? We gotta keep this line clear in case there's a problem."

236

Henry frowned, then slumped back onto the pillows.

"Want something more to eat?" Linc asked.

"Huh-uh," Henry said. "Don't got no appetite."

"I know what you mean," Linc said. "Ain't nothing worse than playin' the waiting game." The M-16 lay on the floor next to him. Two sets of fully loaded magazines, taped together to allow a quick, flip-flop reload, were next to the rifle. He heard a car door slam and went immediately to the window, parting the vinyl curtains ever-so-slightly. "It's Rick."

Linc went to the door and unbolted it. Rick stepped in carrying a large, white plastic bag. He went to the foot of the bed and carefully removed three boxes. Each box was emblazoned with a colorful depiction of a radio headset sending out a bolt of lightning. Rick took out three transistor-sized batteries and tossed one to Linc and another to Henry.

"These are supposed to have a range of five hundred yards," he said, peeling off the plastic sealing the battery to the back of the card. "The guy said to make sure the antenna was up; otherwise you can transmit, but not receive."

Linc took his radio out of the box. It was about the size of a Walkman, with foam earpieces mounted on a thin metal headband. The antenna was on the right side of the headband, just above the earpiece. On the left side a bendable, heavy plastic wire angled downward with a foam-covered transmitter. The wire hook-up for the battery was on a cord about twenty-four inches long and had a clip so it could be secured to a pocket or belt.

"We'd better run some tests on these to determine their capabilities," Linc said, glad to have something to keep them occupied.

"Right," Rick said. "I'll go outside and start a slow count."

"It'll transmit through a building?" Henry asked incredulously.

"It should," Rick said. "Unless there's too much interference."

Henry arched his eyebrows and began ripping open his box. After they all had them on, they decided that Rick and Henry would go outside and walk in opposite directions. There were two channels available on the units and Linc wanted to check out the capacities of each. Rick moved down to the office, counting slowly. When he was about a hundred feet away, he stopped and asked, "How do you read me?"

"Loud and clear," Linc said. "Uncle Henry?"

"Ain't this a trip," Henry said. "I'm all the way down by that bar and I can hear you both as clear as a bell."

"Okay, try to go down about fifty feet more and check back with me," Linc said. As they went farther, their transmissions began to crackle and break up. Henry even began to pick up strange interference: the sound of a baby crying, words from a phone conversation, part of a drive-up order near the Burger King. Linc told them to begin working their way back. After about thirty minutes more, they'd determined that the outside perimeter for understandable transmissions was about five hundred feet.

"That gonna be enough?" Henry asked back in the room.

"It's all we got," Linc said, then realizing that his uncle was fishing for reassurance, he added, "I think it'll be just fine." He slipped the battery out of the radio sprockets and set it on the bed, then glanced at his watch again.

9:07 P.M.

"What I can't understand is why he wanted to meet in Hegewisch," Bobby Mallory said.

"Is that another of the city's predominantly black areas?" Germaine asked.

"Naw, there ain't that many shines around there." He quickly glanced at Gumbo, who sat beside Germaine at the small table. If the big man took offense, he certainly didn't show it. Mallory took a quick drag off his cigarette and said, "I mean, Hegewisch, that's the tenth ward. Mostly Polacks, dagos, and spics. It's Eddie Vrdolyak's turf. You guys heard of 'Fast Eddie,' right? Used to be an alderman. Stirred up a lotta shit back when Washington was mayor." Neither of them spoke. Mallory scratched his nose and went on. "It starts at about 130th and Brainard. This is probably a good place to wait," he said, leaning over to tap his forefinger on the map that was spread out in front of them. "Brainard and Avenue O, which turns into Burnham Avenue once you get down by Burnham Woods."

"Woods?" Germaine asked questioningly. "As in what?"

"You know, woods," Mallory said with a shrug. "Like a forest preserve. Lots of trees and shit."

Germaine nodded.

"You think that's where he's going to set up the meet?" he asked.

Mallory took another drag on his square and blew the smoke out his nose.

"Your guess is as good as mine," he said with a smoky breath.

"Hege-wisch," Germaine said, drawing out the two syllables. "Your descriptions of the neighborhood are very interesting, Bobby. And perplexing as well. I figured that our friend Linc would prefer to stay in the briar patch." He paused for a moment, then said, "Is it an area that's easily accessible?"

"Not really," Mallory said. "Everybody always says, if you

put trains on all the tracks, and raised up all the bridges, nobody could get in or out."

Germaine looked at him questioningly.

"The whole fucking place is surrounded by train tracks and water," Mallory said. "I don't think I've ever driven through there where I didn't catch a fucking freight train. Then you got the Calumet River and Wolf Lake."

"What type of areas are those?" Germaine asked. "Isolated? Deserted?"

"Yeah," Mallory said tentatively. "Hegewisch itself is really just a residential neighborhood, but there are some places I guess that are kinda desolate."

"How about the surrounding area?" Germaine asked, tapping his finger on the map.

"That's the East Side. It's mostly spic," Mallory said. "There's a lot of abandoned areas around there. Used to be lots of steel mills, till the market closed them all. Only one or two still operating now, I think."

"What's your instinct telling you. Gumbo?" Germaine asked, turning to him.

Gumbo studied the map, his eyes seeming not to blink. He exhaled heavily through his nostrils and shook his head slowly.

"Hard to say, but this boy ain't no fool."

Mallory watched Germaine as he considered this. "You have the van we spoke about?" he asked.

"All set," Mallory said, stubbing out his cigarette after one final drag. "A black Ford Starquest. Got a portable TV with VCR all hooked up for a twelve-volt."

"Excellent," Germaine said. "And the men you've got, are they all dependable?"

"The best of the lot," Mallory said taking out another cigarette. "All pros."

"Ain't that what you said 'bout the last group that got themselves all shot up?" Gumbo said, his dark eyes looking directly into Mallory's. The look was pure malice.

Bobby paused with the cigarette halfway up to his mouth. Was this big fucker going to go after him just because he'd slipped a couple of times and said shine or nigger?

"Well, hopefully things will run smoothly enough," Germaine said. "Let's go over the plan one more time, shall we?"

Mallory put the cigarette between his lips and flicked his lighter.

"Okay," Germaine said. "We wait there till our friend Linc gives us the call. Then we begin to disperse immediately. How many men do you have, Bobby?"

"I take ten with me. You take the other five," Mallory said, his voice not betraying the boredom he felt at going over the plan once again. But Vino's orders had been explicit: *Do whatever Germaine tells you to do, and don't fuck it up.*

"Good," Germaine said. "These men coming with me understand that they are to take no hostile action whatsoever. I simply want them there as a show of force. A diversion, of sorts."

Mallory nodded.

"Excellent," Germaine continued. "Now when our friend shows up, Gumbo will bring the young lady just outside of the van. Then we will obtain the tape from young mister Lincoln and explain to him that his lady friend will not be released until we've had time to view the tape." He reached in his pocket and removed a large wad of bills, rolled into an S-shape and secured by a rubber band. The outside bill was a hundred, and its denomination was clearly visible. "We can show him this to put him at ease," he said, holding up the flash-roll.

"What you gonna do if he opens it up and sees that all the rest of 'em are ones?" Mallory said with a chuckle.

"By the time he's had a chance to handle it, Bobby," Germaine said, smiling benignly, "we'll have the actual tape, and Linc will have his real payoff."

"I still think we should just ice him on the spot," Mallory said. "Then we don't have to go through this fucking game of pretending to go along with him."

Germaine sighed. Mallory could tell that this cracker didn't like it when someone questioned his instructions. But what the hell, the guy was a long way from home, and this thing had turned into an extended cluster fuck. He turned a defiant look toward Germaine.

"Bobby, you do understand that he may not bring the real tape, don't you?" Germaine said. "And you do understand how important it is to keep him and the girl, as well as our friend Mr. Fox, alive until we can ascertain beyond a shadow of a doubt that we have all the copies of the tape, don't you?"

Mallory nodded, inhaling deeply on his cigarette.

"Outstanding," Germaine said. "Now let me make one other point before we commence on Operation Trojan Horse." He stood and looked over into Mallory's eyes with that ice-water stare of his. "Don't ever question or criticize my plan or judgment again."

Mallory swallowed hard because he sensed Gumbo staring at him too. Bobby felt his head do a quick nod.

"After we've secured the tape, Mister Lincoln, *and* the girl," Germaine said, "we will endeavor to interview him and find out everything that he knows, in accordance with the final phase of our plan."

"That's the phase I like the best," Gumbo said. "What's that song by Vanessa Williams, 'Savin' the Best for Last'?"

Mallory swallowed hard again, took another quick drag on

his cigarette, and blew out a cloud of smoke. He managed a quick grin, but the only thing he could think about now was getting away from these two crazy assholes.

9:35 P.M.

Tony sat in his living room, a half-empty cup of coffee on the TV tray in front of him, the television playing out the penultimate act of that night's episode of "Knots Landing." He wasn't concentrating on the glitzy plot, though. Nor was he thinking about the upcoming night's surveillance with Ray. That would come easily enough once they were out there listening for the call. Who was to say if they'd even be able to figure out anything? No, Tony's thoughts had turned to Mary, and how much she'd liked this show. That had been some time ago, when the storyline had been a sort of tie-in to her other favorite, "Dallas." But now "Dallas" was off the air, J.R. having apparently made his peace with his guardian angel, and "Knots Landing" had long since turned into its own version of night-time soap. It was too bad that she hadn't been able to see how they'd turned out. Or what they'd turned into. But if J.R. had an angel, then Mary certainly did, too. Maybe she knew after all.

His thoughts turned to Arlene, and he wondered if she was watching the program. No, she probably watched that one about the L.A. lawyers which was on at the same time. That one was probably more to her tastes. He wondered about her tastes, and if the two of them had anything in common. Was Ray right that the age difference was no big thing in these new and enlightened times? But it wasn't just a matter of a couple of years, or even a decade. And although he didn't think of himself as old, and felt in decent shape, he was old enough to be her father. Or, if he stretched things, her grandfather, as Ray had teased. The prospect of the dinner tomorrow night suddenly became more frightening. Perhaps he should call her and back out.

The phone snapped him out of this reverie, and figuring it was Ray calling to tell him that he was on the way, he answered it with a gruff, "What?"

"Tony?" Arlene's voice came through the receiver. "Is that you?"

"Oh, yeah, it's me," he said haltingly. "I thought it was Ray."

He could hear her laugh, sounding once again so much like his Mary's.

"Are you watching 'Knot's Landing'?" she asked.

"Yes. How'd you know?"

"I heard the theme music," she laughed. "I've been following it since I was a teenager. My mom and I both watch it. It's been on so long, it seems like forever."

"Yeah," he said, thinking about Arlene watching the show as a teenager.

"Did you get some sleep? You looked really tired this afternoon, and I was kind of worried about you."

"I slept all afternoon."

"But won't you have trouble getting to sleep tonight now?"

"Oh, Ray and I are going out to check on something," he said.

"Check on something? You mean about the case?"

"Yeah," he said, figuring the less said about Ray's little illegal wiretap, the better.

"Well, I was going to call you earlier, but I figured you'd be asleep," she said. Even over the phone he could sense the hesitancy in her voice.

"What happened?" he asked.

"They found the Mink's body. He's dead."

"What? When?"

"I don't have all the details yet," she said. "In fact, they haven't even made a positive ID yet. They're just assuming it was him because it was in his car."

"Was it burned?"

"Yeah," she said. "The body that they think is his was in the trunk. They found it parked on a road over the expressway on fire at about eight. They'll have to do the identification through forensic dentistry."

"Tell them to ask for Dr. Kenney at the morgue. He's the best there is." He sighed. "You hear from Fox at all?"

"No, he never returned my calls."

"Something's not right about this," Tony said. "Either he was in on the hit, or they popped him too."

"You think they killed Reggie?"

"These are nasty people we're dealing with, Arlene." He realized how avuncular he sounded. "But I don't need to tell you that, do I? I keep forgetting you're a big girl."

"That's okay," she said, her tone sounding suddenly playful. "Just don't forget about tomorrow night at my place. Get plenty of rest. I have a surprise for you."

What the hell did *that* mean? he wondered.

"Oh? What might that be?"

"Well if I told you, it would hardly be a surprise now, would it?" He heard her tingly giggle again, then she said, "Don't worry, I have a hunch you're going to be pleasantly surprised."

Tony swallowed hard. Perhaps this was getting a little out of hand, he thought. He struggled for the courage to cancel the date. To tell her that he appreciated her interest, but that the plain and simple truth was that he felt that he was just too damn old for her.

"Well, anyway," she said, "it makes finding that tape even more important now, right?"

"What? A . . . yeah. Right."

The doorbell suddenly rang about five times in succession. Tony told Arlene that he had to go, and hung up after she'd told him to be careful. He stormed to the front door as the chimes began their second multiple onslaught. Tony ripped open the door and scowled at the surprised Ray Lovisi, who had been leaning forward with his thumb on the button.

"Oh, I figured you were still sleeping," Ray said.

"No, I was on the fucking phone."

"My, my, my, aren't we touchy?" Ray opened the screen door and stepped inside the foyer. In his right hand he carried a Cellular-One portable telephone. "Who was calling you? Arlene about your big date tomorrow night?"

"Will you knock it off?" Tony said.

"It was her, wasn't it?" Ray chuckled, holding up the phone. "This one's set up only to receive Fox's special number; otherwise, I'd let you call her back right now."

"Lovisi," Tony said slipping into his bulletproof vest and securing the Velcro straps, "sometimes you have the knack of being a total asshole."

"It's a gift," Ray said with a wide grin. "You know, I hope you do get laid tomorrow night. Maybe it'll improve your disposition."

"The only thing that'll improve my disposition is getting ahold of that fucking tape," Tony said. "They found the Mink's body tonight."

Ray's grin twisted into a bitter scowl.

"Shit," he said.

Both of them looked at each other without speaking. With the Mink dead, they knew this videocassette was their last chance to nail Costelli.

Chapter 17

Thursday, April 16, 1992

11:20 P.M.

Linc slowed down as he wheeled the big Olds into the dirt shoulder by the drawbridge that marked the east end of Wisconsin Steel. Henry was in the front passenger seat, and Rick, dressed in dappled jungle-fatigues and with his face darkened by camo-paint, was in the backseat. He opened the right rear door and slid out. The M-16 and the loaded magazines were stowed in a laundry bag. The plan called for him to go under the drawbridge and enter the abandoned plant from the east side along the shore. Linc was supposed to wait for twenty-five minutes before making the call to give Rick time to scout the place and set up. He would call Linc on the radio headset when he was ready.

"See you on the other side," Rick said, giving them the thumbs-up sign.

"*Semper Fi,*" said Linc, returning the gesture. He eased the car back on the road and continued over the bridge. Linc took his time, making a right and then two left turns at each new intersection of side streets, using his turn-signals each time. When he was back on 106th Street, he went back westbound, traversing the bridge.

Henry peered past Linc to see if he could get a glimpse of where Rick was, but all he saw was darkness. As they passed gate six at Muskegon, Linc swung around and made a U-turn. He shut off the engine and got out and lifted the hood. Henry slipped out the passenger's side with a pair of large, industrial-strength bolt cutters and quickly set the jaws over the link of chain securing the gates. He forced the long handles together and felt it pop. Then he looped the sagging chain back through the fence to maintain the illusion of security and got back in the car as Linc was slamming the hood. He quickly jammed the bolt cutters under the seat.

Linc took off again, scanning the rearview mirror to make sure nobody was watching.

"No cops in sight," he said. "It's all working like a charm so far. I'll go down and turn around and then drop you off at the tunnel."

Henry nodded. His dark face had been streaked with loam camouflage to break up the highlights, and Linc had given him a black stocking cap to wear so his bald head wouldn't reflect the moonlight.

As they continued east on 106th, Linc went down an extra block and made his series of turns that would put him westbound again.

"Wonder how Rick's doin'?" Linc said. He glanced at his uncle, who was leaning over, his head bowed. "What's wrong?"

Henry raised his head, shook it slightly, then straightened up.

"Uncle Henry, was you . . . was you praying, or something?"

The big man heaved a heavy sigh. "It's almost Good Friday."

"Well I hope it's *good* for us," Linc said grinning.

"Don't you be dissin' me, boy," Henry said. "Your mama

was a good Baptist. Wouldn't hurt you none to pick up on a little of the same."

Linc didn't reply. He thought about the old Marine Corps saying that there were no atheists in foxholes, and how, just before the balloon went up in Kuwait, so many men were praying and attending the field services. Even though the casualties were low, he hoped that those who didn't come back had gotten some comfort from them. For him, there was no solace in religion. What had soured him on it had been a chaplain that he'd overheard in boot camp talking about how all the niggers had ruined the Corps. The minister had been a charismatic phony who rode a motorcycle around the base, waving to all the boots. Nice to your face, but callin' you outta your name behind your back.

They came to Torrence and Linc turned left. He glanced over at his uncle and saw Henry was sweating, his dark face shiny in the moonlight.

"Rick and me, we gonna be okay, Uncle Henry," he said. "Are you sure you want to go through with this?"

"I'm in it, boy. I'm in it."

"Well, I mean, it's important that you know what we're getting into now."

"You think I don't?" Henry said, the anger welling up in his voice. "I know. Believe me, I know." He glanced out the window and wiped the heel of his hand over his forehead. "I'll be okay."

"Well, what I mean is, just stay low and let Rick and me handle most of it. You just supposed to be our back-up plan anyway."

"I'll be all right, boy. Like I said, I grew up on the streets."

But in truth, Linc knew in his uncle's day, things had been vastly different. When disagreements arose, they were settled with fists, or an occasional knifing, unlike the gun-and-gang-dominated ghetto of today. And for all Henry's bluster, Linc doubted that he'd ever really killed anyone. But he didn't want to ask him that. Not now, anyway.

"I'll be okay," Henry repeated emphatically, then glanced out the window again.

Linc came to Torrence and hung a left, running parallel to the railroad tracks. They'd stashed the Talon on the gravel road on the other side of the culvert. Henry would only have to walk a hundred yards or so in the dark to get to it. His radio and twelve-gauge were in the trunk. Linc slowed as the incline for the tracks began to steepen beside the street. Henry gripped the door handle as they got even with the big metal culvert.

"Give me a test on the radio right away, okay?" Linc said.

Henry nodded as he was getting out.

"Uncle Henry," Linc said.

The big man paused.

"Thanks," Linc said, giving him the same thumbs-up gesture that he'd given Rick. His uncle held up his thumb, then quickly trotted across the street toward the circular tunnel. Linc drove down the block and across the bridge with the immense grain elevator on it. He went down a few more blocks, then turned around. Estimating that Henry had had enough time to get to the Talon by now, Linc dug his radio headset out of the box and slipped it on, adjusting the speaker mike in front of his lips. There was nothing on the band but static until he got across the bridge. Then the earphones grew silent.

"Uncle Henry?" he said tentatively. "You read me?"

"I'm here."

"Okay," he said, glancing at his watch. "It's eleven-forty-three. Start moving up. I'm gonna go make the call now."

"Roger," Henry said.

Linc drove back toward the intersection of Torrence and 106th. There was a pay phone farther down the street, by a gas station. As he rode by the west section of the old mill, he said into the speaker: "Rick. You read me, bro?"

Silence. Probably too much interference from the structure, he thought. At least that was all he hoped it was. His plan depended on everything holding together. On him and Rick wasting these dudes before they knew what hit 'em, and Uncle Henry being able to get Diane out of there. But if one part of it went wrong, the whole thing would be blown. He touched the VHS tape beside him for reassurance.

Have to do my best to see that it goes down right, he thought.

As Rick made his way through the rugged underbrush, he paused to wipe off his sweaty hands on his pant-leg. Wet hands, dry mouth—the classic symptoms of anxiety before a fight. But suddenly he began to feel the weak, sickening tingling begin to creep into his legs again. Oh, God, no, he thought. Please, don't let it happen now. He reached frantically into his pants pocket for his medicine, but it wasn't there, and then he remembered taking the plastic vial out when he was getting dressed. He knelt on the ground amongst the weeds, and clutched his face in his hands.

I can't let myself feel sick, he told himself. Linc and the others are depending on me. I can't be sick. Not now.

He breathed in and out. If only he'd thought to bring a canteen to wash down his face a little. Maybe that would help. But it would wash off his paint, too, he thought. Marshaling what strength he could, he got to his feet and headed toward the darkened silhouette of the abandoned steel mill, the huge structure looking like a hulking monster back-lit by the rows of ubiquitous streetlights. He drank in a few more deep breaths of the cool night air, and suddenly, as his adrenaline kicked in, he began to feel stronger. The nausea and weakness were fading, and he knew then that everything was going to be all right.

With trembling fingers, Linc deposited the coins into the pay phone slot and punched in the number. Germaine answered just after the first ring.

"Yeah, it's me," Linc said. "Where you at?"

"Close, Linc. Very close."

"I mean, you in Hegewisch like I told you, right?"

"We're here."

"Okay, good," Linc said. "Then go north on Torrence till you get on up to the East Side. We'll meet inside the old Wisconsin Steel Works at midnight. Come down to gate Six-A. That's at 106th and Muskegon." Linc spoke slowly and plainly. "The gate'll be open so you can drive right in. Go toward the buildings to your left. I'll signal you when you get inside."

"Wait just a minute, Linc," Germaine said. "Where exactly are you going to be?"

"I'll be inside too, driving a tan Olds. I'll flash my lights and drive over to you once I see you inside and alone."

"Linc, we both know I am not going to be alone."

"Say what?"

"I've got Diane with me, and a couple of my associates."

"Oh, yeah, that's cool. What kind of car you got?"

"We're driving a van. A recreational vehicle."

"I want Diane with me 'fore I give you the tape."

"And I want to check the tape before I give you her or the money," Germaine said, but then paused. "But I can understand your anxiety, and I'm prepared to be somewhat flexible on that point." His tone was almost affable. "Are you there now?"

"Close," Linc said, mimicking Germaine. "I'm very close. Midnight." He hung up.

"Goddamnit," Ray swore as he twisted the steering wheel of the unmarked car and shot around a slower moving car on Michigan. Tony grabbed the oscillating red light that was now sliding over the length of the dashboard. "Who the hell woulda figured they'd meet on the fucking East Side, when all the shit's been going down in Roseland."

His hand slammed onto the horn and he whipped around another car, ran the red light, and swung east onto 111th Street at the intersection.

"For Christ's sake, Ray, you're driving like a fucking maniac," Tony said, gripping the dash with his right hand, his left on the oscillating light again.

"Don't worry," Ray said, grinning. "I drive as good as I box."

"Then I *know* we're in trouble. But slow it down, will ya? There's no sense getting into an accident. We'll be there in fifteen or twenty minutes or so, anyway."

"Ten, the way I drive," Ray said. They were shooting by Michigan and heading into Pullman. "We gotta get that fucking tape, Tony; otherwise the whole thing goes down the drain, now that we ain't got the Mink anymore."

"Don't I know it," Tony said grimly. "This is my last shot at Vino, which is why I don't want to blow it by getting into a wreck on the way. Now slow it down, will ya?"

Ray seemed to ignore him at first, then eased off the gas pedal ever-so-slightly. "You want to call for back-ups from District Four on city-wide?" he asked.

"Let's wait till we get over there," Tony said. "We don't

want any blue-and-whites nosing around and spooking them. If we can, we sneak up to the mill, get an eyeball on them, and then call for the cavalry, okay?"

"Sounds good to me, partner," Ray said.

The lights of the Calumet Expressway were just becoming visible up ahead.

Chapter 18

Friday, April 17, 1992

Around Midnight

Rick had used his extra time to move up cautiously from the west side of the building, where he'd made his entrance, toward the easternmost end. Hopefully, the meet would take place there. He used his flashlight sparingly, allowing himself only a quick burst of light through the red lens every few feet. The M-16 was held at the ready out in front of him. Even though he was positive that the enemy couldn't have correctly anticipated the exchange location, he couldn't afford to take anything for granted. Do it by the book, he told himself. The enemy. It seemed a strange designation here in the States as a civilian. In the Corps, things had seemed so much clearer. They had their orders to follow, their mission to accomplish. This time they had a mission, too, but it was different somehow. He felt as if he'd wandered into some sort of "twilight zone," just like on that old TV show. Only this wasn't TV.

He forced his mind back on the task at hand. The inside of the massive building had been gutted, and large sections of the roof and sidewalls removed, showing dark velvet patches of the starless sky. But despite the overcast, a full moon illuminated things through the holes in the roof, and made the movement easier. Only the rusted metal stairways remained, along with remnants of old boilers and partially disassembled platforms.

Rusting chains still hung from anchored pulleys, and heaps of trash had been pushed into piles of various sizes. The shell of the building was at least one hundred and fifty yards long. The floor was cement, but weeds had somehow begun to crop up through the cracks and would occasionally pull at his boots like grasping hands. Rick moved to a position of cover and surveyed the remaining area between him and the open expanse where the two overhead doors had once been.

Take the high ground, he told himself, as he headed for a stairway that wound around to a catwalk above the entrance. The metal walkway extended over the gaping holes of the door spaces and went to the other side of the building. The stairs made slight creaking sounds as he ascended. Rick moved cautiously at first, testing the metal for sturdiness, but it felt pretty secure. He got up to the top of the catwalk and made his way to the opposite wall. A small room, which must have housed some sort of heating unit, was situated in the corner. Rick pushed through the warped door, ducking instinctively as the hinges groaned.

Good thing no one was around to hear that one, he thought. The room was about fifteen feet square, with a large pipe running up from the floor and out the side of the wall near a window. The window was hung from above with a handle that secured it to the center of the base-frame. The glass, which had been lined with some sort of chicken-wire, hung in jagged sections. Rick pulled an old dilapidated metal chair over to the window and stepped up on it. The window slid out from its base and he looked outside. A three-foot-wide ledge ran parallel to the ground just under the window. It spanned the width of the building. Rick slipped the rifle over his shoulder and adjusted the sling. Then he braced both hands on the window frame and boosted himself up. Levering over the base of the frame to the outside, he carefully lowered himself down to the ledge, testing it gingerly with his left foot. The structure felt solid underfoot. He lowered himself the rest of the way down and fell into a crouch, then flattened out. The coolness of the night air felt good against his face. From this vantage point he could keep tabs on the entire situation. The yard was about fifty feet below, and there was a small ridge that ran along the edge of the ledge that even afforded him a modicum of concealment.

Escape would be tricky, but if everything went according to plan, he wouldn't really have to worry about that. Maybe the guy had been sincere and would just trade Diane for the tape, give Linc the promised money, and they could slip out without a shot being fired.

Yeah, right, he thought. Get used to the idea that you're gonna have to take these guys out. Otherwise, everybody down there that I care about is gonna die.

He resolved to wait till Linc made his move, then take out the rest of them. After all, they were dealing with scum. The same kind of assholes who had lain in wait for him and Linc in their apartment. He knew from his previous combat experiences that he couldn't afford to start thinking of his foes in anything that remotely resembled human terms. When it was over, he'd go back up through the window and down the stairs. From there he'd just make his way to the river, ditch the rifle in the water, and wait for Linc to come pick him up at the base of the bridge.

He heard static on his headset and glanced around. Then Linc's voice came over.

"Rick, you read me?"

"Yeah," Rick said.

"I'm coming in the gate now," said Linc.

Rick's gaze moved over to the fence line and he saw the blacked-out Olds pushing back the gate. The big sedan crept around the old crane and went right, toward the eastern section of buildings. When Rick saw the brake lights flash he said, "Better use the emergency brake to stop it or you'll give away your position."

"Yeah, right," said Linc.

The Olds swung around and faced west.

"Where you at, bro?" asked Linc.

"I'm on the roof," Rick said. "Well, almost. Watch for the flash."

He shined his red flashlight again.

"Got you," Linc said. "I'll drive right up under you when they get here."

"I can cover just about the whole yard from up here," Rick told him. "Just watch your asses when I start opening up with this mother."

"Sounds good," Linc answered.

"Where's Henry at?"

"Uncle Henry, can you hear us?"

There was a static-laden, indistinguishable reply.

"He's out there," Linc said. "You hear him?"

"Huh-uh," Rick said. "I must be too far away. Sometimes you're fading in and out too."

"Say, when they get here I'm gonna have to put this headset antenna down so they don't see it and freak," Linc said. "Thinkin' about slipping it down under my collar. That way you'll be able to hear what's goin' down."

"But then you won't be able to hear me," Rick said. "Let's try a couple of test runs now."

"Can't," Linc said, the urgency creeping into his voice. "Here they come."

Rick saw a dark van bumping through the opening. The driver kept the headlights on as the vehicle steered around the fallen crane and proceeded to the left. Rick leaned over the edge and watched the van drive almost directly below him, turn around facing east, and then stop. The vehicle's lights went out.

"Linc, you read me?"

"Yeah, bro. I'm gonna have to make the move now, so I'm tucking this thing down."

Rick's earphones exploded with static and loud scraping noises. He saw the lights of the Olds flash, then the van's did the same. Slowly the Olds started traversing the grassy area between the two buildings. Out of the corner of his eye, Rick caught some movement back by the gate. Another vehicle, some sort of big sedan with no lights, had pulled up and parked parallel to the gate, blocking it. All four doors opened and Rick watched as six figures moved stealthily toward the crane. They all seemed to be carrying rifles of some sort. A second car pulled up behind the first one and parked. Four more men got out of that one and began slipping through the gap in the fence.

"Uh-oh, we got trouble," Rick said into his mike. "You read me. Linc?"

No answer.

"Linc, you read me? There's at least ten other players moving up on you at this time. Do you read?"

Silence.

"Shit," Rick said. "Henry, you picking me up?"

There was a garbled reply.

"Henry, I hope that's a yes, 'cause we got real problems now. We've got about ten hostiles moving toward Linc from the front gate. Looks like they're armed with rifles." Rick tried to speak slowly and clearly. "As soon as Linc makes his move, I'm gonna try and take out the ones on my side. You'll have to open fire from yours, but stay down. When I see their muzzle flashes, I'll spray the area. You got it?"

His earphones began to pick something up, but it was drowned out by a sudden blast of some type of radio signal. Possibly a C.B. radio from a passing truck. Christ, they hadn't even figured on this frequency being so low that it could be stepped on by more powerful waves. In the Marines they'd always had the luxury of having their own nets, and scramblers if necessary.

"Linc, do you read?" Rick's voice gritted into the mike. "You've got hostiles moving up on you from the north, over."

The Olds continued to move toward the van, which had pulled around the corner of the building in the same area where it had stopped. The back door of the van popped open and three men slipped out, flattening against the wall. Rick stuck his head over the edge again and knew he wouldn't be able to take that group out. They were too far under him and too close to the wall. He probably could get them if he were on the ground, but he had to maintain the high ground position to deal with the others moving in from the street.

"Linc, we've got three more, at least, set up behind the van," he said. "I don't know if you can hear me, buddy, but this doesn't look good." He realized with belated regret that they should have worked some sort of distress signal independent of the radios.

Rick's thumb snapped the lever of the M-16 from safe to semi. He had no choice but to hope Linc had heard him, and wait for his partner to make the first move. He'd take out as many of them as he could from the ledge, then move down to ground level and mop up the rest. Suddenly he wished they were back in the Corps, with a squad of highly trained men with them, ready to get the job done.

It'll be a miracle if we all survive this, he thought.

The Heist

★ ★ ★ ★ ★

Linc felt the bounce of the suspension as the Olds went over the grassy area between him and the van. It was parked facing his direction, about twenty feet beyond the corner of the building. He glanced up to the position where he'd last seen Rick and figured to stop about thirty feet this side of them to give Rick a clear field of fire. First, he had to get Diane out. Then take out whoever was in front of him and let Rick do the rest. Hopefully all Uncle Henry would have to do would be to grab Diane and scoot out the back way. Linc felt for the Glock tucked into the side of his pants.

"I'm movin' in now, Rick," Linc said into his mike. He'd heard a constant blare of static from his earphones since taking the antenna down, so he'd turned the volume control way down. Linc flipped on the headlights and lit up the area, then punched the brights-button on the floor with his left foot. He could see at least three heads in the van. One of them looked like Diane's. The other two looked masculine.

As he drew closer he could distinguish that the driver was a white guy, with grayish hair combed back like Elvis Presley. Diane sat in the middle and on her right was the same big, black motherfucker that had tried to take him in the house. He scanned the field before him and thought he saw a flicker of movement by the corner of the building. If he'd been alone, or if Diane hadn't been in that goddamned van, he'd have swung the Olds around and taken off, then called the motherfucker back on his little cellular phone and told him to go pound sand up his ass. But it was all or nothing now. They were in too deep. And there was Diane.

Linc cut his lights and came to a stop, adjusting the Olds so it would be between him and the side of the van when he got out. That would give him a little cover from hostile fire if the thing went bad right away. Now it wasn't a question of whether or not it was going bad, only how soon it would, and if he could extricate Diane before it got hot. The side door of the van slid open, displaying a lighted interior. It was one of those fancy RVs that had a raised roof, plush seats, and a small table with a portable TV and VCR. The white guy got out of the driver's door and ambled around the front of the van.

"You must be Linc," the man said. "I'm pleased to make your acquaintance." It was the same southern accent that Linc had heard on the phone. The guy looked to be a genuine cracker.

The man made no effort to move toward him, and that was good because in the moonlight, Linc could see the butt of a big chrome-colored revolver tucked in the front of his pants.

Linc nodded and said, "I want to see Diane."

"Understandable," Germaine said. "And have you got what I want?" He held up a roll of currency.

"Yeah, I got it," Linc said, holding up the tape in his left hand. With his right, he gripped the Glock and pulled it out from his belt, just letting it hang down by his leg.

"Why, Linc, do I detect a hostile action?"

"Yeah, cracker, just like I detected those motherfuckers waiting over there by the building. You said no tricks, and I took you at your word."

"I am a man of my word, Linc," Germaine said. "And just to show you that, I'm going to give you Diane in exchange for the tape."

Linc saw a sudden shift of movement inside the van and Diane was at the side door, sitting on the big man's lap. His long legs splayed forward, extending almost leisurely out of the open side door. The black asshole's left arm was around her chest, and his right hand was holding a big-bladed knife just up under her chin.

"You motherfucker, let her go now," Linc said, leveling the Glock at Germaine.

"Put the gun down and place the tape on the roof of your car, Linc," Germaine said. "Then come around here and you can have her."

"Fuck you," Linc said.

"You wants to see her guts all over this fucking ground here, boy?" Gumbo asked, his mouth twisting into a leering grin. He pressed the point of the blade into the softness of her neck.

She made a hissing sound and said, "Linc, baby, just do what they say. Please. They promised me. It's gonna be all right."

With his gun still outstretched, Linc moved around the back of the Olds and in between the car and the van. Germaine shifted slightly, a disarming smile on his face, but he was still looking at Linc with that ice-water stare. Then he extended his left hand, leaving his right free to draw the revolver.

"Come on, Linc, don't try to be a macho fool," he said. "Just give me the tape, and as soon as I can verify that it's the real McCoy, you and your lady can collect your money and get out of here."

"Then tell him to take that fucking knife away from her throat."

"Gumbo," Germaine said, cocking his head slightly and speaking over his shoulder. "I think we can lower the knife as soon as Linc here lowers his gun." He looked back inquisitively at Linc, who slowly let his arm go down. Gumbo licked his lips, lowered the knife, but adjusted his hands so that he held Diane's arms.

"The tape," Germaine said.

Linc held out the tape in his left hand, but then brought it back.

"She comes to me first," he said.

"I don't think so," he heard a voice behind him say, then heard the clicking sound of a gun being cocked.

"Just let your gun fall to the ground, Linc," Germaine said, pulling out his own revolver and pointing it directly at Linc's face. "I'd hate for this to be messy, but a man in my position can't afford to take too many chances."

Linc let the Glock slip from his fingers.

"Good," said Germaine. "Now the tape." He moved over and, still holding the gun on Linc, gently helped Diane down from the inside of the van. Gumbo jumped into the open a second later, looking like a refrigerator with arms and legs. Linc handed Germaine the tape, and the southerner let Diane walk over to him. Linc felt Diane in his arms, and he was kissing her and telling her it was all gonna be okay.

"I know it will, baby," she said. "They won't hurt us. I know they won't, now that they got the tape. That's all they want."

She bought into all that shit, he thought. Brainwashed.

Linc just patted her on the back of the head, keeping his arms protectively circled around her.

"I hope, for your sake, this turns out to be the one I want," Germaine said, a sudden malevolence creeping into his tone.

"It's got what you want," Linc said. Suddenly he felt Diane's hands fidgeting with his collar. She was fingering the headset.

"What's this?" she said.

He reached up to grab her hand away just as Germaine had turned, pulling the tape out of the box. The bright flash and accompanying blast, punctuated by the southerner's shriek, startled everybody. Linc took the moment to act, shoving Diane down onto the ground and lashing out with his left foot at the man who'd been standing behind him. He heard a sharp grunt as his boot connected with the guy's gut. Following up, he smashed his right fist into the slumping man's face, and watched him crumble.

"It's show time," he yelled as he stooped, trying to grab the Glock. But Gumbo was moving forward, slashing with the knife. Linc saw a silvery glint in the moonlight, then felt the pain sear up his left arm. Backing away, Linc bumped up against the Olds. Gumbo was still advancing, the knife outstretched. A sudden staccato-burst of gunfire erupted above them, the flame from the M-16's muzzle jumping out half a foot, and looking like a flame-thrower in the reduced lighting. Then Linc heard some more booming pops. It had to be Uncle Henry's twelve-gauge. All this caused the big man to miss a step as he glanced back over his shoulder toward the source of the shots.

That was all Linc needed to grab the huge hand in both of his, twisting and pivoting the way they'd taught him in the Corps to disarm sentries. Gumbo grunted and shifted his weight almost nimbly, getting up under Linc, then using his massive legs to lift the lighter man completely off his feet and slam him against the fender of the car. Linc saw the man's other hand reach across toward the knife. The motherfucker was going to switch hands, then stab him. Linc's right elbow smashed into Gumbo's mouth. The struggle for the knife stopped for a split-second, then resumed, with Linc trying to tighten his grip around Gumbo's right hand so he couldn't transfer the knife to his left. But suddenly the fingers of Gumbo's left hand were on Linc's face, pressing and tearing at his eyes, forcing his head back. Linc's knee came up hard into the other man's groin. Gumbo's fingers stopped for only an instant. Linc brought the knee up again and again, feeling the giant's grip start to fade slightly.

Using the Oldsmobile's fender for leverage, Linc managed

to push Gumbo back a little, but the bigger man shifted his weight again and Linc felt himself being twisted to the ground, the man-mountain following him down, maneuvering himself on top. Linc felt the blade slice the back of his left hand with stinging effectiveness, so he let go. That was all Gumbo needed to rip his hand away from Linc's grasp. The knife flashed down in an arcing motion, which Linc managed to deflect at the last second with his left arm. The point traveled down the length of his arm instead of into his chest. A burst of white-hot flame exploded inside his shoulder, and he saw the blade thrust through his sleeve, buried to the hilt. Gumbo leaned his upper body forward, pressing his face close to Linc's, and said, "I'm gonna do you slow, motherfucker, for messin' with me in that house."

Linc's right arm flew out to the side as he sought stability. His fingers brushed something in the grass. Something hard and smooth. The Glock. Linc's left hand gripped the back of Gumbo's right, which was now twisting the metallic shaft around in a circular motion, sending waves of pain tearing through him.

"You hear me, nigger?" Gumbo snarled. "You hear me?"

Linc brought the Glock up with his right, putting it in nice and close to the giant's belly, and began pulling the trigger. After five successive shots, Linc managed to say, "Yeah, I hear you."

Gumbo reared back, releasing the knife, which was still embedded in Linc's shoulder. Linc brought the Glock up, and the flash of the exploding round engulfed the big man's face. As the huge, lifeless body rolled off him, Linc became aware of more rounds popping around him. He saw an unfamiliar white guy crouching by the side of the van, shooting a rifle up toward the building. Linc leveled the Glock and shot the man in the side of the chest. Two more unfriendlies came into view, gazing intently upward, oblivious to Linc's supine position. He squeezed off two more rounds, dispatching each man. As he moved to get up, he felt wracked with pain, and belatedly realized that the knife was still sticking out of his shoulder. Touching the hilt made it worse when he tried to pull it out. He sat back against the fender well of the Olds, legs outstretched, and tried to catch his breath. Suddenly all he could think of was Diane. Where was she? Had she been hit? Struggling to his knees, he called her name. Crawling toward the open side door of the van, he glanced up inside and saw her. She was scurrying around, holding the scorched tape in one hand and the wad of bills in the other.

"Diane," he said weakly.

"Don't worry, baby," she said, her eyes reflecting an almost maniacal look. "I got 'em. I got 'em both."

He reached for the knife hilt again, but once more the pain kept him from trying to remove it. He heard the sound of fading voices, of men running, then Rick was suddenly beside him, firing the M-16 over the top of the Olds.

I hope he got that cracker fucker Germaine, Linc thought.

"You all right?" Rick asked, then, glancing down and seeing the knife, said, "Oh shit."

Rick set the M-16 against the side of the Olds and pulled out his flashlight.

"Henry. Henry, you read me?" he said into his mike. "We've got them on the run. What's left of them are running towards their cars at the gate."

There was a crackled reply.

"Bring in the Talon," Rick said. "Linc's hurt." His hands probed the wound site, pressing his fingers around the blade to see if it had gone through the other side. "Easy, partner, it looks worse than it is."

"Easy for you to say," Linc said, feeling himself drifting

away from consciousness. Rick was pressing a first aid pad around the base of the wound. Linc started to say something when Diane shrieked. An adrenaline jolt roused him to a full state of alertness. Struggling, he began to get up, only to be gently pushed down by Rick, who stood. Linc twisted slightly and looked over his shoulder as Rick said, "She's okay."

"Look at this," she screamed, holding the burned plastic cassette. "It's ruined. You ruined it. You ruined it all. And the money's gone too." She held the wad of bills toward them. "It's not all here. They showed it to me before, and now it's not all here."

"Woman, don't you know nothing!" Linc screamed. Then he felt Rick's hand on his good shoulder.

"Easy, Linc," he said. "She's been through a lot. Remember the Stockholm Syndrome. She's not thinking straight. We'll—"

A gunshot cracked and something ripped through the front of Rick's chest, his face contorting as the blood gushed out of his mouth with his expelling breath. Tumbling forward, Rick slumped across Linc's legs, pinning him to the ground. Linc glanced to his right and saw Germaine, his face blackened and burned by the powder blast, advancing forward pointing the snubnosed revolver. The white-haired man's steps were unsteady, almost tentative. Linc heard Diane scream. Germaine turned, leveling the gun at her. Linc made a grab for the M-16 which was almost within arm's reach, but Germaine quickly kicked it away. He brought the pistol back around and pressed the muzzle against Linc's forehead.

"It could have been so easy," he rasped in his southern accent. He thumbed back the hammer, then was knocked back by a blast of thunder which Linc felt whoosh by him. Germaine was on his side, blood trickling from his blackened lips, his expression surprised, but determined. With slow determination, he raised the revolver and pointed it at Linc. The gun discharged, blowing a hole in the side of the van next to Linc's head. Uncle Henry was there, jacking another round into the twelve-gauge and stepping over Rick. Henry put the barrel against Germaine's chest and pulled the trigger again. The southerner's body bounced with the impact of the round.

"Linc, you all right?" he said, stooping down next to him.

"I'm okay. Check Rick."

Henry rolled Rick's prone body over. Linc felt the fading warmth of his friend's blood on his legs. From the light spilling out from the inside of the van, Linc could see that Rick's face was ashen, his breath coming in spasmodic spurts, the blood around his mouth already starting to darken and congeal.

"Oh, my lord," Henry said. "I gots to get the other car, Linc. I left it back there by the other building. Don't move," he said, standing. "Don't nobody move. I'll be right back."

"Wait," Linc said. He was going to tell his uncle to just put him and Rick into the Olds, but Henry had already left at a run. Linc stared at the Olds, but his eyes had difficulty focusing. Then he saw that both of the right side tires were flat, apparently having been hit during the firefight. Looks like Uncle Henry was right, Linc thought to himself. He swiveled his head back toward the van. Diane sat a few feet away on the running board by the still-open side door, her head down, silently weeping. With considerable effort, Linc reached out and patted Rick's face gently. He heard the yelp of sirens, then moments later, saw the intermittent flashing of oscillating blue lights. He tried to get up, but couldn't. Adjusting the earphones back over his head, he said into his mike, "Uncle Henry, keep going out the tunnel way. The cops are here. You read me?"

"I'm coming back for you," Henry's voice said through the earphones.

"No way. Too late. Just get out now and I'll call you. We need you to stay outta jail, remember?"

Silence.

"Uncle Henry, you read me?"

"Roger," Henry said.

The next voice Linc heard was from an older-looking white guy pointing a .38 at him and saying, "Police. Don't move."

"Would you please call an ambulance, sir," Linc said. "My friend's been hurt."

Another white guy, younger and shorter than the first, was kneeling next to them, gathering up the M-16 and the Glock. His fingers probed Rick's neck, and he looked up and shook his head.

"Will you call a medic for him, for Christ's sake!" Linc heard himself scream. "Can't you see he's hurt bad?"

"I'm sorry," the kneeling man said, turning his attention to Linc. "Your friend's dead. We'll have to leave him where he is."

"The Marines never leave their dead," Linc heard himself say, just before the world faded away into darkness.

Chapter 19

Friday, April 17, 1992

3:25 A.M.

"Jesus, it's like a fucking war zone over there," Ray Lovisi said, walking over to Tony, who was seated by the nurses' station sipping a cup of black coffee. When Tony didn't look up, Ray's concern deepened. He knew how much cracking this case meant to both of them, but to Tony, it was the last hurrah.

"Got any more coffee?" he asked the nurse behind the partition. She nodded and pointed to a small break room across the hallway. Tony stood and motioned for Ray to follow him. They moved across the hall and entered the room. A stack of Styrofoam cups sat on a small Formica table, along with glass jars of sugar, powdered cream, a well-used plastic spoon covered with a crust of additives, and an automatic coffee-maker. Ray grabbed one of the cups and immediately began shoveling spoonfuls of sugar and cream into it.

"That's a lot of sugar for a man in training," Tony said.

"I need the energy," Ray said wearily. "You'd think for being health care professionals, they'd be more sanitary with things, you know?" he said, looking at the crusty spoon before filling his cup with the dark liquid.

"They probably do it on purpose to keep mooching cops from stealing all their shit," Tony said. "What's the latest from the crime scene?"

Ray drank some of the coffee before he answered; then, smacking his lips, he said, "Got twelve dead and seven wounded, counting our buddy in there. They got the evidence technicians going over everything now. Had to get some portable generators in there to light the place up." He took another gulp from the cup. "How's he doing?"

"They're still stitching him up," Tony said. "The doc says we should be able to talk to him shortly."

"The girl give you anything?"

Tony shook his head.

"Sealed up just like a clam," he said. "In shock. Already called some boys from Violent Crimes to come pick her up and take her downtown. We'll hold her until we get this thing all sorted out."

"I take it she wasn't hurt?"

Tony shook his head as he took a sip from his own cup.

"Looks like she's been roughed up," he said. "She was holding a flash roll—one hundred and ninety-nine ones, and this." He held up a plastic evidence bag containing the charred remains of a VHS cassette.

"Ahhh, shit," Ray said. "Is that the tape?"

"Looks like it."

"What the fuck happened to it?" Ray said, bending close to the bag and sniffing it. "Looks burned or something."

"That's one of the things we'll have to ask our buddy Lincoln about," said Tony. "Maybe the FBI guys can salvage some of it with those new enhancers, or something."

"Maybe," Ray said dubiously. Knowing how much getting Vino Costelli meant to Tony, Ray didn't want to say he thought the chances of getting any images off that tape were slim to none.

"Maybe if either of them watched it, we could get some kind of grand jury indictment."

"Somebody testifying about what they saw on some video-tape?" Tony said skeptically.

"What the hell, it's better than nothing, ain't it?"

"Not much better," Tony said. "The kind of legal muscle Vino'll get, we'll have to have something really solid. Two kids testifying about what they seen on a videotape ain't gonna cut it."

Ray said nothing, knowing that Tony was right.

They stepped out into the hall and talked with the nurses again, talking about all the dead and shot-up bodies that they'd brought into the ER since midnight.

"We've been due for the shit to hit the fan," one nurse said. "Things been too quiet since this flood downtown." She was kind of tall, and had brownish hair with blond highlights. Ray gave her the once-over and liked what he saw.

"How close is the doc to being done with our buddy Lincoln?" Tony asked, interrupting Ray's fantasy.

"I don't know," the nurse said. "I'll see."

She walked across to the ceiling-to-floor curtains on the other side of the room, Ray's eyes on her ass the whole time. Pulling back the edge, she spoke softly to someone inside, then came back and smiled at them.

"You can go in there now," she said. "He's almost done."

They went over to the curtained-off section and stepped inside. Tony held up his badge and nodded to the doctor, who was peeling off some latex gloves. A tray of various suturing instruments was positioned above Linc, who lay on his right side on a gurney. His left arm and shoulder were swathed in bandages. The doctor looked at Tony and smiled.

"Are you guys taking him?"

"Looks that way, Doctor," Tony said. "The nurse said you were about finished."

The doctor nodded and told them he was going to go write

this up. Turning to Linc, he gave him some outpatient instructions that included drinking plenty of liquids because he'd lost so much blood, keeping the wound site clean, and following up with his regular physician on Monday. After the doctor left, Tony stood on one side of the gurney and Ray on the other.

"I'm Detective Cardoff and this is my partner, Detective Lovisi," Tony said, holding up his badge-case. "You know why we're here, right?"

Linc nodded slowly.

"You want to tell us your side of it, Lincoln?" Ray asked. " 'Cause if you do, I gotta read you this." He took out his Miranda card and quickly recited the litany. When he'd finished, Ray asked, "You understand your rights?"

Linc nodded.

"So you want to tell us what happened?" Ray said.

"How's Diane?" Linc asked.

"She's okay," Tony said. "She wasn't hurt."

"Can I talk to her?"

"Not right now," Tony said, shaking his head. "Lincoln, I'll be honest with you. We had to take her downtown. Like I told you, she wasn't hurt, but I think you know that you both have an awful lot of explaining to do, don't you?"

Linc sighed and slowly nodded. "What do I get for talking?"

"Depends on a lot of things," said Ray. "Mostly on what you tell us. You see, we got a whole field full of dead bodies over on the East Side, and we gotta sort this whole shitbox out. We already know they were holding your girl hostage."

Linc looked up quickly.

"How you know that?" he asked.

"It ain't for us to tell *you* how we know what we know," Ray said. "You want to cooperate, we'll do what we can for ya. But if you try running a game on us . . ." He left the threat implied.

"What do I have to do to get out of this?" Linc asked. "And get Diane out too."

"We said we'd do what we could for you," Tony said. "But we ain't miracle workers."

Linc swallowed and then said, "Suppose I had something to trade?"

"And what might that be?" Ray asked.

"Well, it's about this long," Linc said, holding his two index fingers about seven inches apart, "and it's about this thick," he held his right thumb and forefinger about an inch away from each other, "and I guess you don't even need to ask me anymore whether it's Beta or VHS."

"Wait a minute," Tony said. "Don't try to bullshit us. We recovered the tape already." He held up the burnt VHS cassette inside the plastic bag.

"Not the right one, you didn't," Linc said.

"Which one's the right one?" Ray asked.

"The one with that crazy old white dude doing those two cats with the baseball bat," Linc said. He leaned back on the pillows, tried to raise both his arms behind his head, and grimaced suddenly.

Tony and Ray exchanged a quick glance.

"You want me to talk to the doctor to get you something for the pain?" Ray said quickly. His concern level had immediately gone from one of significant indifference toward Linc to one of extreme solicitousness.

"Huh-uh," Linc said, shaking his head. "What pain I got, I earned. Besides, I got to keep my head clear. Now, how soon can you have somebody down here to put this deal in writing?"

"What deal is that?" Ray asked.

"Where Diane and me, and anybody else on my side who's still alive, gets off if I give you the tape."

"We'll get somebody from downtown to discuss it with you," Tony said. "But we're gonna have to see the tape before we finalize anything."

"You really got the tape, Lincoln?" Ray asked, leaning closer to the gurney. "You wouldn't be bulljiving me, now would you?"

"No, sir," Linc said. "All I need to do is make a couple of phone calls. But, like I said, no disrespect intended, I gotta have this deal in writing from a lawyer first."

"I'll go see if I can get ahold of somebody," Tony said. "But like I told you, we'll have to go downtown to discuss it further."

Chapter 20

Friday, April 17, 1992

10:24 A.M.

After getting released from the emergency room, Linc was driven downtown to Eleventh and State by Tony and Ray. They escorted him in the back way and took the elevator to the fifth floor. Then, after sending out for coffee and donuts, the interview began. It was euphemistically called an interview now, but the old term, interrogation, was more applicable: a tedious process of re-advising Linc of his rights, having him sign a rights-waiver form, and then asking him to tell his side of it, going over it again and again. Tony and Ray periodically shot questions at him, balancing their inquiries against facts that they knew to gauge his truthfulness. Occasionally they would make him repeat things, making him think that they knew more than they actually did.

"How does your uncle fit into all this, Lincoln?" Ray asked him. "You want us to call him and tell him where we towed the Olds?"

"How much did Jem Dandy charge you for the M-16?" Tony asked casually.

When Linc's head shot up in surprise, his gaze was met by stony stares. *We know the whole story, son*, they seemed to be saying. *So don't try, don't even try, to bullshit us, 'cause if you do . . .*

The process did as it was designed to do, for the most part.

277

It distilled the truth from what he told them. Not that Linc was a total stranger to interrogation tactics, having been in charge of POWs in both Panama and the Gulf. But that had been different; in those instances, none of them even spoke English, so there wasn't any real attempt to obtain information. And Linc was weary. The strain of the past few days, coupled with the trauma he'd sustained and the loss of blood, made his mind fuzzy. In the end, he decided to stick to the truth, making his judgment on the apparent honor he sensed in the two men before him. He'd served with such men in the Corps, and he believed them.

By the time Arlene arrived with a representative from the State's Attorney's Office and a stenographer, Tony and Ray knew virtually everything. The only thing that Linc had consistently managed to leave out was Uncle Henry's involvement in the final, bloody confrontation. He stuck to his story that his uncle was nothing more than a wheel-man who was supposed to pick them up afterwards.

When they'd finished taking his statement and explained to him that any agreement was contingent on the immediate surrender of the tape, Linc only nodded wearily and told them that he'd need to make a phone call.

"But first, you said I could talk to her, right?" he asked.

They hastily arranged a somewhat unorthodox visit between Linc and Diane in a fifth-floor interview room. Tony and Ray stood outside, looking through the glass window at the two young lovers and drank their umpteenth cups of stale coffee. Although they couldn't hear the words, it was obvious that all was not going well inside the room. Linc was on his feet, gesturing emphatically with his good arm, using his index finger as he spoke. Diane merely sat on the chair by the table, leaning forward dejectedly with her head in her hands.

"Don't look like the reunion of Romeo and Juliet, does it?" Ray said.

Tony shook his head. He brought the cup to his lips once more, only to be disgusted by the bitter-tasting, lukewarm liquid.

"I sure hope they don't start fighting in there," Ray said. "I don't feel in the mood for no domestic at Headquarters."

Just as he said that, Linc moved forward to the thick glass window and tapped on it twice. Tony opened the door.

"We're finished," Linc said. He glanced back at her. "If I can make that call now."

Tony nodded. He held the door open for Linc, then told Ray to call the matron to escort Diane back down to the women's floor. Tony led Linc over to a small office and indicated that he should sit at the desk. Linc grabbed the phone, then looked up at him.

"The agreement stands, right?" he asked.

"As long as we get the real tape," Tony assured him.

The agreement they'd worked out with Arlene and the representative from the State's Attorney's Office had laid it all out for him. He was to get an offer of immunity to testify before a grand jury, detailing his acquisition of the videocassette, and the subsequent events that led up to the confrontation at Wisconsin Steel. Diane and Uncle Henry were not to be involved in any testimony, nor would either one be charged in connection with the incident. This was all contingent upon the government obtaining control of the videocassette immediately. Linc felt comfortable with the deal. He also felt strangely comfortable with Tony and Ray. These two honkey cops had played it straight with him, getting him quickly to the hospital from the battle-site, and letting him talk privately to Diane, and all. Even before they'd interviewed him, he'd pretty much made up his mind to give them the tape. It seemed like his only chance. Besides, the fucking thing had brought him nothing but trouble anyway.

"You mind if I make this private, sir?" Linc asked Tony, adding the polite salutation as much out of sincerity as guile.

He waited till Tony stepped out of the room and then dialed Uncle Henry's office number. He answered on the first ring.

"Yeah, it's me," Linc said quietly.

"Linc? Where you at?"

"I'm in jail. Eleventh and State, but never mind that. I can't say much right now. Are you okay?"

"Yeah. How 'bout you?"

"I been better, but I been a lot worse," Linc said.

Linc gave him the news about Rick, and told him that a deal had been worked out to take them all off the hook. After speaking for a few minutes more, Linc said, "Yeah, I trust 'em. Now just do what I asked you, please." He saw Tony glance his way and figured he'd overheard, but that was cool.

He hung up the phone and stood.

"I guess I'm ready to wait on it," Linc said.

Tony nodded and motioned for him to step back into the hallway. As they walked toward the holding cell, Ray came ambling down the corridor pouring a can of orange juice into a Styrofoam cup. He stopped in front of them and handed the cup to Linc.

"The doc said you gotta drink a lotta liquids 'cause of all the blood you lost," Ray said.

"Thanks," said Linc, taking the cup. "I appreciate it."

"Hey, us ex-gyrenes have to stick together," Ray said and grinned.

The Heist

★ ★ ★ ★ ★

It was forty-five minutes later when the phone rang. Tony picked it up as Arlene came over, and he covered the mouthpiece and said, "It's Kent. He's still at the Federal Building." Faulkner told him in short order that a Dunkin' Donuts bag had been dropped off to the desk sergeant at the twenty-second district with one of Tony's cards stapled to it. Upon investigating, the sergeant opened it and found a videocassette and a hand-printed note saying: *GET THIS TAPE TO THE MAN ON THE CARD RIGHT AWAY*. Faulkner was laughing as he told Tony about the desk sergeant's disappointment.

"Apparently he thought some guy was bringing in some donuts, Tony," Faulkner said. "Maybe he wanted to grab a few for himself."

"Kent, call him back and tell him to make sure nothing happens to that tape," Tony said. "Tell him to guard it with his fucking life, and that we'll be there in twenty minutes to pick it up."

"Roger-wilco, Tony," Faulkner said.

Arlene cocked her head slightly to the side and asked him if that was the call.

"That was it," he said, standing up and slipping on his jacket. "You wanta come with us?"

"Are you kidding?" she said. "You'd have to lock me up to keep me away."

They took the Dan Ryan to 111th Street and were at the Morgan Park Station inside of twenty minutes. The desk sergeant gave them a curious glance when they walked in.

"The bag," Ray said in a low growl.

"I'm Tony Cardoff. Somebody drop something off here for me?"

"Oh, yeah. Lieu," the sergeant said, bending over and coming up with the white paper sack. "Here it is."

"What did the guy that dropped it off look like?" Tony asked, studying his card, which was still stapled to the outside of the bag.

The sergeant leaned back and rubbed his chin.

"It was a big black guy," he said.

"Bald?" Tony asked.

"I don't know. He was wearing dark glasses and a hat."

"That Henry sure likes his donuts, don't he?" Tony said with a grin, holding up the card for Ray to see. The lower right-hand corner had been cut off, but the card itself was stained with dark splotches. Coffee stains.

"You know who dropped it off?" Arlene asked. "How?"

"It don't take Charlie Chan to figure that one out," Ray said. "Come on, let's take this baby down to the office so we can watch it."

"The hell with the office," Tony said. "My place is closer."

1:34 P.M.

They'd watched it so many times, frame-by-frame, that when the chief prosecutor from the U.S. Attorney's Office failed to show much emotion at seeing it for the first time, Ray asked him if he wanted it replayed.

"No, I'm just going to pinch myself a couple of times to make sure I'm not dreaming all this," he said. "I'm going to call Judge Perona right now. Once he sees this, I'm sure he'll issue a warrant for Costelli. We can get a specially-convened grand jury set up for early next week and indict him."

"And we want to serve it," Tony said. He looked at Ray, whose grin was a mile wide. "Right, partner?"

In the hallway, Tony and Arlene gathered around the doorway and exchanged enthusiastic predictions. Ray, who'd gone for more coffee, came back with Kent Faulkner in tow, each man carrying two cups.

"Hey, guess what?" Ray said, handing one of his cups to Tony. "They just found another body, and guess whose it is?"

"Come on, Ray," Tony said irritably. "I been up all night and half the day, and I ain't in any mood for any more Charlie Chan bullshit."

Ray smirked, then said, "Reginald D. Fox. He was in a convenience store lot on the East Side, all neatly folded up in the trunk of his Jaguar."

"He's dead?" Arlene said, stunned. "Not Reggie?"

"Yep, Reggie," Ray said. "And we ain't gonna need Dr. Kenney from the morgue to do a dental ID on this one. Five shots to the head with a .22."

"The classic mob-style execution," Faulkner added, not to be outdone. "Looks like old Vino's getting panicky now that we got him on the ropes."

"Oh, my God," Arlene said. She quickly turned away.

Tony gave Ray and Kent a harsh look, then put his hand gently on her shoulder.

"He was mixed up with the worst kind of people, Arlene," Tony said. "It was bound to happen sooner or later."

"Exactly," Ray said. "He brought it on himself."

"I know you're right," she said, quickly wiping her eyes. "It's just . . . it seems like such a shame. He really was a fine lawyer."

"Ain't no such thing," Ray said, then grinned as he caught Tony's look of disapproval.

"Don't over-generalize now, Ray," Faulkner said in his good-old-boy drawl. "After all, Arlene and I are both law-yers."

"Yeah, okay," said Ray, his grin widening as he nodded his head at Arlene. "I'll make *one* exception to that."

★ ★ ★ ★ ★

4:15 P.M.

Tony and Ray sat in their unmarked squad car down the block from Vino's River Forest home. The radio squawked that the FBI SWAT team was in position. Ray grinned and shifted the car into drive.

"You ready for this?" he asked.

"I've been ready for a long time," Tony said. "Let's go."

He radioed the SWAT team leader that he and Ray were going to the front door.

The unmarked jerked to a stop and they calmly opened the doors and got out. Tony took the time to straighten his coat, and then checked to make sure his pistol was secure in its holster. Ray was already holding his down by his leg, his Chicago star in the other hand.

Two guys in black BDUs, holding MP-5 machine guns, appeared at each side of the house. Tony nodded to them and headed for the door. There was no way he was going to miss the expression on Vino's face. He reached out and pressed the doorbell several times, waited, and pressed it again.

"Hold your horses, goddamnit," a gruff voice called from inside.

Tony smiled. It was here. It was really here.

The door popped open and a big lug with an oily pompadour and black beard stubble glared with an expression he must have thought passed for ferocious.

"Whaddaya want?" His voice was a growl.

"Where's Vino?" Ray said, holding up his star. He started to push his way inside, but the unctuous hood put a hand on Ray's chest and shoved.

"Hey, this ain't Chicago, asshole," the thug grunted. "You got no right to—"

Tony punched the man in the gut with his left, then brought a straight right across that twisted the guy's greasy head. He collapsed in a heap.

"Not bad," Ray said, stepping over the fallen bodyguard. "Maybe you're the one that should be entering the Police Olympics."

But Tony was already moving inside. He took out his gun and held it in front of him as he yelled, "Police. Vino, get your ass out here."

Vino emerged from his den with a look that was somewhere between outrage and amazement. He was dressed in a blue silk bathrobe over some tan pants, and had a glass tumbler filled with amber liquid in his hand.

"Don't you look cute," Tony said, putting on the most malevolent grin he could muster.

"Cardoff," Vino said. "What the hell you think you're doing in *my* house?"

Tony looked at the other man's face, the heavy jowls, the flushed, scarlet birthmark, the mocking smile . . . It took him back all those years, to the time he'd slugged the gangster under the streetlight.

Finally, he thought.

"You eat yet, Vino?" he asked. "Because you're not gonna get any linguini downtown."

The sets of darkly-clad SWAT team members came through the door, pausing to handcuff the fallen punk in the doorway, and then spilling past them into the various areas of the house. Vino's head bobbled back and forth.

"Hey, what the hell is this?" he asked, the cocky smile starting to fade. "What you talking about?"

"This is the future for you," Tony said, holding up the federal warrant along with his handcuffs. "Bring your toothbrush."

★ ★ ★ ★ ★

7:06 P.M.

When Tony had tried to back out of having dinner at Arlene's place, she became very insistent. Finally he acquiesced, and went home for some much-needed rest. When his alarm had gone off at five-fifteen, he felt more than ever like turning it off and going back to sleep. But it was better to get it over with, he thought. On the drive north to Skokie he rehearsed in his mind what he was going to say to put an early end to the evening and to any designs that Arlene might have on him. He'd thought it through, and the age difference was just too great. To think otherwise would be making a fool of himself. An old fool.

He stopped at a corner Seven-Eleven and bought one of those generic bouquets. Something nice, but not overly romantic. Just a polite thank-you-for-having-me-over sort of thing. As he pulled up by her apartment building, Tony was already formulating an assortment of excuses to make an early exit, not the least of which was how bone-weary he actually felt. He sighed heavily as he rang her doorbell and pushed through the buzzing security door. Arlene lived on the third floor of a three-flat, and Tony dragged his feet going up the stairs. He was almost considering not even staying for dinner at all, just explaining how dead tired he was. He gently rapped on the door.

Arlene opened it and smiled. He handed her the bouquet as she opened the door further.

"Oh, Mother," Arlene said, smelling the flowers. "Look at the beautiful flowers that Tony brought us."

Perplexed, Tony glanced over her shoulder and saw an attractive woman smiling at him. She had Arlene's eyes, and her smile, too. But she was a generation closer to his age.

"Tony, this is my mother, Grace," Arlene said, then

286

leaning close, added in a low whisper, "and she's unattached."

The woman held out her hand and Tony took it in his. She had Arlene's face, he could see that now, and the same classic lines of her body, which had been softened slightly by time and motherhood. But all in all, he thought, she was just about the most beautiful woman he'd seen in ages.

"I'm afraid," Arlene's mom said, shaking Tony's hand, "that my daughter inherited all of my late husband's brashness."

Tony just grinned, and suddenly realized that he didn't feel quite so tired after all.

Chapter 21

Friday, April 24, 1992

9:25 A.M.

Linc waved through the tinted window of the bus at his uncle, but it was so dark that he wasn't sure if Henry could see him from the outside. He watched as the big man grinned, waved, then turned and walked slowly back toward the escalators that would take him back up to street level. Linc saw Henry pause and wave once more before stepping on the metal stairs and rising out of sight. Settling back in the seat, Linc adjusted the earphones of his Walkman. In this immense subterranean cavern of the downtown Greyhound Bus terminal, all he could pick up clearly was one of those all-news AM stations and a lot of static. The announcer was talking about the apparently successful efforts now being completed to stem the floodwaters coming from the tunnel system. At the mention of the tunnels, his mind began spinning through the events of the past week and all that had happened: getting out of jail, testifying before the Federal Grand Jury, the final talk with Diane, Uncle Henry in the clear, Mr. Faulkner pulling some strings to get Linc reinstated in the Marine Corps, and the relief that he felt now that the worst of it was over.

Oh, sure, he'd have to come back and testify again, once the Costelli trial started, but that wouldn't be a problem since he was working for the Gee now. Be good to have the government fly him back to Chicago so he could see Uncle Henry and everybody. He thought of Diane and how everything had gone from bad to worse for them in this past week. Maybe they'd been through too much. Maybe, after they'd had some time apart . . . He shook his head. No, it was probably better that it was over with between them.

The darkened cement walls of the terminal reminded him of his and Rick's descent into the tunnel system during the heist. He shut off the Walkman and removed the earphones. Rick. If only that damn white boy had made it, too, he told himself. Then they'd both probably be riding this bus back to Camp Pendleton now. His thoughts drifted back to the funeral, with Rick laid out in his dress blues, and Linc felt his eyes misting over. He'd personally shined up all his friend's brass and spit-shined his shoes too, before giving them to Rick's uncle to give to the undertaker. Even though all of the uniform wasn't visible with the casket half closed, Linc felt that it was the right thing to do. He'd wanted Rick to look strack when he went up to them pearly gates.

"Mmm, mmm, mmm," the woman next to him was saying. She was an older black lady with grayish hair pulled back into an unpretentious bun, and small gold-colored glasses that rested halfway down on her nose. Linc glanced at the newspaper page she was reading. "Ain't this flood terrible," she said. "Sure done closed this city down for a spell." She looked at him and smiled pleasantly.

Linc smiled back.

"Are you all right, young man?" the lady asked.

"Yeah . . . I mean, yes, ma'am," Linc said, quickly rubbing his eyes. "I was just thinking about a real good friend of mine. He just passed."

"Oh, I'm so sorry," she said. Her lips firmed up. "But he is in the Lord's hands now."

She looked at him for a few moments more, then turned her attention back to her newspaper.

"We've certainly got enough people out of work to begin with, without this flood coming along and closin' more things down," she said.

The big diesel engine began to rumble to life. The driver closed the door, and the bus lurched forward.

" 'Course, to look at things down here, you wouldn't even know there was any flooding, would you?" the woman continued.

"No, ma'am," said Linc, thinking that it was going to be a long, long trip to California.

" 'Course, things ain't always what they appear to be," she said, flipping the page on her paper. "Things can look mighty calm, but swirling down deep, there's always some trouble brewing. Still waters run deep, but remember, the Bible says, 'all thy billows and thy waves passed over me . . . yet I will look again toward thy holy temple.' "

"Yes, ma'am."

She folded her paper in half, set it down on her knees, and turned to look at him. He saw that on her lap was a well-worn King James Bible. Digging in her purse, she took out a religious tract from a Baptist church and handed it to him.

"Here, young man," she said. "Something for you to read on the way. We've got a long journey ahead of us."

"Yes, ma'am," said Linc, taking the pamphlet and smiling to himself.

"Sometimes the Lord puts us through some trying times, before He shows us the light," she said. She adjusted the newspaper on her lap and opened the Bible.

Not wanting to encourage any further conversation, Linc turned his face toward the window, catching sight of his reflection on the glass. The bus pulled onto the darkened, winding ramp that took them through an extended tunnel, before emerging up onto Clark, and into the brightness of the April sunshine.

A long journey, he thought. A helluva long one just to end up in practically the same place he'd started. And this time without Rick. *Towards a New Past*, he thought, remembering the title of a book he'd studied in high school. But at least he was getting another shot at zeroing in on the brass ring. And that was all a professional grunt like him could really ask for.

"Amen to that," the woman said aloud, tracing her finger over one of the biblical passages.

Linc adjusted the seat slightly, placed the earphones of the Walkman back on his head, and began once again to try and tune in an FM station. As the bus merged into traffic and began to pick up speed, he finally got one to lock in.

About the Author

Michael A. Black holds an MFA degree in Fiction Writing from Columbia College. He has been a police officer in the south suburbs of Chicago for the past twenty-six years, and has had short stories published in various anthologies and magazines, including *Ellery Queen Mystery Magazine* and *Alfred Hitchcock's Mystery Magazine*. He has also written two nonfiction books for young readers, *The M1A1 Abrams Tank* and *Volunteering to Help Kids*. His first novel, *A Killing Frost*, featuring private investigator Ron Shade, was released by Five Star Publishing in September 2002 and received excellent reviews. *Windy City Knights*, the second novel in the series, came out in May of 2004. *The Heist*, a stand-alone thriller set in Chicago, is his third novel. He has worked in various capacities in police work including patrol supervisor, tactical squad, investigations, raid team member, and SWAT team leader. He is currently a sergeant on the Matteson, Illinois Police Department. His hobbies include weightlifting, running, and the martial arts. He is rumored to have five cats.